PRIMAL RESURRECTION

A WHISKEY TANGO FOXTROT NOVEL

W.J. LUNDY

Edited by TERRI KING

Edited by SARA JONES

Illustrated by AJ POWERS

PRIMAL RESURRECTION

A WHISKEY TANGO FOXTROT NOVEL

W.J. LUNDY

COPYRIGHT

CHAPTER 1

COLDWATER COMPOUND, MICHIGAN SAFE ZONE

The coffee was watered down, but it was hot. The tin cup warmed his hands. As he wrapped his dry and worn fingers around it, he found comfort in the old, dented cup. With the room, he wasn't as lucky. The space was cold and drab, more like a storage locker than a living space. He could see the vapor of every exhale as he fought back the temptation to put his heavy coat back on. Made of cement blocks, obviously not designed for living, it was low-lit and heated by a thick handmade candle. This is what they called a dorm, but to Brad it resembled a cell more than a home.

He looked down at the cup and grimaced. He didn't know what to call this place or what to think of it. Was this what survival meant in the north? Was this survival? It was the closest he'd been to his home in northern Michigan but suddenly, he felt as a far away as ever. He wasn't a prisoner —he was sure of that; they'd allowed them to keep their weapons. They provided them with food and treated them well. Treated them like guests. Even given them clean uniforms and bedding at the entrance before ushering them into this underground sanctuary.

Hearing footsteps outside, Brad looked to the door. He could hear children's voices.

Not a military base—not entirely. A shelter, maybe? he said to himself. *A housing area, in the drab confines of a cement building. This is what passes as a safe area?* In West Virginia, they'd lived in cabins and walled compounds. They were free to move around and to hunt. But here, in this supposedly safe area, they all seemed to be confined indoors. *Is this what safety looks like in the north?*

They'd only been here for hours, less than six, maybe. After crossing the wall, they were quickly brought into a tent, which was dressed in clean white fabric. The room, filled with stainless-steel carts and furniture, had the strong scent of bleach and disinfectants. Brad and Chelsea were inspected for infection and injuries, given a chance to shower and exchange their uniforms for fresh ones, then moved into another waiting area. Soon after, an army officer took a quick statement from them. It was supposed to be a debrief, but the man didn't get far, and it was apparent to Brad that his answers struck a nerve. The de-brief suddenly ended once General Carson's name was mentioned.

The officer appeared worried, and Brad knew this must have been far from the ordinary, not what they'd expected to hear. He'd felt from the moment they arrived that the place was under siege from primals or something else; he wasn't sure. They were moved to a small tent with wooden benches, where they waited until a military ambulance arrived. The vehicle had two windows, both covered with tightly coiled wires. The drive was longer than he'd expected. When he was able to see out, they appeared to be driving down city streets, then onto a narrow county road, and finally to this place.

From the outside, it looked like an old manufacturing plant, tall steel-sided buildings surrounded by chain link fencing. The military had augmented the structure with entry control points and tall watchtowers, complete with spotlights and sandbag barriers. All along the perimeter, the gates were secured and guarded. The sentries were as professional as any Brad had seen in Afghanistan. Whoever ran the place was doing a good job.

Once inside, things were remarkably different; instead of the drab feel of a military base, it looked more like a shopping mall. A long center aisle was lined with market squares where people peddled goods. Behind them, Brad could see living spaces—some very elaborate, others nothing more than cardboard shanties. The micro community seemed to go on for hundreds of yards down the middle of the steel building. He smelled wood smoke and roasting meat and vegetables. Brad had turned to move toward them when the escorting soldiers blocked his path and turned him away.

He was told the town square was for civilians only and was quickly moved around a corner to a guarded steel staircase. They descended several levels before stopping at a deep subbasement. A long hallway with doors on both sides, it was previously used for equipment storage and maintenance but was now utilized as soldier and military family housing.

He took another sip of the coffee, shaking himself from his deep thoughts. He looked at Chelsea asleep in the bed by the opposite wall. Watching her sleep, he wondered if they were lucky, or just another step back from where they had been a month ago. Life had been good at the camp, and they could rebuild it if they put in the effort. He wondered if it was a mistake to come here alone without the others.

He heard heavy footsteps in the hall and the casual banter of soldiers on the move. Yeah, they could have stayed in the free territories, but they would never be safe; someone else would always come for them. He felt guilt at leaving Sean and the others, but they knew how to find him, and if they were smart, they would do the same and pack up. Head for the Safe Zones in Michigan or Texas and abandon the wastelands.

Brad shook his head at the self-doubt. "No, leaving was the right thing to do," he whispered to himself.

There was a light knock on the door, and Brad got to his feet then moved to the entrance. Turning the knob, he pulled the door in and was greeted with the smiling face of a young woman. Her brown hair was pulled back over green eyes. She held a tray of thick-sliced bread and a bowl of hand-churned butter. Brad opened the door wider and allowed the girl in.

"It's not much, but it's the best we can do for break-fast these days." The girl turned and spotted Chelsea asleep on the bed. "Oh—I'm sorry. I didn't mean to disturb you."

Brad smiled and waved her in. "It's fine, miss. She's just tired from the trip; rest when you can."

The girl smiled again and extended her hand to Brad. "Please, call me Maria."

Brad accepted her hand and nodded. "My name is—"

"Sergeant Brad Thompson; yes, I know. We haven't had a survivor from the south in quite some time. Especially a military man still in his uniform. Most of the formal military is gone outside these walls."

Brad attempted to shrug off the comment before she

continued. "Can you tell me what base you came from? Are there more soldiers there?"

He shook his head and looked away. "I'm sorry, no. But there are more soldiers in Texas, and there is an outpost in the Carolinas." He immediately recognized the woman's disappointed expression. "But, hey, why worry? You have plenty of soldiers here. I saw the wall; it's impressive."

This time it was the woman who shrugged. "The wall..." she whispered, turning away. "Yeah, it was great against the infected. The senator's council saved us all by constructing the wall. We owe a lot to them." She looked off into the corner and then dipped her head. "But it didn't do much to save us from ourselves."

"You mean General Carson and his raiders? I wouldn't worry about him anymore."

She reached out and took Brad's hand. "Carson..." She frowned. "I know the name. He's a monster, but the movement against us is far larger than just one man. We are constantly under attack. Without help, we won't be able to stay here much longer."

"Stay?"

She nodded. "Most of the safe zones in the east have already been vacated."

"Vacated?" Brad asked, still not understanding.

She nodded. "Yes, when the Alliance began breaking apart, a new government began to form in Pennsylvania. It goes by many names, but some of the people call it the New Republic. They pretend to be patriots, but I swear to you they aren't."

Brad scoffed. "If Carson was a part of it, then I believe you."

Her brow tightened. "Our senator refused to join with them. He refused to give in to their demands." She turned away then looked back at Brad. "Texas was our only hope to hold out against them. When you arrived—well, we'd hoped you were part of them."

There was a stirring from the end of the room. Chelsea rose up on an elbow as she looked at them, overhearing part of the conversation. "I don't understand. They said Carson was in charge of the resistance. He's dead. It's over."

"Dead?" Maria pulled back her hands, embarrassed when she realized she'd held Brad's for so long. She moved to the wall and checked the coffee pot, finding it nearly empty. "I heard what you told the soldiers at the gate. If Carson is dead, things will only get worse."

"Worse? How?" Brad said, a puzzled expression building on his face. "I thought Carson was the one causing all the problems. With him gone—"

"I shouldn't have said anything; it's not my place." Maria turned away. "I'll have more supplies sent to your room. But you should dress and take advantage of this time to clean up."

"Wait," Chelsea said, moving to a sitting position. "The soldiers, they said this is a safe zone."

Maria nodded. "Safer than some, but we don't know for how much longer."

"I still don't understand," Chelsea said.

"It'll all be explained soon enough. Please get cleaned up; he will want to see you as soon as he arrives from the capital."

"Who?" Brad asked.

"The senator, of course."

CHAPTER 2

The scent of bacon woke him. He pulled the tattered wool blanket away from his face as he looked into the hazy room. Brooks was standing over him with a porcelain plate. He angled it down just enough for Sean to see the strips of glistening bacon.

"Are you kidding me?" Sean asked.

Brooks took a long strip of bacon, folded it in half then pushed the entire thing into his mouth, grinning, before handing the plate to Sean, who quickly stood upright. "Where in the hell did you get bacon?"

"You can thank Texas; those boys know how to live," Brooks said, taking a step back. "Seems even with the Primal holocaust, the wild boar population is thriving. One thing Texas has plenty of is pork." The big man opened a knapsack, removed a large slab of cornbread and tossed it onto the bed next to Sean.

Sean nodded at him. "You bring coffee too?"

Brooks shook his head. "You can get your own coffee." He moved across the room and dropped to a stool near a glowing woodstove. "So, what's the plan?"

Shrugging, Sean broke off a corner of the cornbread and stuffed it into his mouth. "The Rangers are setting up here. By the sounds of it, they have no intention of surrendering this ground now that they've taken it."

"Surrender it to who?" Brooks asked.

Sean shrugged. "I don't know. Makes no difference to us; we're headed back out—"

"After Brad," Brooks said, interrupting. "That's what I'm talking about."

"I figured you were anxious to get moving," Sean said. The younger SEAL had been harassing him to track down Brad and Chelsea since they'd been separated on the train just days earlier. It took them the better part of two days just to get all the civilians back to Crabtree in one piece. The long walk put a beating on all of them, and now Sean was wary about asking his men to turn back around and head out without any rest.

"What's the plan then?" Brooks asked. "You want me to get our crew gathered up?"

"No," Sean said between mouthfuls of cornbread and bacon. "We'll take Joey. I won't ask the others to leave their families again; they've risked enough. Besides, we can move faster with a small group."

Sean finished the last of the bacon and tossed the empty plate at the foot of the bed. He turned out and grabbed his trousers hanging off a hook and quickly dressed. "And keep it to yourself; outside of you and Villegas, I haven't told anyone about our plan."

"So just us and Joey? What about Hassan and the others? They'll want in."

Sean shook his head. "I know they would demand to come if asked. That's why we can't tell them. They all have families now; we're the last bachelors out here. If we're going to leave, we need to keep it quiet. And as far as Texas is concerned, their mission has to come first. They won't approve of us slipping out of camp."

"What the hell are you talking about? Mission, my ass."

Sean laughed. "Come on. Burt has called a morning briefing. Cloud is supposed to be coming down out of the mountain so we can talk things out. I'll bring up our excursion to him there."

Brooks shook his head. "What is there to bring up? It doesn't matter what he thinks."

Sean made his way to a weapons rack by the door and slung his rifle over his shoulder. "Well, we kinda entered into an alliance with Texas, and we have a previous obligation to Cloud. Or did you forget that? They won't be pleased with us just running off. We have commitments to these people too."

"You're shitting me, right?"

Seeing he was starting to rub a nerve, Sean looked back. "Just relax, brother. We're going, but we have to be cool about it. We need to stay on good terms with the guys now that they are providing the bacon," Sean said, throwing another wink. "Now, come on. Let's go have this meeting."

Sean opened the door and stepped outside. Snow was coming down and blowing across the frozen muddy road. Most of the tent city built by the raiders was still intact but was now supplemented with more tents constructed by the Rangers from Texas. Men were positioned all along the walls, and the watchtowers had been rebuilt or repaired. The doors to the large barn stood open, and supplies were being unloaded from a large flatbed truck.

Sean waited for Brooks to fall in beside him then, without turning his head, said, "They are intent on staying. No doubt about it." He pointed out the activity in Crabtree.

Brooks grunted. "All of our civilians were moved back to Camp Cloud or farther south to the main farm sometime last night. There ain't a damn thing keeping us here," Brooks said, his voice now lower. "Our troopers left here can handle themselves. I heard some talk that they have another company of Rangers moving in tomorrow. Might even be regular Army troops out of Fort Hood on their way up." Brooks paused. "Don't sound like this all ended here; they're prepping for something big."

Sean shook his head and continued walking toward a building marked *Horton's Sundries* on a tin sign over the door. The raiders had previously used the building as a meeting place—a sort of headquarters—and it appeared to match the requirements of the Rangers, as well. Sean opened the door and felt the warmth of the fire as he entered, stomping his feet to loose the mud and snow from his boots.

The room was filled with talking men in mixed uniforms. Either none of them noticed Sean's entrance, or they were just not concerned with it. He looked to the woodstove and spotted a steaming coffee pot on the top. He made his way straight for it but was cut off by Colonel Cloud before reaching his destination. Blocking Sean's path, the man grinned and turned to pour himself a cup. He then turned back and smiled before handing the filled ceramic mug to Sean. "I was just catching up with Burt. He says you were an immense help in getting our people back."

Brooks grunted behind him. "If by 'help' he means us doing all the heavy lifting, then I'd agree."

Sean frowned and stepped in front of Brooks. "What's going on out there? Looks like they are staging for some- thing big. This is a hell of a lot more than I expected."

Cloud looked over his shoulder toward a group of

Rangers positioned around a large map table. He leaned in and hushed his voice. "Things are a lot worse than they led us to believe."

Brooks chuckled, drawing Cloud's eye, before Sean shot the younger SEAL a glare.

"Am I missing something?" Cloud asked.

Sean nodded. "The Rangers seem to have a habit of leaving out details. If they had been forthcoming from the start, we could have saved a lot of people. It was on Burt's word about the treaty mission that we took that party out of Camp Cloud. We left the place defenseless on his instructions. He failed to mention anything about this Carson character."

Cloud used a hand to rub his chin and grimaced. "I see, but I'm afraid that's all water under the bridge now. As far as those out east are concerned, there is no distinction between us and Texas anymore."

"That's all old news, with Carson as good as gone, isn't it?" Sean questioned.

Cloud raised his eyebrows. "Are you sure?"

Brooks pushed his way back into the conversation and nodded. "Hell yeah. Brad went after him, and he wouldn't have missed the opportunity. Which brings me to ask—"

Sean raised his hand, cutting off his partner again, then looked at Cloud. "Sir, we still got people out there, and—like you said—the disposition of this Carson is unverified. I'd like to mount a party to go check it out."

Cloud rubbed his chin and stared at a far wall, considering his options. "There's a problem with that. It seems the original mission we agreed to... well, things have changed. These people aren't here to stage for an invasion of the North; they're here to build up a defensive perimeter."

"Against what?" Sean said. "But if we confirm Carson is dead—"

"That's only part of it. Carson was a big shot with this group here, but as far as the larger picture, it sounds like he was just another bully that was looking for a land grab," Cloud interrupted. "One of many."

"The hell you mean 'one of many'? Wait... all of this? What they did to the camp? All the dead?" Brooks said. "*Carson* was the one behind it all."

Cloud looked back at the table of Rangers again. "There's a lot of stuff they held back. Carson was only a chunk of what's been moving against the Midwest Alliance —and he wasn't even a key player, as far as I can discern. Sounds like messing with Carson was just a distraction from what they've really got going on up North."

This time Brooks pushed ahead. "Finding our people was a distraction?! Going after Carson was a distraction?!" The pitch in his voice rose as he spoke. "With all due respect, sir, we wouldn't have even been in this mess if it wasn't for Texas."

Cloud raised a palm, silencing Brooks. "Relax, I get it. But there is more to it... a lot more."

"Then let us in on it," Sean said.

Looking behind him, Cloud pushed the two SEALs to an out-of-the-way corner. "Texas is saying there are hordes of infected massing in the north. They are looking to setup defensive lines to keep them from moving south."

"We've dealt with hordes before," Brooks said.

"Not like this. We're talking about massive amounts moving in from New York, Indy, Chicago... everything that was dormant has been activated by all the infighting. Not only that, but Burt says they are hungry and erratic. It's as bad as the days after the fall. The doctors at Fort Sam

Houston are scared, and if they are scared we should be too."

Sean rubbed his chin. "All the more reason for us to go after Brad; hell, we can do a bit of recon for you in the meantime."

A Ranger behind them started barking for the men's attention. Cloud leaned in closer to Brooks and Sean. He took in a deep breath then let it out slowly. "I don't have confidence on where this is going, so if I were you—" Cloud paused again and looked back toward the men gathering at the front of the room. "If I were you, I'd pack my gear and get out on the trail before I'm ordered to stop you."

CHAPTER 3

Henry used a stick to push the coals together at the edge of his fire-pit. He watched as the flames nipped at the carcass of the rabbit hung on a spit. The old man sat on a high overlook, positioned in the shadows of tall pines so the smoke from his fire broke apart and dispersed in the wind as it wended through the trees. He picked this spot intentionally so he could look down over the camp of Crabtree, and this morning the view was providing plenty of entertainment.

Men were moving in fast; they'd been pouring into Crabtree all morning long. As civilians loaded in the backs of covered trucks and moved south—presumably back toward Dan Cloud's place—military vehicles were convoying in and staging on the main road. From the looks of it, they were setting up for something big.

Henry heard a whinny behind him and turned to see his horses, as well as two new ones, tied amongst the trees. He'd found the four of them sitting at the crossroad, kicking at the snow to get at the grass beneath. He knew his girls and knew they would follow the trail that led back to his cabin higher up in the mountains. The horses had been making their way home the way they'd been trained, which is exactly what he should be doing now. Being a loner had kept him alive during the fall, but that was the extent of it. After his wife passed, he'd been nothing more than a shell, and it was no way to live. The last week, being back with the men and making a difference, had sparked something in Henry. Now, with everything that had happened, he wasn't sure he could bear going back to his solitary existence.

Still, looking down at Crabtree, he wasn't sure what that meant. Maybe he'd invite folks back to live on his farm. Maybe he just needed to spark up some sort of association with those people down there. But maybe it was more than that. The way he felt knowing his friend had been murdered for nothing... the way those poor people below had been treated. It all sparked a fire in Henry, one he wasn't sure he could soon extinguish. Maybe he'd just continue on alone, looking for something else, anything else.

A snapping branch and the locking back of a hammer caused him to freeze. He dropped the stick he'd been probing the fire with and raised his gloved hands into the air. Henry looked toward his right boot and could see the lever-action rifle. Its stock was within arm's reach, but he was certain it would be the last reach he'd ever make.

"No need to shoot; I'm friendly," Henry called out. "It's just me alone here. I've got some food and water if that's what you're after."

Henry held his position and listened intently to the sounds of shuffling feet and heavy footfalls in the brush behind him. The horses whinnied again before snorting at the unknown person intruding in on their space. The stranger crossed into view, circling around the fire and stopping to Henry's front. Big and burly with a red beard and a black watch cap, the man pointed an old .357 Colt revolver directly at Henry's chest. His chapped lips pursed, and his eyes widened before lowering the pistol. "Hey, wait a minute; I know you," the man said.

Henry nodded, grinning. He recognized the stranger from the gate watch at Crabtree. Henry slowly lowered his hands and spoke. "You were workin' the gate the day I rode into town."

The bearded man nodded and moved closer to the fire. "Yeah, that's right—the bounty hunter. You rode in with that kid." The man's head swiveled then looked back to Henry. "Where the hell is he, anyhow?"

Henry shrugged and retrieved his poker stick, adjusting the roasting rabbit. "Not sure. We got separated out there in the bush. Came back this way hoping to meet up with him in Crabtree; that's when I saw the place been overrun. Figured I should keep my distance for a bit. Least till I can figure out what's going on down there." Henry reached into the fire and lifted the rabbit. He tore off a hind quarter and tossed it to the man across from him. "What the hell happened down there, anyway?" Henry asked.

The bearded man shook his head and scowled. "I don't know. They come in at night. Attacked us right after General Carson arrived on the train." The man paused, taking a hearty bite of the rabbit. He looked off in the distance, contemplating as he chewed. He nodded his head then looked back at Henry. "They were ready for us, almost like they were looking for us. They hit hard and fast. We lost control of the walls then everyone kind of just let out.

"Carson abandoned us by knocking the wall open. Busted right through the gate, leaving us all exposed. What was we supposed to do? Them infected were inside and men was attacking from the back. Carson gone on his train. I lost sight of Gus and the others, and once the infected started in, I made a break for it." The man again lifted the rabbit to his mouth. He took a bite and pointed the leg bone at the dancing flames "You know burning a fire so close to the camp is taking a risk. They got a lot of men down there; they'll be patrolling soon. Those boys from Texas get a hold of you, they liable to hang you on sight."

Henry nodded as if considering the suggestion. "Yeah, I reckon you're right on that." He took a bite at the meat and washed it down with a swig from a canteen before tossing it across the fire to the bearded man. "So, tell me, big man—"

"Name's Riley."

Henry dipped his chin. "Okay, Riley, so what was to have happened if you didn't recognize me from the camp? Were you figuring to shoot me?"

The man shrugged. "Nah, nothing like that, old timer. Look." Riley lifted the pistol back from his lap and flipped open the empty cylinder. "I ran empty during the fight. Been out here just looking for a way out... my chance to get away. If I didn't know you, I imagine things would go similar. I'd get some of this here rabbit and some of your water and let out. I'm not fixing to kill anyone that ain't looking to kill me."

"So, what's your business then? You headed back east? You looking for Carson? Gus maybe?"

The big man looked at Henry, trying to study his expression, before shaking his head no. "Screw Carson. To hell with Gus. I've never been interested in his shit. Only reason I'm here is because they were holding my family hostage." The man turned and looked over his shoulder toward Crabtree then back at Henry. "I figure with all of that down there in Crabtree, maybe I can get back to my family. Get them out while Carson is busy with problems of his own."

"Sounds reasonable to me," Henry said, smiling. "Where would you take 'em? After you fetch 'em, of course."

The man frowned and gazed back into the fire. "Not sure. Anywhere free, I guess. Michigan, Texas... hell, I'd take a cave if it meant seeing them again."

"You think they would take you in Texas after what you've done?"

The man looked at Henry, his face turning hard and cold. "And what exactly have I done, old man? I watched a gate, I trained people on how to secure a compound; I never had a part in any of the other evil shit Gus and his people were up too." The man took a long drink from the canteen and wiped his chin with his sleeve. "What the hell was I supposed to do? Carson had my family. Said he'd kill them if I didn't go to work for him."

Henry raised his hands and smiled. "Hey, partner, I'm not judging you. I was just saying."

The old man worked on a shirt pocket and retrieved his pipe. He tapped it against his knee before stuffing it with tobacco. He grimaced and placed the pipe between his teeth. He lit it, puffing until smoke drifted from the end. "You say you trained folks? You military or something? A policeman maybe?"

The big man let his head hang as he looked down and into the fire. "Nah, nothing like that. I worked in the steel-works until it shut down. With nothing else to do, I caught me a security job guarding the same damn mill I used to work in. You know, I hated that job. But that factory, the steel buildings, and tall fences are probably what saved my family."

Henry nodded, puffing on the pipe. "How so?"

"When people started getting sick, when things went to hell, others went to the shelters; not me. I had the keys to the steelworks, and there was plenty in there. Plenty to keep us alive while the rest of the country went to shit."

Henry puffed on the pipe, nodding his approval. "And no problems from the infected?"

"Some, but we were able to harden the fences and seal the gates. For the first few months, it was mostly a game of hide and seek. We stayed quiet and hoped the infected outside wouldn't hear us. We made it one month, then two, and before you know it, it was winter. We did good, considering. We'd go out during the day, find survivors and bring them back. We saved lots of people; we really did. We had a good thing going until Gus and his group came along."

"What happened?"

"We were naïve. They came under the flag of the Midwest Alliance, said they wanted to trade, to work with us. Hell, you know, we had it bad enough just trying to keep people fed; we let too many in, got overextended. Seeing Gus and his men roll up in them trucks and eighteen wheelers full of goods... we kinda thought we'd been saved."

Henry took a long puff on his pipe. "When did it all turn on you?"

"First evening they was there." Riley looked across the fire directly at Henry, trying to read him. "They waited until nightfall. We'd only let a handful of them stay inside, so one of them must have killed the man at the gate and let the rest in. They took it all, killed many of us, then those of us he could leverage, he made us join up with him. Took our families and left some of his own scum behind to take over the place."

"That easy?" Henry asked.

Riley bit at his lower lip. "I know you must be thinking what kind of coward runs off and leaves his family with folks like that."

Henry shook his head. "I wasn't thinking no such thing. I reckon they didn't give you much choice."

"No choice that ended above ground. There was ten of us when we left the mill. I'm the only one of the group left."

"And now you want to go back?" Henry asked.

Riley nodded his head. "I'm going back. I have to try."

Henry took a final puff from the pipe then tapped it against the log he was sitting on, knocking loose the ashes. "Well, if you're looking to travel east into trouble, then I reckon I should go with you."

Riley looked at him, his face scowled. "And why would you do that?"

The old man stood and pointed out and across the valley at the gates of Crabtree. He watched as three men left the gates of the compound below. They rode stiff-backed and high in the saddle. Instead of rifles in sheaths, they carried them across their chests. Henry smiled, knowing who the men were and thankful they were still alive. He watched as they guided the horses down the road and up an embankment toward the railroad bed. He stood and pointed toward the men on horseback. "See those riders down there? I know 'em and I reckon they'll be going east too. I think they'll be good ones to join up with."

"And why is that?" Riley scoffed.

Henry laughed, kicking snow over the fire. "Let's just say we hate a lot of the same people."

CHAPTER 4

They were escorted down a tight corridor, past hallway intersections and unmarked doors. Light bulbs hung from the ceiling by thin wires. The walls were drab and made entirely of concrete. At the end of the hallway, a uniformed soldier removed a keyring from his pocket and unlocked a thick, steel door. The soldier pulled down on a heavy handle and swung the door open, revealing a staircase leading up. Before Brad could ask where it went, another soldier stepped into view. The man was carrying an MP5 close to his chest. "Sergeant, if you could follow me," the man said, looking Brad in the eye.

Brad turned his head to look at Chelsea, giving her a reassuring smile before stepping through the doorway and following the guard up the stairs. There were no windows in the stairway and, as before, the passage was dimly lit. The soldier spoke over his shoulder without turning his head. "This was once a cable conduit for the plant's servers. When we moved in, we ripped it all out to make room; now it's a fast track to the control room."

"Interesting." Brad looked at Chelsea and rolled his eyes. "Where exactly are we going?"

The soldier stopped at another locked door and turned back to face him. "The senator has been eager to meet you."

"He's in there?" Brad asked.

The soldier grinned and rapped his knuckles on the door. After a brief pause, there was the clunking of a lock, and the door pulled out into a larger room. The soldier waved Brad and Chelsea ahead then secured the door behind them. Brad turned, watching as they quickly relocked the door.

"It's all for our safety," an older white-haired man said from the front of the room.

Brad took a side step and scanned the space. They were in a large rectangular office. Workstations covered with dust spanned the room, and dead computer monitors covered the desks. Old whiteboards and faded engineering charts were pinned to the walls. Brad examined the white-haired man, who stood in front of the large window at the end of the room. Wearing burgundy slacks and a grey jacket that didn't match in texture or color, Brad found himself thinking the man looked more like a high school math teacher than a senator.

"We learned the hard way that locked doors are the best way to prevent the spread of infection. You'll find a lot of barriers here." The old man waved Brad forward. "Welcome to Coldwater Station. I don't normally greet visitors up here, but I thought you'd want to see this." He pointed toward the window. "What do you see down there, Sergeant?"

Brad stepped closer and looked through the window. He was in a high control room that overlooked the former factory floor. He could view the open market he'd seen the night before when they'd arrived. He looked to the old man and said, "A refugee camp?"

The old man shook his head. "No, Sergeant, this is a community... a chance at a fresh start."

Brad frowned. "You can call me Brad. I'm not sure I'm a sergeant anymore."

"Oh, I would have to disagree; we can't afford to lose anyone from the ranks right now." He looked at Brad's soured expression and quickly changed course. "Men like you, people like us, are the only chance those people have. The infected are now a greater threat than ever, Sergeant. How do you suppose we fight it without soldiers?"

Brad rubbed his chin and took a quick look at Chelsea before turning back to the senator. "I think there has been a misunderstanding on why we are here."

The senator turned away and walked toward a desk. Removing a stack of papers, he flipped through them before identifying a page and separating it from the stack. "There is no confusion as to why you are here. You claimed to have been working with Texas; you said you killed the one they called General Carson."

Brad sighed and moved to a wall, leaning against it, still looking down into the community below him. "Yeah, Carson is dead. But I wouldn't say I was working with Texas. They just happened to be a part of it."

"Where are they now?" the senator asked. "We've been waiting on their arrival. They promised us help."

Brad tilted his head toward his shoulder. "I don't know. Virginia, I guess. Look, we didn't come here as any sort of emissaries for Texas. We came because we heard Michigan was safe. If I was wrong about that, then just turn us around."

"No." The senator shook his head, suddenly aggravated. "You said you were with them, that you killed General Carson. Listen, maybe you want to put all of that behind you, but this is important to us." He pointed to the market below. "It's important to them."

Chelsea—having remained quiet the entire time—finally stepped forward and looked at the senator. "There is something you aren't telling us."

The senator put his hands up in frustration. "What do you want me to tell you? It's no secret that we've had problems with raiders from the East. The infected are back, massing all along the wall. You see that down there?" he said, pointing to the window. "A month ago, I had over forty colonies just like it. Now I have half of that. If Texas doesn't get here soon, I don't know how long before we are all gone."

"But, Carson is dead," Brad said.

The senator laughed. "Son, I'm starting to think your cornbread ain't all the way cooked in the middle. I don't know... maybe you're tired from the travel or maybe it's the stress, so I'll slow down and spell it out for you." He took steps closer and faced the window. "Without the help from Texas, all of those people down there are going to die. This New Republic—or whatever they're calling it today—in the East, it's planted and rooted in deep and has destroyed what we once called the Midwest Alliance. They've caused damage to the walls and have the infected spun up, leaving nobody left to guard them. They have raiders out there raising hell, trying to get whatever they can from us. Carson was just part of it, drawing a path of destruction to the south. His death won't even slow them down."

"What do they want?"

The senator let out a long sigh and pursed his lips.

"They aren't like us; they want it all. They want the land, the resources, the people. There is a misunderstanding amongst the citizens here. They think I refused to surrender... refused to join the Republic. They think that's why all of this is happening." He took in another deep breath and clenched his fist. "There is no surrender, only submission. Ohio tried to surrender to those animals, and they are gone now. Same as Indiana—all of it is gone. They don't want surrender; they want us to give up what we've made here and move east."

Brad's jaw began to hang with the realization of the trouble they were in. "How much time do we have?" he asked, his voice low and serious.

The old man rubbed the stubble on his chin. "Their scouts have been spotted on the highway less than twenty miles from here." He turned and looked Brad hard in the eyes. "It's not only that. They've broken parts of the wall and led infected to it. The infected we can handle in small groups, but in the massive numbers we've spotted, it's impossible. It keeps us behind the walls and inside, unable to support the colonies farther east."

Brad looked at Chelsea then back at the senator. "If the enemy can move with Primals on the loose, then so can you. Are you saying you abandoned the positions east of here?"

"We were cut off from them," the man said, his voice growing angry at the accusation.

Brad scoffed. "Whatever helps you sleep at night. Like I said, I think there has been a misunderstanding as to why we are here. I'll be gathering my gear and departing soon. I'm sure Texas will be sending people here shortly; you can explain your failures to them."

Before the senator could respond, sounds of automatic weapons fire echoed from somewhere outside the building.

As if someone had pressed a mute button, everything became silent—including the crowd below on the floor. There were two loud mechanical clicking sounds, and the lights went out. A third click, and the room lit with a low red glow.

"What's happening?" Chelsea asked.

Brad moved to the overlook window. In the crowded market below, he couldn't see a single person. Lights were cut off, the shanty doors all closed and secured. The large entry doors at the end of the factory floor were sealed shut. Brad panned the shops; goods still lay on tables and shelves, but it was like the people had vaporized. He spun toward the senator, looking at him for a response.

"It's the attack protocol," he whispered, holding a finger to his ear. Soon the sounds of weapon fire were joined by the pitch of a siren. "It's the infected," he said, letting out a sigh of relief.

"How do you know?" Chelsea asked.

The senator looked to the guard at the back of the room. The uniformed man put a hand to the door and rattled it, confirming it was locked. "It's the attack proto-col. We cut the lights, get quiet, and lock the doors. The sirens are let off to guide the infected into a designated kill box."

Chelsea moved closer to Brad. "Why lock the doors?" she said.

"It's like protecting the compartments of a battleship; we seal everything off to limit the spread of infection."

"And just like the colonies to the east, you sacrifice parts of the body to save yourself."

The man shook his head furiously. "It's not like that at all."

The gunfire outside raged and was soon joined by

explosions. The senator's face went pale. Brad quickly recognized the fear. "What was that? Not part of the protocol, is it?"

The senator ignored the question, shook his hand at the guard, and pointed to a different bolted door on the far side of the room. "Open it; we have to go."

"What happened to the battleship?" Brad said sarcastically.

"It doesn't work against people. People have always been more dangerous than the infected."

The guard unbolted the door and swung it in, revealing a set of stairs going up. The senator looked back at Brad and said, "My men will escort you back to your room. You'll be safe there."

Brad could see in the man's eyes that he was lying. "And what about you?"

An explosion shook the building, and more gunfire ripped from outside. The senator shook his head. "I have to get back to the capital. We'll talk again." The man stepped into the stairway, his guards rushing in behind him. The door shut, and Brad heard the bolt clunk. For a moment, he thought he'd been abandoned with Chelsea in the control room. He heard movement in the other stairwell, a clicking of the lock, and a screech as the door pushed in.

A burly soldier pushed through, his rifle in his hands. Brad recognized the man from the night they'd arrived—Sergeant Rufous Brown from the watch at the gates. The soldier stepped into the room and scanned left to right. "I see our fearless leader has already left us."

Brad was taken aback by the comment. He pointed to the second sealed door and nodded.

Brown scowled. "He'll be back on his helicopter, headed north. We'd all be dead out here if he had his way.

He wants the territories, just doesn't want to defend—"
Another sustained burst of weapons fire turned Brown's
attention back toward the windows. He moved forward and
looked over the encampment on the factory floor then
rushed to the door. "Come on; we have to hurry," he said,
running into the stairwell.

CHAPTER 5

Sean pulled back on the reins, slowing his horse atop the railroad bed. In the distance, he spotted the silhouettes of riders, two men standing aside their mounts, two other horses behind the men carrying packs. Brooks move up beside him; Sean held his position, not speaking and knowing the younger SEAL would make a quick evaluation. Brooks grinned then made a clicking sound with his teeth and used his heels to nudge the horse ahead. "It's Henry," Brooks said.

"Fuckin' A. I like that old man." Joey Villegas called out, rushing his horse forward to greet the newcomers.

Sean grimaced and snapped the reins of his horse, allowing it to follow the others. For a moment, his mind told him it was Brad and Chelsea—and he had been just tired enough to believe it. He was disappointed in it not being them, but still happy to find the old man. They were moving on into unknown territory, and Henry knew the local terrain better than anyone else. Sean followed the group closer and watched Henry stand alongside his horse, holding his pipe between his teeth.

"Was wondering when you all would show up," Henry said, grinning.

"If we knew you were waiting on us, we wouldn't have stopped for breakfast." Brooks eyed the new, red-bearded man up and down. "Looks like you made yourself a friend."

"Yeah, that I did." Henry removed the pipe and tapped ash into the pristine white snow. "He's okay. Name's Riley, survivor from Crabtree; he's just looking for answers, same as us."

Sean rode his horse up alongside the others and stopped. "Survivor, you say?"

Henry licked his teeth and placed the pipe back into his shirt pocket before stepping into the stirrup and mounting his horse. "He's missing people out east, and I offered to help him out. I reckon'd you all would be traveling the same way, so no reason we can't ride together."

Sean cast suspicious eyes on the stranger. As the big man mounted his own horse, he looked back to Henry. "He got a voice of his own?"

The red-bearded man grinned. "I got plenty to say, if you want to hear it."

Sean looked the man up and down, his eyes stopping on a revolver carried in a gun belt. "You some kind of cowboy?" Sean said, pointing at the handgun.

"It ain't loaded. You all don't happen to have any .357, do ya?"

Sean ignored the question and locked eyes with him. "If you're a survivor, why are you out here beyond the walls of Crabtree?"

Riley shrugged his shoulders and shifted his weight in the saddle, the leather creaking as he moved. "I used the attack to escape and found the old man here up in the mountain this morning."

30

"Escaped? So you were a prisoner then?" Brooks asked, moving up beside them.

The man nodded. "I was taken from my home out east and used as a laborer. They told me they'd kill my family if I didn't go with them."

Sean eyed the man, his teeth clenched before relaxing and dipping his chin. He turned toward Henry. "If you vouch for him, then I guess there is no reason we shouldn't ride together. But tell me, how do you know we're headed in the same direction?"

"Just a hunch," Henry said, turning his horse onto the railroad bed, the others falling in with him. "I figured you'd be going east to finish what you started. Why else retrace your steps from a few nights ago?"

Brooks spat on the ground and let his horse move up beside Henry and Sean so they were now riding three abreast. Joey lagged back, covering the rear, and Riley rode in the front with the pair of pack horses. "We were separated from a man on the train; we're looking for him," Brooks said.

Henry lifted his brow. "Yeah? Which one?"

"Brad," Brooks answered quickly.

"The soldier, aye? Well, he seemed capable enough. I'm sure he'll be okay."

"Yeah," Brooks said, adjusting his rifle in his grip. "What about you? What's the story, old man? Where you been holing up?"

Henry let the reins lie across his lap as his hands rested in his pockets. He spoke slowly, explaining how he'd met Riley up on the overlook and how Riley was in search of his family. He omitted any parts about working for the raiders, not sure of how the boys would react. The men rode on in silence, following the tracks, until Riley stopped ahead, pulling back on the reins of his horse and holding up his hand.

"What do you see?" Henry asked, moving up.

Riley pointed to the low ground to the left of the raised railroad bed they were traveling on. Below, the snow and vegetation were trampled and packed hard. Henry slid off his horse and pulled his rifle from its scabbard. As he moved toward the spot, he could see that the other men were already fanning out, posting for security. He grinned, knowing he was traveling with professionals. Stepping closer, he took a knee at the embankment. The snow was white and wet with the temperatures rising, allowing him to see boot prints and markings from bare feet.

He felt Brooks move up beside him. "There's a lot of them," he whispered. "All headed east."

"Primals." Henry bit at his lower lip. "Fresh too; the tracks aren't covered up from the snowfall yesterday."

"How many you think?" Brooks asked.

"A hundred, maybe more."

Brooks scratched at the back of his neck. "Something I don't get though. Why are they all going east? Crabtree is just a few miles away; why not go there?"

"Chasing raiders," Riley called out.

Henry turned and saw the big bearded man standing behind him, looking over the same trail. Brooks rose from his crouch and walked closer to him. "What raiders? I walked this same railroad bed with women and children days ago. We didn't see anyone out here."

"Yeah," Riley muttered. "Carson's men—or what's left of 'em. They were probably hiding in the woods waiting for things to cool down some then headed out, same as us. I imagine some will be bleeding and wounded. Probably picked up a tail, and you know how the infected are: where there's one, there's always more."

Brooks nodded his approval at the assessment. "How do you know so much about Carson's people? You said you were just a laborer. Is there more to it than that?"

Riley turned and looked at Henry who shrugged. "I spent enough time with his people to know they're cowards, and to know they'd run."

"Time?" Brooks said.

"Yeah, *time*," Riley spat back. "They took my family hostage and held me prisoner for close to a year."

"I see." Brooks turned back to the packed trail in the snow. "This family... it's the same one you're after now?"

Riley didn't speak, looking away from the trail.

"And you know where they're at?" Sean said, moving up behind them.

"I got a good idea," Riley grunted. The man pointed down at the trail below them. "So, what about that?"

Brooks shrugged and re-slung his rifle, moving back to his horse. "Well, this doesn't change much. We keep in the same direction, but you hold back with them pack horses; I'll ride point now."

CHAPTER 6

COLDWATER COMPOUND, MICHIGAN SAFE ZONE

The sounds of the fighting were muffled in the subbasement. Brad had his rifle again and was running down the hallway with Chelsea, following other soldiers to the end of the corridor. "Where are we going?" Brad shouted. Brown slowed as they reached a locked door at the end of the hallway. Soldiers were stacked up against it. One of the men pounded on the door and waited for the coded response from the other side before turning a key and unlocking it.

As soon as the door was opened, others filed into the stairwell, moving up. Brown turned to Brad. "Something has the infected riled up; they're hitting us all along the east perimeter. What's worse though, someone is out there lobbing mortars at us. My men can keep the infected at bay, but those damn mortars are punching holes in my security fences."

Brad scowled. "Where does this put us?" he said, glancing at Chelsea.

"I have to get back to the Tactical Operations Center, and I plan on bringing you two along with me. The captain says not to let you out of my sight, so I guess you're stuck with me."

Chelsea hit the bolt release on her rifle, racking a round, and looked back at Brown. "Can we just get to wherever it is we're going?"

The sergeant cracked a smile. "Stay behind me," he said, moving into the stairs.

Brad went to move, but Chelsea pushed in ahead of him, leaving Brad to close the rear. Inside the stairwell, the gunfire was amplified, and in addition, he could now hear the infected. Daylight burst into the stairwell as they turned onto the last landing. Brown took a bounding step outside with Chelsea close on his heels.

Outside, Brad could see uniformed men pressed up against a log half-wall. They were firing into a series of chain link fences that were lined with twisted bodies of the infected. Some were farther up the fence, tangled in strands of heavy barbed wire. A shrill whistle and the crack of an explosion to their front spit dirt, snow, and blood at them as a mortar round impacted in the middle of the horde just feet from the perimeter fence. Brad crouched down and looked forward. He could see there wasn't just one fence—or hadn't been. The men were at a log wall; beyond that was a twelve-foot-tall chain link fence, a short snow-covered dog run, then a second chain link that was currently bowed in and full of holes.

A corporal on the wall saw Brown and turned toward him. "Sergeant, they've breached the outer wire; they're inside the dog run, and they'll have us surrounded soon. We'd like to pop the fire pots to draw them away."

Brown frowned and rubbed his forehead. "What's the captain have to say about it?"

The corporal shook his head. "Sergeant, the TOC was

hit by direct mortar fire. We haven't been able to reach them."

"Well, hell." Brown ducked as another mortar struck to their front. "Get the pots ready to go on my word. We only have one go at them, so we have to make sure we have their main body in range before we use it. Get the fifty cal teams set up and standing by."

The corporal clenched his teeth and nodded. "Roger that." The man turned away and ran along the log fence.

"What's going on here?" Brad asked.

"Primals have breached our fences, they're filling the dog run, and we've lost contact with the TOC."

"Sounds great," Brad said.

Brown grimaced. "Yeah, that's terrific, but don't sweat it. We've got a contingency plan, and it's time to use it."

Brad stared at him. "I picked up on that, but exactly what the hell is it?"

Another mortar went off to the front, kicking mud and Primal parts into the air. Brown guided them closer to the low wall and took a knee. "The infected are attracted to bright lights; for whatever reason they love a fireworks show."

Brad shook his head in frustration. "I'm aware. I was born during the day, but it wasn't yesterday."

The big sergeant sighed. "We have pots buried all around the perimeter. They're filled with gas and oil, triggered by artillery simulators. We light off one of those bad boys, and it's like ringing a dinner bell. These things drop everything and run at the pots. Attached to every pot we have a pair of heavy machine guns dialed in for intersecting fire."

"You've done this before?" Chelsea asked.

Brown nodded. "A couple times. It's really messy, but it works."

"Won't it attract even more of them?" she said.

Brown nodded. "Yeah, but not any more than a full-on gunfight. We've never had an infected attack like this before, though—an attack supported by whatever it is out there shooting at us. If we can't get those mortars to stop, more will just come in and replace the ones we kill."

There was another impact, this one right on the inner fence. The steel bar holding the fence bowed in but still held back the mass of infected. Brad turned away as he was pelted in the face with bits of frozen dirt. "Hold off on lighting the pots. From the frequency of those blasts, there can't be but one team out there. You have any armor?"

Brown nodded his head. "I've got a police MRAP. No crew-served weapons, but it'll still stop bullets."

"Put some troops on the roof and see if they can get us a location on the mortar team, then get me a couple shooters and that MRAP. I'll stop those mortars for you."

Chelsea put her hand on Brad's shoulder. "What are you doing?"

"Keeping us alive. If that fence falls, we're all dead." He turned back to Brown. "You going to get me that truck?"

"Roger that, Sergeant. I'll take you to it."

BROWN HAD BEEN HOLDING BACK... they didn't have an MRAP—they had a fleet of Mine Resistant Ambush Protected vehicles. At least a half dozen in a mix of differing configurations. Some painted black, others olive green with a variety of police markings on them. Brad walked down a darkened aisle in the basement converted into a below-ground parking structure. A man in green coveralls was wrestling with a compartment on the side of a black painted vehicle with "Special Response" painted on the side in bold white letters. "It's a six-by-six Cougar. You familiar with it, Sergeant?" Brown asked.

"Yeah, I know what makes it tick." Brad looked left and right for a garage door. "How do I get it out of here?"

The man in coveralls turned around, wiping grease from his hand with a rag. "There's a dugout at the far end of the structure. Get mounted up, and I'll show you the way."

"You?" Brad asked.

"Yeah, you ain't taking my girl unless I come along. I spent almost a year tracking these down, wandered over half the state; I'm not about to lose one."

Brad looked up and down the row of armored vehicles. "You found these?"

"Yes, Sergeant." The man pointed to an armored Humvee with plates welded to the windshield. "It started with *Sue* down there on the end. My team's been hitting up every police station in the directory, looking for these old battle cats."

Brown laughed, moving in from out of the shadows. "Don't let Palmer scare you off. He's a good wrench, and he knows his way around outside the wire."

Brad nodded and extended his hand to the mechanic. "Okay then, get everyone on board, and let's get outside. Palmer since this is your *girl*, you drive."

The man smiled with stained teeth. "I wouldn't have it any other way. Don't want any of you grunts rolling my girl over again. Last time she was out of commission for a month."

"Whatever," Brad said, moving to the passenger door. He swung open the heavy door and pulled himself into the seat, a sudden case of déjà vu coming over him. For an instant, his mind was back in the deserts of Afghanistan. He closed his eyes tight and opened them slowly. He wasn't in Afghanistan, and it wasn't Primals lobbying mortars at their Forward Operating Base. He was as close to home as he'd been in years, and people were still trying to kill him.

"You okay, Brad?" Chelsea asked from the compartment behind him.

He nodded. "Yeah, just thinking about the good old days." He looked to Palmer beside him, who already had the vehicle started. Brad leaned left and surveyed the space, watching a well-worn soldier enter from the back and secure the rear hatches. The big soldier didn't speak, but he carried himself like a veteran, and he had the scars and the stare to go with them. He had long black hair falling from under his Kevlar helmet. His MultiCam uniform was faded and patches covered the elbows. Brad squinted, looking for a name tape or rank insignia but found none.

Chelsea was just behind him, with Brown in a drop seat across from her. The soldier in the rear took a back seat, sitting with his rifle near an open firing port in the sides of the vehicle. Brown caught his confused stare. "Palmer removed some of the exterior armor and cut in those firing ports."

Palmer looked back and nodded. "Removing larger armor plates opened up the vision ports and lightened her up. But don't worry, Sergeant. The infected won't never get in Bertha; she's a mean girl, and even though we don't have a big gun mounted up top, those firing ports are a game changer."

"I see," Brad said. "You got us a location on those mortars?"

Brown nodded. "Our spotters on the roof gave us a good

direction, and I have an idea of where they're set up. There's an old corner market about 1,500 meters in that direction, beyond the high trees."

Brad put a hand to the stubble on his chin and turned back to the front. "Sounds about right for a sixty mike-mike. Palmer, take us out."

"On it," the man said, rolling the heavy vehicle forward. Taking a left, he drove down the drive to a narrow ramp built of earth and old lumber. He centered the Cougar and beat the horn until a man opened a door and ran out, waving at the vehicle. He grabbed the pull handle of a sliding door and ran it open. Light poured into the basement and Palmer mashed the accelerator, launching the Cougar up the ramp. Just as the last of the vehicle cleared the exit, the door was shut behind them. The Cougar raced out onto a gravel road then made a hard right onto a snow-covered access road that put them in the dog run between the two perimeter fences.

Surveying the area, Brad could see they'd left the factory somewhere on the back side, away from the attack. He couldn't see an exit. "How do we get out?" Brad asked.

"We have a sally port on each end of the fence," Palmer answered. "It'll be dangerous opening the gate with the wire breached and the outside full of them zombies, so I have a proposal."

"Yeah, why am I thinking it's going to be something stupid, or you wouldn't be asking?" Brad said.

Palmer smiled and looked over his shoulder at Brown. "I like this guy." Palmer's face turned serious. "I intend to drive Bertha around to the front and run her right through the breach in the wire."

Chelsea gasped. "Are you crazy?!"

Palmer nodded. "Well yeah, but that's beside the

point." He slowed as he made another hard series of turns within the fenced area. "We have at least three breaches in the outer wire, one big hole right in the front. We have zombies in the dog runs; they'll be all over those gates, and why risk getting out of Bertha here to open them? Or worse, destroying the gates by ramming them."

Chelsea shook her head. "There has to be a better way than ramming through the gate; what if we get stuck?"

Brad stared ahead, seeing the mass pour through the hole in the outer fence. "He's right. And it'll lead the Primals away; they'll follow us," Brad said.

"Ha!" Palmer exclaimed. "Told you I like this one. Exactly... it'll lead them away. Those fire pots and machine guns help lure them into kill zones, but the fires always bring in more. We can do better; we can grab the attention of the mass and lead them right back to that mortar team."

"Let's do it," Brad said.

CHAPTER 7

After several miles, Brooks paused and rode back toward the team. They were at a tall bend in the railroad tracks. The men recognized the area from traveling through the low canyon days earlier, and it also being the place where they'd attacked Carson's train. Brooks held his position at the bend and waited for the others to get in close before he spoke. Joey and the new man, Riley, stayed back covering their trail.

"It's gone," Brooks said in a low voice.

"What's gone?" Sean asked.

"The train; it's gone."

Sean looked toward the path they were riding. "How far ahead did you ride?"

"A mile, maybe a bit more. It's gone. I know where we left it; I remember the spot where we unloaded the civilians. I'm telling you, it's not there."

Sean laughed, shaking his head side to side. "Well, I'd hope you wouldn't accidently go past a big ass train, but it didn't just vanish."

Moving his horse to the outside of the others, Henry

looked down into the low ground. The others followed his eyes and could see where the snow was trampled from the infected horde traveling in the same direction. "When you left the train, did you damage the locomotive?"

Brooks shook his head. "We got separated. The bastards put a bomb on a coupler somewhere ahead of us. Brad was on the front when it went off. The rest of us got cut loose from the engine."

"I see," Henry said. "So it appears, whoever took off with that engine came back for the rest of their train."

Brooks scowled. "You saying Brad is dead, old man? You think he failed to accomplish his mission?"

"Not necessarily," Henry said, reaching into his shirt pocket for the pipe. He went to pack it but looked down at the Primal tracks in the snow and thought better of it. He put the unlit pipe between his lips and looked to Brooks. "He might have finished what needed doing, stopped that train, and moved on. I imagine locomotives ain't easy to come by, so whoever owned it, probably came looking when it never returned home."

"So, what do we do now then?" Brooks said, this time looking at Sean.

The SEAL chief shrugged his shoulders. "Nothing's changed. We came looking for Brad, so let's keep looking." Sean's horse whinnied and spun around. Sean grabbed at the reins and dug in his heels to straighten it.

"You okay there, Chief?" Brooks said with a grin.

Henry put a finger to his lips. "The horse is telling us something."

Sean's mount calmed, but took steps back, nervously snorting. "And what exactly is she telling us?" he said in a low voice, his free hand rubbing the horse's neck.

Henry shook his head and pulled his rifle from the sheath. "No quick movements, but we ain't alone."

"Primals?" Brooks said, tightening the grip on his own rifle.

Casually looking up at the high ridge behind him, Henry squinted and said, "I had a feeling about something for the last mile or so."

"A feeling?" Sean asked.

Henry nodded and pointed to a pile of broken ice and snow where the canyon met the railroad bed. "These clumps of snow on the ground? They came from up there... Could be natural, just normal snowfall, sliding off the edges above—"

"Or could be someone knelt there and knocked it loose," Brooks interrupted.

"People then?" Sean asked.

Henry smiled and looked up again before turning back to Sean. "Yeah and more just ahead of us. I caught a glimpse of him just as your horse stirred. They're watching us."

Sean rubbed his chin. "I got it. Thoughts, Henry?

Without turning again, the old man tilted his head toward the high ridge. "Worst case, something is up there. And if it's hostile people, they've got the high ground and we're trapped."

"So... what? We just keep moving?"

Henry nodded his head. "We're in a canyon, only one way in or out, and I have no intentions of turning back."

"Push through then?" Sean whispered.

"Yeah, but call your boys up and have 'em ride two-by-two," Henry whispered. "I'll be leading the way now. You all see me run or go down, you better be ready to fight."

"What are you planning?" Sean asked.

Smiling, Henry said, "Not much daylight left. We need

to find cover and get off this trail. I plan on seeing who's hiding around that corner, or keep riding until they stop us."

Brooks spoke low. "I don't know, Chief. What's to stop them from killing us?"

"They could have already shot us, if that's what they wanted." Without waiting for a response, the old man nudged his horse forward with a click of his mouth. Sean turned to Brooks. "Tell the boys to stay close; I'll take slack behind the old timer."

Sean kicked his horse, moving ahead and riding wide to the left so he could keep his eyes on Henry as the old man rounded the bend in the canyon. He expected to see a roadblock or a man blocking their path, but there was nothing, just more snow. Sean rode on and moved his horse right as he turned the corner. He looked at the ground near the canyon and could see dry patches where a man could potentially walk and avoid leaving tracks in the snow.

Ahead, Sean saw Henry's posture change. The old right man's elbow pushed out as he let his lever-action rifle hang unthreatening, low in the pocket of his arm the way a duck hunter would carry a shotgun. Sean scanned up and could see why. There were silhouettes high on the ridge above them. Two, maybe three, men dressed in flannel and hunting camo were attempting to stay hidden, but with the sun low in the sky, they were sky lining themselves on the high ridge. Sean never would have seen them if he wasn't looking.

Just fifty feet ahead, Henry pulled his reins back and sat high in his saddle with the rifle across his legs. Sean cautiously closed the distance until he was right beside him. He dropped his right arm and flashed a palm to the riders behind him, signaling for them to keep their distance.

"What is it, Henry?" Sean whispered.

"I think we're about to find out," the old man replied. "They're just to your left."

A twig snapped and three men holding rifles stepped from the thick cover of the trees. Sean cursed himself; he'd allowed his eyes to focus so much on the high ridge that he'd missed those in cover. Sean let his horse turn naturally to face the men on the ground. They were tall but not husky. One was older with deep lines at the corners of his eyes, the other two, far younger and maybe in their twenties. They all shared a family resemblance with narrow cheeks, rusty-red hair, and green eyes. The men eyed him suspiciously, but they carried their rifles at the low ready.

"You're a long way from your mountain, Henry," the eldest of the three said.

"I see even Armageddon can't kill off you damn gingers." Henry grunted then pulled out his pipe and placed it in the corner of his mouth.

The man on the ground grinned. "Not all of us, anyway. You know you shouldn't be smoking that. The zombies can smell it for miles around."

"You see it smoking?" Henry scoffed, rolling his eyes.

Sean looked at Henry quizzically. "You know each other?"

Henry sighed. "Yeah, I know him." He moved his rifle and let it drop back into the leather sheath. "This is Eli Baker and his sons." Henry turned back toward the man on the ground. "If I had to take a guess, those are your shit head nephews up on the ridge."

Eli laughed. "You'd be guessing right. Who you riding with Henry? You looking for trouble?"

The old man spat on the ground. "Screw you, Eli." He shifted in his saddle, looking behind him then ahead on the trail. "So, you going to take us back to that dump of a ranch of yours? I got some hungry soldiers from Dan Cloud's place. We could use a place to spend the night."

The red-haired man locked eyes with Sean then turned back to Henry. "I reckon I can spare a meal for your horses," the man said with a grin.

CHAPTER 8

The MRAP lunged forward into the dog run, impacting hard with the crowd ahead of it. Primals bounced off the tubular steel brush guard as others were caught in the heavy-tread tires and pulled to the ground. The MRAP slowed but continued to lurch forward as the vehicle's big wheels ground through bodies and caught traction on the frozen ground. Brad flinched at the sounds of bones breaking and skulls popping under the weight of the seventeen-ton vehicle. He cringed, knowing that each of the snaps and pops was a once-human body being destroyed.

"She does okay in hordes of zombies if you keep the speed up," Palmer said, not taking his head off the Primal-covered path ahead. The man held the wheel steady like he was driving through thick drifts of snow as they approached the break in the wire. "The turns can get tricky; these vehicles have such a high center of gravity they want to tip on ya in a sharp turn."

Brad grunted and reached out for a handhold to steady himself as the vehicle bounced over another bunch of infected. "Well, let's not roll over then," he said, gasping for air after being thrust back into the seat.

Palmer made the turn through the break in the fence and had begun to straighten the wheel when a mortar struck just to their front, tossing mud and blood across the windshield. Palmer flipped on the wipers, and when the grime cleared, Brad saw a bit of wire frag embedded in the glass block to his front.

"Son of a bitch!" Palmer shouted, pointing at the chunk of broken glass. "You know how hard it is to find replacement glass for these things?" He cussed again. Mashing the gas and cutting the wheel through the mob, he navigated into the open ground before cutting back toward the field full of infected. Another mortar struck just to their right. Palmer ignored it, keeping the MRAP on course. He shook his head saying, "It's a real cowardly way to attack a place, letting the zombies do all the heavy lifting."

Brown pulled himself into the cab. "Can those bombs hurt us?" he shouted over the roar of the engine and screaming infected outside.

"Nope," Palmer answered without looking back. "Even a direct hit from those little mosquito bombs won't hurt this girl. It would take some real arty to penetrate big Bertha— No offense, ma'am," he said, throwing a halfhearted nod toward Chelsea. The driver cut the wheel again; this time Brad felt it lean to one side before Palmer corrected and straightened them out. They approached a snow-covered incline and Brad could feel the wheels slip as they pushed through the mass of Primals and deep icy snow.

The ride grew smoother and, leaning forward, Brad could see they'd moved over the high embankment and onto a blacktop road covered with a thin layer of snow. Palmer kept the bearing for another two hundred feet before he pointed at the door mirror on Brad's side of the MRAP. The factory was fading behind them.

"They're following just like we wanted," Palmer said. "Market is just ahead. You want me to pull right up on it?"

"You sure they don't have anything that can hurt us?" Brad asked.

Palmer shook his head. "Only thing I'm sure of is if you unass this truck, them damn zombies will be making a quick meal out of you."

Brad acknowledged the comment and dipped his head forward. "Hell then, yeah, take us right up to it. Getting smoked by anti-tank weapons gotta beat getting eaten by a Primal."

"I knew I liked you." Palmer laughed.

The man slowed the vehicle as he approached an intersection that was only identifiable by a stop sign flapping in the wind. Palmer came to a hard stop, ensuring the Primals were still following, before he cranked the wheel hard and turned them onto a road heading north. "Store is just ahead. Used to be a Mom and Pop gas station. Pumps are all dry now. Store was picked over for anything useful months ago. Mostly zombies will be lurching around, but keep an eye on the tree lines for the fast ones."

Brad looked in the mirror and could see that the mass of infected were still pursuing them when the vehicle again slowed and veered into the market's parking lot. It wasn't much: a blue-sided building with a pair of gas pumps out front. Every window in the place was broken. A pair of burned-out cars sat rusted in parking spaces. In the front, the large storefront was destroyed, the doors missing and shelves knocked over so that it was possible to see deep into the building. Even the glass doors on the coolers were shattered, allowing a clear view behind them.

Looking to the roofline, he couldn't see any movement. Brad ordered Palmer to stop, and he climbed into the back of the MRAP.

"We can't hold long," Palmer said. "Bertha has got horsepower, but let too many of them things wrap up around us and get to pushing and grinding... well, too many of these things and she starts to lose traction in the gore, if you know what I mean."

Brad frowned. "Yeah, I think I know," he said, moving to the center of the MRAP and reaching up for the hatch. The military-issue turret had been removed, and what used to be a glass-block-covered cupola had been replaced with a simple steel hatch with three hundred sixty degrees of viewing ports.

Brad took a quick scan and couldn't see any infected closer than a half mile, although they were closing on them fast. "We clear?" he called out to those below him.

"Shit no!" Palmer screamed back. "Those things are getting closer by the second. If you're intending on doing something stupid, you only a got a minute or two before they're all over us."

"Okay. Well, cover me from those firing ports; I'm just going to open up for a closer look." Brad waited for a response from the veteran trooper looking through windows below before he pulled back on the lock bar and pushed the hatch up behind him. Slowly, he lifted his head up and into the brisk cold air. He could only hear the distant gunfire and the screams from the approaching Primals. He panned left and right and saw sets of heavy vehicle tracks in the snow.

He dipped back into the compartment and pointed. "Palmer, take us over there."

Leaning forward to see the ground ahead, the driver did

as instructed and stopped just over the tracks. Brad took another scan of the market. The building was a total loss and empty. He could see all the way through to the back walls. There were multiple tracks where at least three trucks had turned around. No boot prints on the ground, so they must have parked close to the building's walls then climbed directly to the roof—maybe using a ladder. Finding no sign of the mortar team, Brad pulled back into the vehicle, slammed the hatch shut, and returned to his seat.

"What do you make of the tracks, Palmer?" Brad asked.

The driver strained against the windshield and said, "Pickup trucks, civilian, probably 4x4 and loaded heavy if you wanted my full opinion."

"You think it's the mortar crew?"

"Who else would it be? They probably saw us coming and hauled ass. Which also indicates they ain't got weapons that can kill us when we're all buttoned up," Palmer said. "You want me to follow them?"

Brad shook his head. "Not a good idea to follow them. They'd lead us into an ambush. They had to have seen us coming, and it's what I would do."

Brown leaned forward again. "But like the man said... we're armored up. They can't touch us."

The soldier in the back laughed. "Yeah, frigging armor, something as small as a bucket of paint thrown at the windshield can blind and disable us. If they left tracks it's because they wanted to be followed," the man grunted. "They're gone; let them run."

Brad pursed his lips and nodded at hearing the solider speak for the first time, agreeing with his assessment. "He's right. We've lost the element of surprise, and we're too small to go after them."

Palmer pointed to the slow-moving zombies that were

beginning to fill the lot and surround the MRAP. "Well, we can't go back to the factory, not for a while anyway. Not till we lose this herd."

Brad exhaled and nodded his head in agreement. "You have a suggested hide spot? A place we can hole up in until things die down?"

Palmer grinned. "I know a spot."

"Good, take us there but follow those vehicle tracks for a bit. Cut the trail in a good spot where we can lose this pack. These boys want to be followed, let the creepers follow them. With any luck they'll chew them up in their sleep."

The driver laughed again, shaking his head. "That's savage, Sergeant, downright savage. You sure we ain't related?"

CHAPTER 9

SOUTHERN OHIO, THE DEAD ZONE

The strangers led them beyond the narrow railroad pass and deep into the woods to the north. The trail narrowed to where the horses barely fit between the thick pines. Sean was riding with his rifle cradled in his arms, Henry on the horse just behind him. "Where the hell we going?" Sean asked.

"It's not much farther," Henry answered.

"You trust these people?"

Henry laughed and shook his head at the comment. "What right do we have to be asking for trust? These people don't know you, and you don't know them. If I was in your shoes, I wouldn't trust a one of 'em, because I guarantee that's exactly how Eli's boys are thinking about you right this minute."

This time it was Sean who laughed. "Well, hell if that don't give me a warm and fuzzy feeling."

"Regardless of your degree of fuzziness, their place is just ahead."

Sean watched as the trees began to thin, and they were led down an incline and onto a blacktop county road where grass and small trees were sprouting up through the cracks. They passed several empty and burned-out homes overgrown with weeds and unhedged bushes. Mailboxes sat on the side of the road with doors closed; he imagined what he would find if he opened one. Would there be anything inside? Bills? Birthday cards? How long did life go on before the mail stopped? They passed a house that looked almost completely untouched. A car on flat tires sat in the driveway, and leaf-covered windows reflected light.

"All dead or gone," a man said behind him, looking at the same house. "No point in wondering."

Sean turned to see Eli moving his horse close. The man had been following Sean's stare toward the home. "Did you know them?" Sean asked.

The red-haired man frowned. "Not directly, but we shared a road. I have a ranch just back in those woods. It's no secret to anyone that lived on this road. My place is plenty big enough to support a hundred men, but outside of my family, nobody came knocking on Eli Baker's door."

"Nobody?" Sean asked suspiciously.

Eli shook his head. "Not a one."

"I find that hard to believe," Sean said. "You must be some kind of asshole to have people avoid you even at the end of the world."

Eli laughed and pulled a canteen from his belt. "Hell, you might be right about that. You can believe what you want, mister," Eli said. "I'm telling you, when things went to hell, I called for all of my kin to come join me at the ranch. I sent my son up and down this road telling folks to pack up their shit and come stay with us until things calmed down. I got everything out there... beef, water... plenty for anyone that wants to contribute."

Sean looked at the man, his brow tightening. "Why

would you invite so many? Most folks I know would want to stay hidden."

Shaking his head, Eli continued. "I saw what was going on, saw what was happening on the news. This wasn't some flu that we could hide from. No, I knew right away this was something different. I took inventory of my own situation. I had plenty of food, I had plenty of beds, and I had plenty of guns and ammo, but what I didn't have was people."

"So, you thought you'd recruit them?"

"Nah, nothing like that; just figured the more people I could get on the ranch, the more manpower we'd have. Strength in numbers and all that."

"And you said nobody took you up on the offer?"

Eli took another drink from the canteen before offering it to Sean, who declined. "It was that damn army of yours," he said, putting the canteen back in his belt.

"I'm Navy, not Army," Sean said.

The man grinned and nodded. "Fair enough, but still they're responsible for a lot of dead, if you ask me. They came down this same road in their big covered trucks, rounded people up, and left with 'em. When they were done, there wasn't a single occupied home on this road. Said they were taking folks to a FEMA camp up by Athens, Ohio."

"But they skipped over you?"

"Mostly. Guess with everything that was going on, they didn't have time to argue with a bunch of hillbillies back in the sticks. Their commander told me about all the bad things that would happen to us if we refused to go with them. Told us how if the infected didn't get us, we'd prob-ably starve. Yeah, that son of a bitch all but promised me my family wouldn't survive the winter."

"Well, guess you proved him wrong," Sean said.

"Yeah, hell of a prize, right?" Eli mumbled.

"The FEMA camp... you ever find out what happened to it?"

"Yeah, last spring I took a couple boys up to try and find out." He dipped his head and looked to the shoulder of the road. "The place is a graveyard. Nothing I'd recommend visiting."

Sean nodded. "I don't need the details. I've seen enough overrun camps to last me a lifetime."

Eli sighed and pointed ahead. "We're here."

Sean could see where a trail broke off the blacktop and wound down to a shallow stream hardly a foot deep. One of the younger Baker boys was already leading his horse down to the water. "We use the stream to cover our tracks."

Sean nodded then took his horse onto the narrow path to follow the boy. They turned and rode downstream for close to a mile before exiting onto another trail that jutted out of the water. Sean saw a wooden gazebo, a set of polished picnic tables, and a pair of armed men on the shoreline. Beyond the table were half a dozen RVs and kids running through a field, kicking a ball. One of the Baker boys rode up to the field and dismounted from his horse, laughing with the children.

Eli waved to the guards then pointed to the field. "We got nearly ten families here. Most of 'em my kin; others are friends from up north that came in with family of their own."

Sean looked left and right. "I don't see any walls."

"Don't need 'em; it's the creek. Something about the zombies—they don't like water. The ranch here is set up on a sort of island. The river makes a V about five miles north of here. The creek running along the west side and a wider river to the east join back together about a mile south. All that fresh mountain water wraps right around this ranch like a soggy blanket. We got water on all sides, and we knocked out the only bridge crossing the river. Unless the zombies are actively pursuing someone, they won't cross the water. Only time we got to worry is when it freezes up, but we been lucky so far."

"They're hydrophobic," Sean said.

"Hydrophobic? What? Like rabies?"

"Yeah, something like that. Met a doctor couple years back; he said they share traits with the rabies virus. Mad as hell, but they hate the bright lights and water. Like a rabid wolf, all they want to do is kill and feed."

Eli nodded. "Guess that makes enough sense to me." The man stopped his horse and dismounted, waiting for the others to do the same. They were on a short rise now, and Sean could see a pair of red wooden barns next to a long, two-story ranch house. On the roofs of the buildings were men with scoped rifles. Sean noticed them but didn't comment on it.

Handing the reins of his horse to a younger man, Eli looked at Henry and pointed to the barn farthest from the house. "You can put up your horses and men there. I'll have the boys bring you out some warm water so you can get cleaned up before supper."

Sean went to speak, not liking the idea of being separated and confined to one space, but he could tell from the look on Henry's face that they should just head to the barn. Sean buttoned his lip and stayed put until the Baker men moved off toward the ranch house. Henry looked around then pointed to the barn before leading the way. "He's telling the truth, you know," Henry said.

"About?" Sean asked.

"The Army and the FEMA camps. It's not the first time

I've heard Eli's story. I bumped into him about a year back. He was out looking for survivors. I was out looking for deer. I give Eli a load of shit, but he's good people. 'Bout like Dan Cloud, I reckon."

"How many other people like this are out here?" Sean asked.

Shaking his head, Henry stopped and turned back. "To be honest, I didn't even know the Bakers were still out here. Most of the holdouts are dead or gone, moved on someplace to the north in search of safe areas. I used to know of a half dozen families. Most are gone now." Henry walked into the barn and moved his horse to an empty stall. "I used to drive out this way quite often when the roads were still open. I guess I just stopped after a while."

Sean and the others followed the old man in, beginning the process of clearing gear and saddles from their horses. "What happened to them?" Sean asked as he tossed a heavy saddle over a rail. "The holdouts, I mean."

Henry tipped his head to a side as he thought about a response. He bit at his lower lip and removed a flannel blanket from his horse's back without speaking.

Sean grimaced, saying, "I'm sorry. I guess I know what happened."

The old man turned back, pulling the pipe from his pocket. This time he lit a match to it before putting it to his lips. "It's okay. I don't mind talking about them," he said between puffs. "You know, to be fair, I was spared most of the details. It's like them folks down in Crabtree: one day it was a bustling community, next time I rode past it was gone." Henry left his horse in the stall, then he walked across the barn and found a spot on a bench carved from a wide log. He looked down at his boots and frowned. "But there were others, you know. I wasn't always so lucky. I've lost good people and good friends."

Sean finished with his horse then dropped beside the old man on the bench, waiting for the rest of the men. "I've lost people too; a lot of 'em."

"Aye," Henry said, exhaling smoke. "Let me ask you, Chief—"

Sean shook his head. "Please, call me Sean."

Henry smiled. "Okay, Sean, let me ask you—what the hell are you doing out here?"

With a puzzled expression, Sean tipped his head before looking toward the door at two young boys running into the barn. The kids greeted Henry by name before filling grain sacks and attending to the horses. Henry waited until the boys were out of earshot before looking at Sean for an answer.

Sean shrugged. "What do you mean? You know I'm looking for my man."

Grinning, Henry shook his head. "No, that's bullshit. You could send someone else to do that. You're a capable man; you don't need all of this. You could leave at any time and make an easy life, even in the middle of all this. I don't think you're just looking for your man."

"You don't?"

"Nope. I don't know you very well, but I know your type. I think you're hooked on it. You don't like it none, but you can't rest. Because it's in the downtime that you really consider just how lost you are, just how much you've lost."

Sean forced a laugh. "Why would you think that?"

Henry smiled and looked out the barn door, squinting at the sunlight. "Us warriors all have a type. Like those boys that used to kill each other in Northern Ireland, maybe like them British fellas against the Zulus, or even our own

General at Custer's Last Stand. We always seem to be doing the wrong thing because we can't help but be led into a fight. I tell you what, son, maybe I didn't go off to war like you did, but I still managed to find one. It's just what boys like us do."

Sean stood and rolled his shoulders. "Maybe you're right; guys like us are just drawn to the fight."

Nodding, Henry turned back toward the others. "Come on, fellas. Let's see what sorta grub that ginger is keeping from us," he said loud enough for the others to hear.

CHAPTER 10

NORTHEAST OF COLDWATER COMPOUND, MICHIGAN SAFE ZONE

It had begun to grow dark before they reached Palmer's hiding spot—an out-of-the-way strip mall. Surprisingly, the shop windows were covered with sheets of plywood. The parking lot, instead of being filled with burnt-out and rusted vehicles, was completely empty. Palmer drove into the lot and then circled around to a back-loading dock. He reversed the big vehicle into an elevated bay that had been modified to marry up with the armored vehicle perfectly. "This is my home away from home," he said.

Palmer pulled himself from his seat and moved to the rear compartment. Brad could see that the rugged soldier in the back was closing the firing ports but keeping his weapon ready. "The strip mall is sealed up tight, but you can never be too careful out here in Indian country. I don't worry about the zombies breaking in. They don't have much need for spare parts and diesel, but there are looters out here and the scumbags have been known to leave the gate open when they leave." He chuckled.

The driver gripped a heavy bar and looked to the soldier beside him. The man nodded, expressionless, and Palmer pulled the lever then let the door closest to him swing out. Cold, musty air quickly filled the compartment. The soldier exited, wearing a night vision device lowered down from his helmet. Palmer stayed in the vehicle, waiting until the soldier called the all-clear from inside, and a warm yellow light filled the space outside.

"They've got power?" Brad whispered.

Brown unbuckled himself. "Palmer's got more than that in this little *He-man Primal Haters Clubhouse,*" the big man grunted, working his way to the back and leaving the vehicle.

Chelsea turned and looked at Brad. "You regret volunteering for this yet?"

Brad smiled. "I regret everything I volunteer for. Never again, right? Come on, let's see what I got us in to."

He climbed over the seat and moved through the vehicle, pausing before stepping down onto the concrete floor. He turned back as Chelsea moved in beside him, carrying her rifle and looking deeper into the building. Brad could see that the doors of the MRAP were pinned back and chained to the walls of the building then heavy canvas tarps had been pulled over the doors in a sort of airlock. It wouldn't stop an armed entry, but a Primal would have a hell of a time trying to chew its way in. He turned back and could see that the soldier was gone, having moved out of the empty room they were in.

With the rest of the group, they moved out and into the larger room. It was long and deep, filled with rolls of carpet and flooring samples. The walls were lined with boxes of supplies and random goods—everything from large cans of fruit to motor oil. Palmer was in a corner feeding bits of wood into the mouth of a steel drum converted into a stove. The other soldier was back pulling boxes down from a high shelf, rummaging through canned goods and MRE packets. He came walking back toward the stove with a coffee pot and a sack of ground beans. Brad saw Brown leaning over a desk in the corner, working the controls on a SINGARs radio set.

Chelsea looked at Palmer and called out, "Is there a head?"

Palmer looked at her confused.

"A bathroom," Chelsea said.

"Ahh, yeah, through that office; use the rain barrel to flush," Palmer said before getting back to building the fire.

Chelsea turned to Brad. "I'm going to go clean up. Make sure I get some of that coffee."

Brad nodded and moved to the desk where Brown was working the radio. He was wearing a headset and talking into a microphone. The big man looked up as Brad got closer; he removed the headset and flipped a switch, diverting the sound to a small speaker.

"The attack has stopped, but we can't get out to repair the fences until daylight. Over."

Brown lifted the handset and spoke. "Understood, we are holing up at site Tango with six souls. We ran off the raiders but made no contact. Over."

"Roger that, Rodeo Five. Oscar Rodeo is activating Operation Juliet. Hold position and contact us at daybreak for instructions. Over."

Brown pulled the handset away from his mouth and looked at the other soldier then looked back at the mic. "I'm sorry, Rodeo Six; did you say Juliet? Over."

"Affirmative, Rodeo Five, Operation Juliet is active. Check your timelines. Rodeo Six, out." The radio transmission clicked back to white noise.

"Rodeo Six?" Brad asked. "Who's the commanding officer at the factory?"

Brown shrugged and pulled an old office chair from the wall before plopping into it. "I wish you'd had more time to get a read on things before this happened. It would have been a hell of a lot easier to understand."

"What's Operation Juliet?" Brad asked.

"The senator is evacuating civilians from the camp. They'll convoy north within seventy-two hours. Only a small military presence will stay back to maintain the compound and the gates."

"The senator ordered?" Brad said. "Who exactly is in charge out here?"

"Well, we've got military, local authorities, state government, and then the folks that think they are Feds just because they came up with a title."

Brad rubbed at his chin. "But who is in charge?"

"We've all got responsibilities. When shit goes sideways, they blame us," the man replied. "The man on the radio—Rodeo Six—is the captain you met at the gate a night ago. He's good people. The military runs all ground operations and security for the camp. We also are charged with protecting this sector. The civilian leadership is charged with the people and making sure they stay happy and that the camp doesn't go hungry. They've elected their own little government of sorts. They do a good job of keeping the peace, so us Joes can stick to doing our jobs."

Brand nodded. "And the senator?"

Smirking, Brown shook his head side to side. "Yeah, the senator... Well, he's supposed to keep us resupplied. Sort of acts like a trade baron between colonies, tasked with keeping this fragile thing from falling apart. Now don't get me wrong, he's done a great job, and I can't fault him when he's gotten us this far."

"But?" Brad said, finishing the man's thought. "Don't hold out on me, there is always a but."

"I don't know. Maybe there was nothing he could've done, but some of us think he's been too weak in dealing with the East. Maybe if he'd been stronger from the start, we could've avoided all of this."

Brown looked up as the rugged soldier approached, carrying tin cups and a pot of coffee. "Hot Joe, fellas?" the man said with a deep voice, setting the cups on the desk and topping them off.

Brad asked for an extra for Chelsea as she returned from the back of the room. Then he took his cup and backed away from the desk, surveying the space that was filled with shelves full of goods. He spotted chairs near the now-glowing wood stove.

Brad moved and pulled up a chair near the stove before looking back to Brown. "What do you mean if he'd been stronger? You mean like not evacuating your compound at the first sign of trouble?"

The big sergeant frowned and crossed the space, finding a stool of his own. "It's a lot to explain. When we first set up here, things were okay; nothing to brag about, but at least everyone was trying. We all pulled together to survive. We all shared a common goal, and it wasn't hard to convince people to work together. We constructed the barriers, we took over large grocery stores, warehouses full of food. Took control of fuel stores and power plants. Hell, we had a gravel pit and a cement factory working around the clock. At one time, eighteen trucks and five hundred workers were assigned to building that wall."

"And a beautiful wall it is," Brad said.

Brown shrugged. He took a sip of his coffee and continued. "We got people safe behind fences and then let the military and the locals loose on the Primals."

Chelsea took a sip of her coffee then looked at Brown sideways. "You set the locals loose on the Primals? What does that mean?"

"Excuse me, Corporal, but where are you from?"

Chelsea looked puzzled by the question. "New York, why?"

"From the city, I guess?"

Chelsea shook her head. "I'm not from Manhattan, if that's what you're asking. But yeah, I grew up in *a* city, lived in apartments most of my life."

Brown nodded and rubbed his chin. "No offense, Corporal, plenty of my soldiers grew up the same way. But here in Michigan, we've got loads of local boys that grew up in the woods hunting deer, and I'll tell you, they were pretty damn effective at clearing out the Primals. Hell, if the senator hadn't authorized it, they probably would've gone and done it anyway."

Brad grinned, knowing exactly what Brown was talking about, having spent most of his own youth in the woods with a twelve-gauge or a .22 rifle. "So, what went wrong?" he asked.

Sighing, Brown took another long sip from his coffee. "Even with Primals growing scarce, the concrete walls up, and the security fences keeping folks safe, you know there will always come a time when people wear out. It was all holding together until supplies dwindled and people got hungry."

Brad frowned. "The bad thing about taking food from warehouses and off the streets is it's a finite amount."

"Exactly," Brown said, nodding in agreement. "And

apparently, conditions were even worse in the East; they had more people and less reserves."

"So, they came for what you had here?" Chelsea asked.

Shaking his head, Brown looked down. "No, too cowardly to face us head on. They opened the walls out east and moved south. Claimed they were looking for survivors. The leaders in Philadelphia said they were going to expand the safe zones. It started small; first they took over smaller communities just beyond the wall, requisitioning supply stores. Relocating *survivors.*" Brown paused on the last word, locking eyes with Brad.

"Let me guess—women and children," Brad said.

Brown nodded. "I swear we didn't know. I read your brief. If we'd known, we would have done more to stop it."

He took another sip of his coffee, looking at the glowing fire in the stove. "We had people show up at the wall. They started telling stories of raiding parties, attacks on settlements, the burning of the gated communities in Indiana. We still didn't want to believe it was the East. The captain sent a request up to the senator, asking for formal permission to send a recon team out south of the wall, but the old man shut it down."

"You went anyway," Brad said.

The big sergeant clenched his jaw as the other men moved closer to the fire. Palmer opened the stove door and filled it with wood. Brown nodded and pointed to the rough veteran soldier who was sitting just across from him. The man was young, but his face was leathered and serious. "Captain wasn't having it. He gave me three vehicles and provisions for a week; he wanted to know what was going on. I took this man here and a few others, and we rolled south then cut east toward the reports of violence.

"Not fifty miles beyond the wall, we came upon a turned-out village... buildings burned, bodies on the street."

Brad sighed. "Places like that are a dime a dozen in the wasteland. How do you know it was raiders?"

Slowly dipping his chin, Brown again pointed to the soldier across from him. The rugged man removed his patrol cap, exposing dark hair and piercing blue eyes that stared into the darkness beyond Brad. Eyes that Brad recognized as having seen their share of violence.

Brown sighed and continued. "It wasn't circumstance that I asked him to come along. He knows the wasteland. Because of him, I knew it was raiders... because we had Gyles. This fella has spent more time outside the walls than any of us. Maybe even more time in the wild than you."

Gyles shook his head. "Not by choice; I was just surviving," he said in a low voice that rode on the edge of anger. "But I know that place was standing six months earlier. And unless some shit has changed, I don't know nothing about these zombie dicks clearing out supply cellars. They don't steal casks of homemade wine, and they don't shoot men execution style in the back of the head."

Chelsea's expression softened. "You knew them?"

Nodding, Gyles reached into a pack and removed an amber bottle. He popped a cork and poured a bit into his coffee cup. He looked at the bottle and handed it to Chelsea. "It's local-made and horrible, but you all are welcome to it." He waited for Chelsea to add a bit to her cup and pass the bottle to Brad before he nodded his approval and continued. "I knew them. Had family there once."

He saw the expression on their faces and waved off their concern. "It's not like that. They didn't survive the fall, but folks in the community still knew me. They took me in when I was making my way north. I spent close to eighteen months moving from settlement to settlement, ever since the meatgrinder. They were smart, good people, and somebody killed them for a cellar full of canned goods and some shitty homemade wine."

Brad sat up. "You were at the meatgrinder?"

The soldier nodded. "Yeah, I was there; not part of the defense, but I was there." The man's eyes seemed to burn as they focused on something against a far wall. His voice dropped low. "A lot of shit went on during the fall. Nothin' went the way it was planned—the way *they* planned it. But yeah, you could say I was at the grinder. I managed to link up with some other units, and somehow we survived." He paused again, and his jaw hardened. Instead of speaking, he took a sip from his mug and looked away.

Brown cleared his throat and, getting back on topic, said, "It didn't stop there. We cut a trail east and hit several places, following along just south of the wall. Every place we found told the same story. Cellars cleared out, dead men in the street, burnt structures. It was all the same until we came across an old nuke plant near Toledo. Big place on Lake Erie; they had walls and the lights still on."

"I know the area. Was it a settlement?" Brad asked.

Shaking his head, Brown continued. "Not a settlement. Not like any you would imagine, anyway." He swallowed hard, looking down into his coffee cup. He took a long sip then continued. "It's a massive compound built up around the power plant. We kept our distance and watched them. It was built up like a base: lots of activity, convoys coming and going. There was a lot of traffic for the place being so remote. Trucks came in from the south and rolled out, headed east. They were processing people, but they weren't survivors. It was like a prison. Women and kids under guard... they were driving them up from the places they hit then shipping them back up north, along with all of the goods they stole."

"What did you do?" Chelsea asked.

Brown's face drooped, and he looked away. "What could we do? The place was heavy with armed men. What were we? A heavy recon team—a squad at most."

"I'll tell you what we did," Gyles said, his voice low and cold. "We waited for their patrols to go out, and we followed them. We headed south down that main road. We dropped a tree across the street—a spot where the shoulder was low and tight to the trees—and then we waited for them to loop back." He took a drink from his cup and smiled sadistically. "It didn't take long before they returned. Three big moving trucks and an old ambulance.

"Those trucks stopped just short of the tree. A man got out with a length of chain like he was going to pull the tree out of the road. Like it was a task he'd done hundreds of times before. But this time they would find things a bit different. They found out the hard way when Sergeant Brown boxed them in with an armored Hummer in the back."

Brown cleared his throat, picking up the story. "I called out for them to surrender, but they weren't having it. Told us they were traveling with survivors from camps in Indiana and Ohio. Said they were taking them back east to the safe areas. One man in particular, a big man with a grey jacket, said they were under protection from the Midwest Alliance. I asked the man to show us the survivors, to open the truck doors... well, that's when he went for his gun."

"You killed them?" Chelsea asked.

Gyles nodded. "Every damn one of 'em."

Chelsea glanced at Brad then looked back to Gyles, his

eyes now hard and cold like he was reliving the event. "You didn't take any prisoners?"

He locked eyes with Chelsea. "Why let 'em live? We knew who they were and what they were up to. Do you want to know what we did after that?"

Chelsea slowly nodded her head.

"We split our force in two; half the crew escorted those trucks and civilians back to our lines. The rest of us that stayed behind, well, we loaded that ambulance up with their dead and a few drums of gasoline. We drove it all the way back to Toledo, and we crashed it right into the gate of that damn power plant. At first they reacted all dumb, like there must'a been an accident. Men spilled out of the plant, looking at the ambulance and pulling open the back door, examining the dead that we'd stacked inside.

"But they didn't get much of a look. Once they began to figure out what was going on, we lit that ambulance up with the fifty-cal then rained hell on them with the MK19 grenade launcher until we were out of ammo. Didn't take long, and the entire front of that place was spewing flame. The gate was off the hinges and half the place burning. But that wasn't enough; we could still hear them inside yelling for mercy. We popped every flare we had, and we hid in the tree line while the zombies did the rest.

"We let a few vehicles escape to the East to get reinforcements. It took the rest of them all night, but they eventually got the fires under control and their gates re-locked. Yeah, we could have done more; probably could have killed them easy, but we needed to send them a message. We put those bastards on notice that we were aware of what they were up to, and that Michigan wasn't standing for it."

"At least that's what he thought we were doing," Brown scoffed.

"He?" Brad said. "You weren't there?"

Brown shook his head. "No, I returned with the first group. Sergeant Gyles led the attack."

"Sergeant?" Brad asked, looking at the spot where Gyles's rank insignia should have been.

"Sergeant First Class," Gyles replied. He waved off the comment with his hand. "Screw that noise. I'm in no man's army now; no matter how much they try to pull me back in."

"Well, you're here now; that still says something." Brad looked at Brown. "So you went back to Michigan with the survivors. That's when the senator could have been stronger."

"I did. I told them what was going on, and he ordered us to stand down. Said anything outside the walls wasn't our fight." Brown clenched his fist. "And by the time they started coming after us, they'd grown too strong, and we didn't have the resources to fight back."

"The senator told us earlier that you were losing colonies," Brad answered.

"Shit," Gyles scoffed. "Colonies? Is that what he called them?! We're losing the whole damn state. The alliance is gone, and he isn't doing shit about it."

"How far has it gone?" Brad asked, looking back to Brown.

The big sergeant shrugged and considered his response while gazing into the fire. "We started a one-sided war with that raid on Toledo. What was once a shady operation in the shadows went full scale. We lose more every day. Recon says they cut a hole in the Detroit containment wall and let the hordes out."

"Containment wall?" Brad asked.

"Yeah, the DCW we called it. Back when all this was

going down, Primals were infesting around the city; most of them stayed there. Instead of trying to root them out, we built barriers to keep them safely contained."

"And they knocked it down?"

Gyles grunted. "Blew a big hole in the wall on US12 where it crosses the Rogue River. They let nearly a million Primals out of the city and back into the safe zone. Smaller communities started to drop communications. Supply convoys left warehouses and never returned."

"What have you done about it?" Chelsea asked.

Gyles laughed sarcastically. "What have *they* done? Well, for the most part, the Primals stayed in the area of the hole, so the senator didn't think it was vital. They sent out a few teams, tried to shore up the wall, reported back on the estimated the numbers of zombies released into the safe zone, kept track of the number of communities we were losing; they've done every damn thing except fight back. They pretty much did nothing to retaliate."

"They?" Brad asked. He pointed at Gyles's uniform. "Aren't you one of them?"

Gyles grinned before Brown answered for him. "Gyles doesn't play well with others. He's not active anymore; guess he's like a contractor now."

Laughing, Brad shook his head. "Not active? Hell, me either then, I guess. When did you get your discharge papers?"

Reaching across the fire for his bottle, Gyles poured more into his coffee cup then pointed the bottle at Brown. "*Active* was his choice of words. I'm here just like you. But I won't claim to be any part of that senator's mess. He was almost apologetic when he talked about the breaches—like we deserved it for attacking that Toledo power plant, like this was payback."

A loud bang at the front of the building caused Palmer to put up his hand. His face showed concern, but he wasn't panicked. "We're fairly safe in here, but we should keep it down, especially considering the number of them and the activity."

Brad nodded. "Yeah, they're particularly fired up, aren't they?" He rubbed at his chin. "So, the numbers are up, and the colonies are dropping. Is there any order to all of it?"

Reaching for the bottle, Brown dipped his chin. "They've been moving out from Detroit. Pushing those mobs ahead of them. I'm sure they can't really control the smart ones, but the others... you know, the ones that plod around when it gets too damn cold."

"Creepers?" Chelsea added.

Brown shrugged. "That's a good word for 'em. Anyhow those" —he paused and looked at Chelsea— "*creepers*, well, they can be predictable; they move in big swarms. But the Primals... they're a little different. They'll pull back into hiding, ambushes even. They've gotten more conservative. It's hard to estimate how many of them are out there."

Chelsea nodded her head in agreement. "We've seen the same things down south."

"But what about the attack today?" Brad asked. "In the past, I've seen them drawn to flares or fighting. But your place is locked down tight. It's quiet and behind double layered fences. Nothing drew them in."

"The mortars?" Chelsea said.

Brad shook his head. "I don't think so."

"You're right by that," Gyles said. "They use the mortars to keep our heads down, to attack our barriers. But the horde, they push them ahead then let 'em go crazy on a colony."

"Push? How do you know this?" Brad asked.

Gyles looked at Brown, who nodded his head. "I've watched 'em do it," Gyles said. "They have guys on ATVs—snowmobiles sometimes. They'll ride close to the big cities and population centers, make noise to draw them out, then head toward whatever place they want taken. The hordes of creepers, like Sergeant Brown said, can be predictable, and they'll follow a meal.

"More than likely last night—or early this morning—a pair of riders led those things to within sight of Coldwater Station. Then they vanished, leaving the pack of zombies to collide with our fence lines. From there, the things probably spotted a guard or maybe smelled the smoke from the cook fires.

"The zombies will swarm over the outer fences, but one thing Sergeant Brown left out, is where there are zombies, the Primals are usually close by. And they got more than one type of Primal too."

Brad nodded, having his own experience with Primals, but he wanted to keep the man talking so he held his tongue.

Gyles took a sip from his coffee cup and continued. "There are these ones we call hunters. Mainly because in the early days when we set out to thin out the Primals, and the local boys went to killing them, some of the more advanced ones would track down our boys and turn the tables on 'em. The hunters became the prey and, well, you know how it goes.

"You get a pack of Primals out in the woods. You can still do all right. Enough bullets and the right position, hell, you could probably kill a pretty decent sized group of 'em, but you get a pack of Primals being led by one of them hunters? Well, you better get your ass to someplace safe, and do it quick."

The rough soldier looked Brad up and down and grinned. "Why am I telling you this? You didn't just wake up and walk out into the apocalypse. I can tell you been around."

"True enough," Brad said. "I've done my share of the killing. You said you've watched them. How?"

"I get claustrophobic," he replied. "I can't stay locked up in that compound."

Brown laughed. "Claustrophobic, my ass! He likes to chase tail. This one probably has a girl in every colony between here and Traverse City."

Gyles shook his head. "All lies." He reached to Brown to retrieve his bottle. "But what is true is I've visited those communities—damn near every one of 'em. And I happened to witness more than one attack."

"Were they like this?" Brad asked.

"Give or take. Only here, we were able to stop it. Coldwater Station has high walls and a military to back it up," Gyles said. "The last attack I saw was on a holdout just north of Marble Lake—it's a good ways east of here. I spotted the horde on US12, and I knew they were headed toward the Quincy Gap. It's not a big holdout, but I've stopped there several times on my trips east. I knew the people."

"Did you warn them?" Chelsea asked.

"I couldn't," the young man said just above a whisper. "I didn't have a radio, and by the time I spotted them they were already too close to the outpost for me to try and stop it. I watched the zombies move to their walls. Quincy had a good setup... completely boxed in with shipping containers, even double stacked in some places. They held for a few hours, but that's when the shooting started.

"They hit 'em with more than mortars though. A truck

bomb came right at their gate. I don't know if someone was driving it or if it was just a lucky shot, but that thing blew the doors wide open. It blasted a hell of a hole in the zombies too, but not enough to deter them; they bounced back and moved on. And that's when the howling started. Before long, those Primals were all over the place. Coming out of the woods, like they been watching and following the entire time just waiting for their chance."

"Any survivors?" Chelsea asked.

Gyles shook his head. "I didn't stick around."

Rubbing his forehead, Brown spoke. "He came back to get us. We sent out a quick reaction force, but by the time we got there it was over."

"They'll be coming back to Coldwater Station," Gyles said. "The East has been filling the wall with Primals. I think they plan to let us die off then move back in later for the resources."

Brad nodded. "I think you're right. We need to get back."

Palmer stood and rolled his shoulders. "Well, we ain't going anywhere tonight. I suggest you all get some sleep, and we'll roll out at first light."

CHAPTER 11

H e woke just before dawn to the sounds of the other men snoring loudly in cots along the wall. A warm fire still glowed from a potbelly stove. The men had eaten well the night before, the hospitality of the camp more than what he'd expected. Sean stepped across the room and dressed quietly. After pulling on his boots, he grabbed his rifle, walked to the end of the room, and slid open a double door. A cold damp air hit him as he looked over the dew-covered pasture.

Stepping away from the barn, he heard a series of muffled pops from above. Sean instinctively crouched and looked over his head. He stepped farther out from the barn so he could view the roof. At the top, he spotted a man holding a scoped rifle to his eye

The door slammed at the ranch house just across the way. Eli came out holding a rifle of his own. He looked from left to right then up at the man on the barn roof. The man pointed out toward a distant tree line, showed two fingers, and then sliced across his neck. Eli spotted Sean and made his way toward him. "Looks like we had us some company—

probably stumblers," he said, looking across the pasture. "The river usually keeps them away from here."

"Creepers is what we call 'em," Sean said. "The infected ones that are just too stubborn to die."

"That's a good way of looking at it," Eli said with his eyes sweeping the horizon. "We didn't have many of them types—creepers, as you say—until last winter. Now we been seeing more and more of 'em."

"I'm sure the trouble with the raiders didn't help. But there is something else..." Sean said.

"Oh, and what might that be?"

Sean paused, second-guessing what he was about to say. "Hell, no reason to keep secrets on the frontier," Sean said. He looked Eli in the eye. "I was told by reliable folks that the Primals are massing again. That they are moving the way they did during the fall. It's got a lot of folks scared."

"Well, we didn't see many during the fall, so guess I have nothing to worry about." Eli looked at Sean and asked, "You mind taking a walk?"

Sean nodded his head. He could tell that Eli was set in his ways, and there would be no getting his people off this farm. It was better to let him do what he needed to survive. He exhaled and waved a hand, signaling for the red-bearded man to lead the way. "So, you have boys on watch with squirrel guns? Even considering suppression, that couldn't have been more than a .22 I heard."

Eli dipped his chin. "Yeah, does the job most times. We got bricks of .22s, and like you said, it's quieter. As long at the brain gets dented, they seem to fall okay. We keep a .308 up in the crow's nest for the faster, meaner ones."

Sean spotted the pair of bodies and moved in close. He stood over one and kicked at it to make sure it was down, then reached for the shoulder of its shirt and pulled the creature to its back. The once middle-aged man had long, mangled hair and an overgrown beard. There were defensive wounds on its arms that were partially healed, or at least a purplish scar of healing. He knew from experience that the Primals didn't heal up the way people did; the wounds would instead gel over like a big disgusting scab. Just below its collarbone, there were several gunshot wounds. He lifted the thing slightly but couldn't see an exit wound on its back.

Sean spotted the small entry wound above the thing's right eye. It was recent and what brought the creeper down. "Good shooting. Clean head shot." Sean pulled at the thing's shirt collar, looking at the pale skin on its chest and the bullet holes again. "This one appears to have only been creeping for a while. These gunshots brought it down, killed the Primal in it. Probably took hits back at Crabtree, enough to turn it, anyhow."

"How can you tell?" Eli asked.

Sean pointed at the purple goo on the arm wounds and the skin around the Primal's neck. "They really start falling apart after they go into this creeper phase; this one is still kinda fresh. Those marks on its arms are probably what originally infected him. See how they started to scar over? Poor bastard must have survived the initial fight with whatever got him, only to go Primal later.

"From what I know about them, the Primals can keep kicking for a long time. They get into some good hunting grounds, they can thrive even... well, unless the elements or some other sort of injury gets to them. I've shot some dead through the chest, knocking them off their boots, only to find them creeping in the woods weeks later." Sean pulled back the collar again and pointed at the bullet wounds. "Something put it down, but it wasn't enough of an organ strike to kill it. You have to destroy the heart, lungs, or brain.

"This one probably died, or at least slowed down, from blood loss. See how the wound hasn't healed? Once he started creeping, all that healing stuff stopped; you can tell because there's very little blood and no signs of scabbing. It's like a zombie mode for these pricks. Their bodies start to shut down but the primary organs like the lungs, heart, and brain keep on chugging, like they didn't get the message that it's time to die."

Shuddering, Eli looked away. "Just when you think it can't get any worse."

"You said they couldn't get across the river?" Sean replied, looking at the thing's wet clothing and the distant river bed.

"Didn't say they couldn't; just that they don't. This pair might have stumbled too close the bank on the far side and fell in. They tend to roll and kick about until they find the bank and get back out. Sometimes they find our side."

Sean rubbed at his chin. "Or maybe they were pushed in and guided to your side."

Eli tipped his head to the side and looked off at the bank hold. Sean was surprised to see the man's reaction. It wasn't surprise; it was like confirmation. "What else aren't you telling me, Eli?" Sean said.

The man waved a hand out toward the trees. "There's someone out there working against us, something stirring these things up and leading them into the valley. I've been sensing it, and I've seen it with my own eyes. It's the reason we were out scouting the railroad pass. Before a month ago, we rarely saw any infected up here. Never in the deep river to the east or this shallow run to the west."

"Then the train came?" Sean said.

Eli shook his head. "This happened before all of that." Eli looked back behind him at the man on the barn roof then pointed his hand toward the north. The man on the barn nodded his head in understanding. "Walk with me," he said.

Sean stood and followed the man closer to the river's edge where a dirt path ran parallel to the water. Eli slowed his pace and let Sean walk beside him. "We send hunting parties out all the time—just a few of the boys—after deer and rabbit. They do okay by us. About four weeks ago, maybe a bit less, a pair of my sons stumbled upon something out of the ordinary."

Sean remained quiet, holding his questions and allowing the man to speak. They passed a bend in the river, and Eli stopped. He pointed to the opposite bank. Sean could hardly make out the shapes of vehicles covered in brush and tarps. Eli walked toward a tall oak and leaned back against it.

"They found this little campsite here. My boys thought maybe they were survivors. We've stumbled upon small groups from time to time, offered them what we could. Only this time, these folks weren't camping, and they were all men—six of 'em, to be exact. At first, they didn't appear to be no harm to us, so my boys left them be, just kept a close eye on them. We never approach strangers unless we identify one, like ol' Henry back there, or we for sure know they're friendly."

"It's a good policy," Sean said.

Eli nodded and smiled. "Well, they watched them for a couple hours, sent another boy back to the farm to get me and some of the others. By the time we got here, things had turned from odd to sinister." He pointed to the center of the cluster of vehicles. "Now what we got here is two SUVs and a U-Haul truck. Well, when I come up on them, that truck was backed up facing the river. The doors were closed shut, but there was an awful ruckus coming from inside."

Sean shook his head. "You got to me be kidding me."

"I wish I was, friend," Eli said, looking down. "One of those men rolled that door open, and the inside had about fifty of 'em packed in there. Every one of them was hooked to a series of chains bolted to the floor. One of those boys had a pair of bolt cutters. They were fixing to cut those things loose and let drop into the river. They would have washed downstream a bit then stormed my farm. Even with shooters on the roof, I would have lost people."

"I'm going to go out on a limb and say you didn't let that happen."

"I sure as shit didn't."

"You leave any alive?" Sean asked.

Eli shook his head and started walking back toward the barn. "Intended to, but it just didn't work out that way. Frontier justice and all."

Sean shrugged. "It happens." He looked back toward the vehicles one last time. "And nobody ever came looking for them?"

"Nope; which made me think this was the entire party —at least until all those people showed up at Crabtree, and then the activity at the railroad. My best guess is these guys were out foraging or scouting ahead and stumbled on my place. With the way that truck was set up, they'd used the technique before. I feel no guilt in killing them."

Sean nodded. "No judgments from me." He didn't care about dead raiders, and he could tell by the look in Eli's eyes that the old man didn't care about them either. "What else? Don't hold back on me."

Eli sighed, letting out a low cough. "There was a leader

... wore a grey camo parka ... barked orders like a boss. I only remember the details because it was his face I put the first bullet into. There were a couple others, some fought, others fled, but they all died in the proximity of those vehicles. City boys are no match for my kin."

Sean locked his jaw, hearing the details of the leader's description. "I know all about the ones with the grey ponchos; this is the same group I'm hunting. And the Primals in the truck... what's the disposition on them?"

"Yeah, we took care of 'em. Them and the raiders are all buried out in my hay field. I figure they make as a good a fertilizer as anything. When you say hunting, you mean you got questions to ask of 'em?"

Sean shook his head but didn't speak. Eli nodded knowingly and said, "I know where you're headed, and that terrain ain't suited for your mounts. I'll give you a couple of vehicles. I have a nice Ford Ranger and a Tahoe back in one of the barns. I want you to take them."

"Why would you just give us trucks?"

"Those are solid vehicles to get you where you need to go. Those mounts you have are fine, but they won't take to the pressures like sheet metal can. But hear me out. I ain't after your horses either. You come back for them when you return; vehicles or not, I'll still give you the horses back."

"Where is the but?" Sean asked.

Eli smirked. "I need you to take a couple of my guys with you. Couple of the young men are eager to get out and see the world. I can't have them going it alone."

"I'm not a babysitter," Sean said suspiciously.

"Don't expect you to be," Eli said frowning. "These are good boys; they can take care of themselves, and if you tire of them... well, point them back this way and give 'em a boot in the ass. Regardless of that, we haven't heard much from the world north of the Ohio River in months, and I'd like to get details back from my own kin. No disrespect."

"I see," Sean said. "So... you want me to escort some of your people to go out and take a look around. You know we've already got a mission of our own."

Eli rubbed the back of his neck. "This won't be no babysitting trip. My boys can hold their own, and they know that country far better than you do. That, and I know where your man left the train. My people can get you there; you just make sure they get back here."

"You know about the train? How?" Sean asked.

"We heard it headed to Crabtree that night. We sent a party to find out what it was all about. That's when we heard the fighting. My boys laid up in the woods where they could oversee the rail and avoid the infected. Later that night—early morning maybe—that engine and only a couple cars came flying past here, burning up the tracks. I sent my nephews to follow it. They found that engine and a sleeper car, but everyone was dead or gone. Lots of food and stored goods still left inside."

"Everyone?"

"My people scouted out a road and saw a pair of tracks headed north. I suspect that would be your people. If it was the raiders, they would have stuck by the train and waited for their friends to come fetch them, if not drive it all the way back east. Either way, they wouldn't have left their supplies."

They continued walking and had circled all the way back toward the ranch buildings. Eli stopped and turned back to face Sean. "My only role here is to take care my people and this ranch. I want you to take my boys and find out what's out there. You keep 'em as long as you need them, just get them back to me." Eli sighed again. "No secrets on the frontier, right?"

Sean shook his head and said, "None."

Eli grinned. "If you don't take the boys with you, they're bound to go anyhow. Can't keep young men locked up on a farm forever, ya know."

Sean looked at the man and noticed tired eyes, something he hadn't recognized before. He nodded and offered his hand. "Okay, I won't turn down more help—and more people that know this land, the better." When Sean turned and looked back toward the house, he saw big open barbecue fires. Women were cooking meat, and pots were smoking over the fires. Kids were chasing each other in a field, playing. Sean saw Eli staring at the children.

"We've got to find a way to live out here," Eli said just above a whisper. "I don't have the people to fight raiders and the infected. It won't work; I can't protect them like this."

Sean swallowed and sighed. "Send word to the south," he said. "Cloud and the others at Crabtree will help you. They'll reimburse you to use this place as a staging area. I'll write orders for some of your men to deliver to Colonel Cloud and verify who you are. A working farm's got to mean something."

Eli turned back to face Sean. "Okay, I'll accept that. It's time for us to join up with what's left of the world," he said. "Now go gather your men; I'll ready the vehicles for your trip east."

B rad stared up at the stained ceiling tiles in a cold sweat. He could hear a persistent thumping from somewhere in the building. Not remembering where he was, his eyes searched the surroundings. He closed them tight and then opened them slowly to adjust to the light and found himself still in the strip mall building. He pulled the blanket away from his chest and turned to see Chelsea on a cot beside him. She was asleep facing the wall, her rifle leaned up next to her.

Sitting up, he swung his legs off the cot. There was a low glow from the woodstove at the far end of the room, keeping the room at a comfortable temperature. He could see Gyles standing watch at a barred door where the front of the store would have been before the place was boarded up. Brad turned back to the MRAP behind them. He could still see the vehicle's sturdy hatch shrouded in heavy canvas. He leaned forward and focused on the lone night watchman, Gyles, in the low light. The man held his rifle in one arm, his head turned like he was listening to something outside the wall.

Brad slid his feet into the worn leather boots, lacing them up just tight enough so he could walk. He took his rifle and walked to the front of the space to join Gyles. The thumping remained, a steady cadence of what sounded like a fist hitting the boards outside.

"When did it start?" Brad whispered.

Gyles looked at him. "About an hour ago."

"Any idea how many?"

Shaking his head, Gyles whispered, "One too many, I suppose." Gyles held up his hand, pausing as another loud bang hit the wall. He sighed and looked back at Brad. "I know they always come—they come every night—but that doesn't mean I have to like it. No matter how many I kill, they still freak me out."

Brad frowned and moved away from the wall. Looking straight down a blacked-out hallway, he could see that where this building ended, someone had cut a hole in the wall to enter the shop next door. Through squinted eyes, he saw a dim light at least two shops down. Brad pointed and Gyles nodded at the light. "It's Palmer; he's got a peephole down there. Checking things out on the far end."

Brad patted Gyles's shoulder then moved toward the passageway, ducking to enter the next building. It looked like a tax or insurance office, decorated with typical wooden desks and fake plants. Following the light, he moved to the next hole cut in the wall, past an electronics shop, and finally to what was once a small market. A battery-powered lantern was sitting on a store counter. He could see the remains of looted store shelves and a turned-over soda machine.

"I'm over here," a voice called out.

"Hell, man, you scared the shit out of me," Brad said, spinning on his heels. He spotted Palmer behind the counter watching a small black-and-white TV monitor. "You got cable out here?" he whispered.

Palmer shook his head. "This is the old store security monitor; they've got two cameras out front, more out back and along the side. They don't use much juice, so I've got them tapped into a battery pack I set up on the roof. The owner of this shop must have owned the strip mall. They had a good eight cameras hanging. I moved a few, but he had the place pretty well covered as it was."

"How are they still on?" Brad asked.

"Like I said... batteries. Whoever he was, he was prepared for the usual blackouts. I plugged in some solar chargers to keep them up and going, and I've added more cells. If I'm careful, they'll run most of the night."

"See anything good out there?"

"No, but lots of bad," the man said, not taking his eyes off the monitor.

Brad stepped closer; he couldn't see much through the hazy black-and-white picture. Palmer pointed to what looked like snow or normal broadcast interference. The man pressed a red button on a bar below the TV, and the camera angle changed and focused to view just beyond the parking lot, into tall uncut grass fields filled with overgrown bushes. What Brad first thought were sparkles of static snow on the display, quickly materialized into glowing eyes.

"There's got to be a hundred of them," Brad said. "How can so many have found us?"

"They doubled back and led them to us."

"Raiders?" Brad asked.

"Can't be the Primals alone," Palmer said. "We drove too fast, and it's beyond their range. Someone led them here."

"And the creepers?" Brad asked, still focused on the cold eyes seeming to stare back at him through the camera.

Palmer pulled away from the camera bank and opened a drawer. Inside was a stack of old flip phones. "No, no creepers yet, but they'll be coming up behind them; we'll be surrounded soon. The raiders probably led them here going fast enough to stay ahead of the Primals. The mass of others will be just behind them, but not far. I suppose we only have an hour or so before they spring whatever attack it is they have planned."

Brad pointed. "What's with the phones?"

"They look like phones, but I have them plugged into the strip mall's Wi-Fi router. Think of each of these phones as a clacker on a claymore. Phones obviously have no cell connection, but the shop's Wi-Fi is still online."

"Clacker? Well, if that's the trigger then where is the claymore?" Brad asked.

Palmer grinned and hit the camera bar again, flipping through displays until one stopped on a boarded-up building across the street. He pointed at the first flip phone. "I have a pair of homemade bombs setup. One is out back on the approach road; another set is daisy chained and hidden up on the roof, angled down toward the front parking lot."

Brad looked at the last phone on the counter. "And that one?" he asked.

Palmer pointed at the building in the monitor. "Fifty gallons of old gas and diesel with a block of C_4 is in the basement of that old bookstore over there."

"And why over there?"

Palmer shrugged his shoulders. "Logical assumption. I figured if outsiders ever came and put me under siege, they would most likely set up in that building over there. It's taller than this one, it's made of concrete block, and the windows are all boarded up. If they got on the roof, they would have good fields of fire over the parking lot and us—logical spot, really. They could hold off well against the Primals and keep us pinned indefinitely.

"Sergeant Brown said I should tear it down. But I figured it would do better as a trap."

"Did it?"

Palmer changed camera angles again and stopped on one that looked at the side of the bookstore. The place appeared completely empty. "Not certain, but do those look like tracks in the road to you? And that—" Palmer hit a control, zooming the camera to the sidewalk near the store's boarded-over front window to where there was a lump in the snow. "Now that right there is a body. I'd say our bad guys are in there."

A loud explosion and flash of light flickered the camera monitors. Brad stumbled back as dust and ceiling tiles fell from above. He turned back toward the passageway, where he could see orange light and smoke filtering in. Spinning back to Palmer, he could see the man was flipping switches. "I've lost the back cameras," he shouted. "What the—? How did they sneak up on me?"

Gunfire erupted from deep in the building. A second, larger boom shook the structure, causing more of the ceiling tiles to break loose and fall all around Brad. He staggered back and pulled his rifle close.

Scooping the flip phones into his hand, Palmer turned toward him. "Go!" he shouted, eyes fixed on the monitors.

Brad stared at him with wide eyes, still confused about what was happening.

"I said go, damn it," Palmer yelled again. "They're hitting the back; if we lose that MRAP, we're screwed!"

Brad ducked away and stepped hard, backing toward the passageway. Looking ahead, he saw the path was already filling with smoke, the toxic gasses flowing from one storefront to the next through the holes in the wall. He let the sounds of gunfire lead him as he ran crouched down —ducking through the last passage—then turned back toward where he'd left the others. He looked to the corner where Chelsea had been and found her empty cot. There was a bright flash, then an explosion knocked him off his feet. When he rolled off his back and pulled himself up to his knees, the room was filled with smoke. Brad crawled forward and saw the back of the MRAP engulfed in orange flame, roiling with black smoke. He crawled ahead to a makeshift barrier where his group had been returning fire.

Gyles was staggering to a knee, dragging an unconscious Chelsea by her wrists while firing with his free arm. Brad ran to his side. "What the hell happened?"

"Take her; we've got to get the hell out of here," Gyles said, staggering back while choking and coughing on the thick smoke.

"Where's Sergeant Brown?" Brad asked.

Frowning, the veteran soldier shook his head. "Come on; we've got to go."

Brad looked back toward the MRAP. The bay was completely engulfed in flames, which were working to hold back the advancing Primals. As Brad looked up, he could see that the fire was spreading across the ceiling, the heat igniting plastic and the rolls of carpet as it spread. He grabbed Chelsea's wrist and hoisted her into a fireman's carry as he followed Gyles back to the storefront. On his right, Brad spotted Palmer ducking through the passage, still holding the flip phones. He pointed at a long wooden shelf, and Gyles nodded. The young man ran directly to it, pulling it down and away from the wall.

Behind the shelf was another passageway. This one didn't lead into a store, but was instead a void space, lined with cinder blocks that ran between the store's Sheetrock and the outer wall of the building. At nearly a run, Gyles stepped in first with Palmer trailing close. Brad moved quickly to avoid being left behind. The air was hot and dry but clear of smoke. Brad could feel the intensity of the fire radiating off the interior walls. The men ahead broke to the right and then down a long corridor that must have run the length of the building. The farther they moved from the fire, the cooler and darker it got.

At the end of the passage was another open space. Inside sat several red toolboxes and a dark, armored HUMVEE. Palmer caught Brad staring at the equipment and the closed-in room. "I found this place by accident. It used to a boiler room, but the wall was never bricked up, just covered with flimsy sheet metal. Probably from when they replaced the boilers at some point. I removed the bits of sheet metal and made a swinging door that, from the outside, still appears to be a wall. It's a solid workshop." Palmer moved around to the back door of the vehicle and swung it open then ran around to the passenger side. He looked back at Brad. "Get her inside and buckled in. Can you handle a Mark 19?" Palmer asked.

"Does Grizzly Adams have a beard?" Brad answered, elated to see the armored vehicle.

"Hell yeah, he does," Gyles shouted, pulling chocks from the wheels and running to the front cab.

Brad moved to the truck and eased Chelsea inside, crawling into the compartment as Gyles secured the door behind him. The engine came to life. Brad pulled Chelsea into a seat and secured her harness. For the first time, he looked her over; her face was bright red, her forehead and nostrils covered with black soot, but she was breathing, and he couldn't find any blood.

"We gotta roll, soldier. Keep your head down until we break through," Palmer shouted from the front passenger seat.

Before Brad could ask what they were breaking through, Gyles had the pedal down, and the HUMVEE crashed forward, exploding through the external wall and running head on into a horde of creepers that had the structure surrounded. The things crunched under the vehicle's wheels and spilled up over the brush guard and onto the hood.

"Okay! Go to work, hero," Palmer said, looking back at him and pointing at the turret ring.

"What's the target?" Brad shouted back.

"Target? Just kill shit," Palmer ordered.

Brad nodded and shifted his body into autopilot. No time to attach a gunner's harness or seat, he unlatched the hatch and threw it open. When he stood, his mind screamed for him to return to the safety of the compartment. The parking lot was filled with bodies, and rage-filled eyes focused on him. Brad racked the MK19 and let loose a three-round burst less than a hundred meters ahead of their direction of travel. The rounds exploded in a flash of light and body parts.

Behind him, gunfire erupted, and he saw where rounds sparked off the vehicle's armor. Brad spun in the ring. The two-story bookstore Palmer had talked about earlier was also surrounded by Primals, and the roof had a line of shooters firing at them. Brad lined up his sights on the building, but before he could fire, the place exploded into a blinding fireball that expanded out and over the surrounding Primals. Brad reeled back, the heat hitting his face. Soon after the first blast, a second flash erupted that daisy-chained down the front of the strip mall, exploding and sending shrapnel over the infected-filled parking lot.

Brad grabbed the edge of the ring and pulled himself back behind his weapon. Looking over his sights, he could see that the bookstore was gone and the parking lot was now littered with writhing bodies.

"We could use some support up front!" Gyles shouted from below.

Brad spun the ring back to the front. The road ahead was still congested with creepers moving in. He elevated the barrel and let loose with several barrages, watching rounds explode and blast holes in the mob. Something in his peripheral vision caught his eye, and he swung the barrel thirty degrees to his right. He spotted them: a group of Primals standing on a cleared narrow rise in the terrain. A male and two females. The things were standing out of the fray, just watching the one-sided battle play out below them. It reminded Brad of the way ancient generals would sit on hilltops and watch their armies below.

Brad grunted and rotated the gun, elevating it as high as it would go for the estimated range. He pushed down on the butterfly, keeping the weapon on target as the HUMVEE raced down the road. Brad watched rounds arch out toward the rise. Falling short, he cursed himself at wasting the ammo as the Primals turned away and vanished into the darkness, the 40-millimeter grenades harmlessly exploding along the ridgeline.

The vehicle bucked and rocked as it crunched over more of the infected before smoothing out. Rotating back to the front, Brad could see the road was clear. He looked behind and lost sight of the Primals in the darkness. With the soft red glow of the taillights lighting up the snow, the distant eyes of the creepers reflected back at him. He shivered and ducked back into the vehicle, closing the hatch behind him.

"Where are we going?" Brad asked, looking to the front.

Palmer kept his eyes focused on the road and shook his head in frustration. "I'm running out of hiding spots."

"Yeah, but you're not completely out, right?" Brad asked.

"Go to the Zoo," Gyles said.

Palmer's head turned sharply toward the passenger seat. "The Zoo? You're kidding, right?"

"What's wrong with the zoo?" Brad asked.

The driver shook his head. "Because it ain't a damn zoo. It's filled with those Primals, and the only reason they're there is 'cause they own the place, and we can't figure out a way to get 'em out."

Gyles grinned. "We don't call it a zoo 'cause it's filled with fuzzy animals; it's 'cause it's filled with primal animals."

"Yeah, I get it... you two are a riot. So what is it then?"

Gyles grunted. "Back in the day it was a high school— that was before FEMA converted it to a camp. Now the place is overrun with infected. It's become a bit of a hive for the crazy bastards. And whatever the East has going on, it's bringing in more and more of them."

"And why in the hell would we want to go there?" Brad asked.

"Because I know the place, and those cocksuckers out there hunting us don't."

Brad rubbed the back of his neck then nodded. "Works for me; let's go to the Zoo then."

CHAPTER 13

ELI BAKER FARM, SOUTHERN OHIO. THE DEAD ZONE

Sean walked around the back of the vehicle. The Ford Explorer had a luggage rack loaded down with boxes of gear on top. Towed behind it was a small two-wheeled trailer filled with more equipment. Ahead of them was a Chevy Tahoe, more gear on the top but no trailer. Henry was off to the side of the narrow drive, talking with Eli and two younger men Sean hadn't seen before. As he approached, he caught Eli's eye and the man pointed at him.

"This here'll be your boss. You boys make do as you're told, and don't embarrass your uncle now," Eli said. The two young men gave Sean a look of appraisal. Sean tried to ignore the inspection and extended his hand to them, the handshake readily returned.

"I'm not so sure about 'boss,' but your uncle tells me you boys are decent scouts and trackers. If that's the case, and you can live up to the expectation, I guess we'll get along just fine."

The men nodded, holding their tongues, and exchanged

glances with each other, avoiding eye contact with Sean. The senior military man had seen looks like that before from new recruits, and it didn't concern him much. "How old are you two, anyhow?"

The boy to Sean's left—wiry and lean, with red hair to match his uncle—spoke up first. "I'm seventeen, and my brother Gage" —he pointed an elbow at a second boy— "is sixteen." The younger boy resembled his older brother but had a stocky and sturdy body like a Nebraska football player.

Sean laughed and shook his head. "Damn, Eli, you weren't kidding when you said *boys*."

Eli chewed at his lower lip and put his hands on his nephews' shoulders. "Now don't you go doubting these two. Lucas and Gage have grown up on this ranch during the fall. They've been strong assets to us, and they have as much time out there in the wild as anyone."

Sean stepped back and placed his hands on his hips, looking the two over. Both boys carried short-barreled carbines that were painted an olive green and covered with strands of burlap cloth. The two had small nylon backpacks at their feet. "You two can shoot?" Sean asked.

Lucas smiled and looked back at his uncle, who returned the smile, before looking back at Sean. "Yes, sir, we can shoot."

The rest of Sean's party had gathered around him, looking at him to see what he had to say about the new recruits. "Well, if you can shoot, that's good enough for me. But let's cut the *sir* shit. Get your gear loaded. I'll have you two ride in the lead vehicle with Henry."

The old man nodded his approval and guided the two new men to the vehicle. Riley, the red-bearded stranger, began to walk toward the lead vehicle with them when Sean put up his hand. "Hey, big man, I think I'll keep you in the back with me."

Riley grinned and shrugged. "Whatever you say; you're the boss."

"Brooks, you drive the Ford. Joey, you've got shotgun."

"So, I'm the back then?" Riley scoffed.

Brooks laughed and gave the red -bearded man a sideways glance. "Did you just do that math in your head?"

"Screw you." Riley scowled and turned away, moving to the Explorer and strapping his pack on the top with the others. When the rest of the men had moved out of earshot, Brooks reached out and grabbed Sean by the elbow. "I don't like that man. There's something off about him."

Sean stopped and turned back. "Did you see something?"

Brooks shook his head. "Nothing like that; it's just something about him. Last night at dinner, he took his chow and kept to himself. But later, he came by my cot wanting to chat. He was talking about the women and how he was looking to track one down and wondering what it might cost him. Like he was going to go have him some midnight fling with one of these farm ladies."

Shrugging, Sean turned back toward the now-loaded Ford. "Well, maybe it was just banter; the guy doesn't know anyone and he's still trying to fit in."

Brooks grimaced. "Yeah, maybe. I just don't know many guys who cry about wanting to rescue their wives one minute, then want to go and chase tail the next."

"Whatever... how many married guys you know these days?"

Brooks nodded, keeping his eyes on the vehicle. "Yeah, I guess."

"I hear ya though. I'm not all that sure about him either. That's why I stuck him in the back with me. Let's just get on the road, and we'll figure the shit out later," Sean said, reaching down for his pack. He moved along the side of the vehicle and strapped it to a rail on the top then opened the door and dropped into the leather seats. He sat and waited for Brooks to get in behind the wheel before he looked around then turned to Riley beside him. "Hell, is that you or did something die in here?"

Riley laughed. "Chief, I hate to be the bringer of sad news, but something literally did die in here; the old man said they found this ride up on the highway with the owner over the steering wheel. Matter of fact, if your boy gets to sweating, he'll probably get some dead guy juice from that seat."

With that, Brooks leapt out of the vehicle and stomped off to the barn. Returning with a horse blanket, he opened the door and draped it over the seat. He then got in and started the truck up, which purred like it was brand new off the lot. He looked back at Sean in the rearview mirror, receiving a nod, and then tapped the horn. The Tahoe in front of them flashed brake lights then pulled ahead.

They moved quickly down a rutted trail that eventually ran parallel to the stream. After less than a mile, the truck ahead slowed and dropped into the water. Sean was expecting them to sink but, looking out his window, could see that rocks had been piled just below the water level to create a hidden crossing. The trucks easily forded the stream and entered a field. After less than a hundred yards through tall grass, they cut onto a blacktop road and turned east.

It was an old country road, not many homes to be seen, and what were there were old farmhouses with broken windows or burnt barns set far apart. Occasionally, they slowed to pass an abandoned vehicle until they moved toward an intersection where a gas station sat back from the road. All the pump handles were removed and lying on the ground. The convoy slowed, and they turned their heads to examine the station windows as they passed.

Primal eyes looked back at them through dirty glass. The things didn't move to attack; they just watched the passing vehicles. Riley laughed and reached for a knapsack between his knees as they left the station behind them.

"You find something funny?" Sean asked.

Riley shook his head. "Nah, just the way them things look at us now. I remember when they'd attack on sight. Day when they would have come through that window to get at us." He unzipped the bag and pulled a Mason jar from inside. "But look at 'em now. It's like they're learning to pick their battles."

Sean nodded in agreement and looked at the jar. "What do you got there?" he said.

"Apples," Riley answered. "The barn back there had a storeroom full of 'em. I figure we ain't hitting that gas station for snacks, so what better time to get into them."

"So they gave you their canned goods?" Brooks asked, looking at him in the rearview mirror.

Laughing, Riley unscrewed the jar and fished out an apple slice. "Shit, they didn't offer, but I wasn't going to pass up the opportunity for some fruit."

"So you stole from them?" Brooks asked. "You stole from folks that went out of their way to help us?"

Sean could see Riley's jaw stiffening at the accusation. He locked eyes with Brooks in the mirror and shook his head no. Brooks took the hint and set his eyes back to the road. "I'm sure a missing jar of apples won't hurt anyone. You take anything else?" Sean asked.

Riley grunted. "Nah, I wanted to though. Jars are too damn heavy and last thing I want is them breaking open on me."

Sighing, Sean turned back to the window. "You ever been out this way?"

Slurping down an apple and placing the lid back on the jar, Riley leaned forward and looked out Sean's window. "Yeah, we took the same road when we moved west." The red-bearded man strained and pointed to a distant ridgeline. "The railroad tracks are just over there."

"So, you didn't come out here by train then?"

Riley shook his head. "Nah, laborers like me rode in covered trucks. Others on horseback."

"You say Carson and his men took you captive. Big man like you, what did they have you doing?"

The man wiped his face with the sleeve of his jacket and turned his head, looking away. "I just helped at first. You know, cutting lumber, building fences, loading trucks..."

"At first? So, then what?"

"Carson—well, Gus really, he had a way for promoting people. Like trustees, I guess you could say. I worked hard, I kept my head down, and did what I was told. Eventually, I was removed from the labor teams. They made me a lookout, then a runner, and eventually I worked a gate with some others. But they never put me in charge or left me alone."

"So, you became a collaborator?" Brooks said.

"Man, what's your problem with me?" Riley spat back at him. "I did what I had to, did what I needed to do to survive. I was just trying to work my way up to where I could escape. Do what I could to get back to my family."

Sean could see Brooks smiling in the front seat and knew the man was intentionally pushing buttons—truth tended to fly out of pissed off people. But right now, Sean wasn't sure if they could afford too much truth. He could tell that there was no trust between the two men, and probably never would be. He grimaced and looked back at Riley. "So, you were part of their security; tell me about them."

"What's there to tell?" Riley said. "I wasn't part of their army. I just stood watch in a tower or along a gate. We opened a gate or closed a gate. Let some folks in, told other folks no. Not much to it."

"So, tell me about the army then. How many?"

Laughing, the man looked back at Sean. "A lot. What you saw back at Crabtree was nothing. All of you? You're like pissants compared to what they got back in Pennsylvania. They got outposts between here and there and each one of them is fully manned and stocked. Not dirt bags in camo either; like real soldiers."

"Numbers," Sean said, not impressed. "How many men in an outpost?"

Riley shrugged. "Hundred, two hundred, maybe. Depends on what kinda spot it was."

"Spot?" Sean asked.

"Well yeah, you know... a place like Crabtree, right on the rail line. Hell, could be upward of five hundred, including civilians. But get farther out, the little satellite spot—trading posts, or places they just use as lookouts to keep an eye on settlements—could be as little as fifty. Hell, sometimes no soldiers at all."

"And you know where these places are?"

The man pursed his lips and looked away. "I know

where a few of them are." He sighed and looked back at Sean. "My family is in one of them. But there were more like it all along the rail line."

"We're stopping," Brooks said as he slowed.

Sean could see the truck ahead was slowing. They were at railroad crossing.

CHAPTER 14

B rad had fallen asleep, and when he woke, the Humvee was nestled between tall snow-covered pine trees. He heard the dripping of water smack the roof armor as snow melted from the pine boughs. He lifted his head and looked around the vehicle. Chelsea was still asleep in the seat beside him, wrapped in green poncho line. He removed his glove and put his hand to her cheek, feeling the warmth of her skin.

"She's okay," Gyles said from the front. "She woke up a bit ago and asked for water."

"You should have woke me up," Brad said, putting his glove back on.

Gyles shook off the comment. "It was my watch, and I'm perfectly capable of serving water."

Brad nodded his head and leaned forward to look out the front windshield. Palmer was in the driver's seat wrapped up tight in woolen army blankets. He turned back to Gyles. "Where the hell are we?"

"Just outside the Zoo. The school's over that ridgeline."

"Then why are we here?" Brad asked.

"We can't approach it at night," Gyles said. "It's too dangerous."

"Why don't we just drive back to the camp and—"

Gyles raised his palm and pointed a finger at his ear. "There's something else."

Brad listened and could hear a faint buzzing sound. "What is that?"

"We think it's a drone," Gyles whispered. "We saw the flashing red light last night. It's gone down this road at least twice since the sun came up."

"That's how they tracked us to the strip mall."

Gyles nodded his head. "But I think we lost them after the explosions. The drone doesn't have us located in the trees; it's probably just following the road, trying to pick up our tracks again."

"How do you know?" Brad asked.

"It's not stopping. It moves up and down the road in a search-like pattern. I was just about to wake Palmer here and have him move out next time it goes past us."

Brad sat back in the seat. "It makes sense. That's how they called in the mortar fire. How they knew we were coming after the market, and how to follow us. All this time, they saw everything we were doing."

Gyles nodded and took a sip from a water bottle before checking his watch. He reached over and shook Palmer, who woke with a start. "What the hell, man?" the driver grumbled.

"Drone just went by; it should be moving back up the road any minute on the return route. You need to be ready to go."

Palmer stretched his arms in the tight space and yawned. "Fine, man, whatever..."

He pulled the blankets away from his body and stuffed

them back into a nylon sack. He then adjusted his seat and leaned over the wheel with his finger on the starter switch, listening. Just as Gyles had predicted, the buzzing sound returned and grew louder before fading again as the drone moved past them on the road.

"Okay, hit it," Gyles said. Palmer started the engine and pulled out of their nest tucked into the pine trees. Back on the blacktop road, Brad could see they were in a populated area. There were houses pressed tightly together and burned-out and rusted cars in driveways. Farther ahead, they saw stoplights still swinging from their lines. At the intersection, Palmer took a left turn, and Brad spotted a school zone sign then made out the ruins of a military tent city in the distance. The olive drab remains of general purpose tents were crushed in the snow, edges and flaps blowing in the wind.

Humvees and ambulances sat parked side by side, while the burned-out skeleton of a Black Hawk helicopter sat alone in the middle of a football field. Palmer steered clear of it all, navigating his way onto a back-access road then along a narrow chain link fence. The school was large and shaped like an H, with one set of long legs facing the main road, and the back legs facing a rear parking lot. Palmer took them all the way around the bottom of the H. Tucked between the rear extensions of the building was a courtyard, and in that sheltered space were more tents and an old wooden sign denoting the headquarters of some now extinct Michigan Army National Guard unit.

Palmer moved past it all and up the back leg before stopping at another chain link fence. He turned to Gyles. "You're up."

Gyles grunted and shook his head. "You mind giving me some cover, Sergeant?"

"Cover?" Brad asked.

"Up in the turret, but whatever you do, don't shoot. If you see something coming, give a brother some warning."

Brad gave him a thumbs up, popped up the hatch, and returned to the turret. He spun a quick three-sixty. They were on the back side of the school, in a large, snow-covered lot littered with garbage. Brad turned and saw a row of yellow school busses on flat tires then rotated back to the front where Gyles was working the lock on a chain link fence. Looking it up and down, Brad inspected the fence. It didn't belong there; it was new—probably constructed by the military when they built the camp—but it didn't connect to anything. It was just a large square that encapsulated a back area of the school.

Why would they build a fenced-in yard back here? he thought. *Maybe it was for later expansion.* Gyles freed the lock and waved the HUMVEE through the gate then quickly shut it behind them. Brad spun in the turret as Gyles returned to the vehicle. "What is this place?" Brad asked him.

Gyles looked up at Brad and grimaced. The man shook his head slowly side to side then turned and pointed at lumps in the snow. "It's a morgue, man. They stacked bodies here until they could be moved to the landfill to be burned."

Brad focused on the lumps of snow that he'd earlier thought were just drifts. "My God, there are hundreds of them."

"Try thousands," Gyles said. "They go all along this side of the school." He returned to the vehicle and shut the door, leaving Brad alone outside in the turret.

For hundreds of yards in both direction he could see the mounds in the snow, but now focusing, could make out the blacks, blues, and olive drab greens of body bags. He closed his eyes, not wanting to think about how many must be out there. He'd somehow thought, because of the wall, that this area had been spared the worst of it. Palmer eased the HUMVEE ahead and toward a back-loading dock. He turned the vehicle around and then backed it in.

Brad dropped back inside and secured the hatch shut. He turned and could see that Chelsea was awake. She looked at him and then out the window. "Where are we?"

"At a school. We're going to hole up here for a while," Brad said. "How are you feeling?"

Chelsea closed her eyes tight then slowly opened them "I feel hungover without the pleasure of a night out. But I'll be okay. I must have gotten my bell rung."

Brad smiled at her. "Yeah, I'd say you did." He turned and could see the other men with their packs on their backs, waiting for them. "Come on, we gotta move; I don't know how safe it is here."

Chelsea nodded and reached for her pack and rifle in the space behind her. Together, they exited and stepped into the cold, brisk air. Brad looked left and right, trying to determine where they were headed.

Gyles caught his search and pointed to a narrow pedestrian gate that led to a black steel door with a pane of shatterproof glass imbedded in the center. "Through there. It leads to a maintenance room, boilers, circuit breakers... that sorta stuff."

Brad waved a hand. "Lead the way."

Gyles acknowledged him and stepped forward. Brad had Chelsea and Palmer move ahead of him as he took up the rear. They moved along the fence and to the gate, stepping into a narrow walkway between the red-brick building and the chain link then up a set of poured concrete steps to a walkway that led to the door. They reached the door, and while Gyles worked the lock, Brad's eyes searched the ground. Most of the snow was undisturbed, but there were places where old boot prints had been made then melted, turned to ice, and snow-covered again.

"You come here often?" Brad asked, pointing to the old tracks.

The door clunked and Gyles pulled back on it, signaling for the others to step inside. He turned to Brad. "It's on the route. I come here at least once a month."

Brad shrugged at the answer and stepped inside. Gyles closed and locked the door behind them then hit a breaker. A buzzing sound was followed by the flicker of some sharp, white, LED lights from the ceiling and walls. Palmer looked up at them. "There's a solar cell on the roof and a bank of batteries in the next room over. It's nothing like the setup at the strip mall, but at least there are lights."

"Thought you didn't like it here," Brad said.

"I really hate this place." Palmer scowled. "But I owed this asshole a favor, so I wired him up some lights last year. I haven't been back since."

Chelsea stood and turned toward them. "Is it really that bad? Aside from the morgue outside?" she asked.

Palmer shook his head. "Young lady, you ain't seen shit. That was nothing."

Laughing, Gyles grabbed a large Maglite from a shelf and led the way into a dark hall. "Everything on this side of the school is secure. There are two doors that separate us from the instruction and admin side. Whatever you do, don't go near them or open them."

"Why?" Chelsea asked.

"Oh, cause the neighbors will eat you."

"Wait—" Chelsea said, stopping. "There are Primals in here?"

"Tell her," Palmer said. "The place is full of them; hundreds of them."

Gyles shook his head at them and kept walking. "I told you it was the zoo. Don't worry about it; they're contained," he said, still moving down the hall with Palmer behind him.

"And you all said the same thing about Detroit." Chelsea turned and grabbed Brad's arm. "Are you sure about this guy?"

"I don't know that we have a choice," Brad said.

She nodded and looked at the secured door behind them then turned back and followed the others down the hallway. The hallway floors were dusty linoleum and the walls, rough cinderblock. At the end there was a set of double doors that were propped open by cardboard boxes. The next hallway had more light, and the walls were painted an off white with blue, steel cabinets mounted on them. The doors of the cabinets were opened, exposing worn coveralls and mop buckets.

At the end of the space was a break area—a long table surrounded by chairs and a small kitchen space, complete with a pair of sinks and a refrigerator. A toaster oven and microwave were hanging from the bottom of a long wooden shelf. Brad moved around the table and checked the faucet out of habit.

"No water, but there's beer in the fridge," Gyles said as he dropped his rifle on the table and moved to one of the blue, steel cabinets.

"Seriously?" Brad asked, looking at the refrigerator. "I'm not going to open this thing and find it full of rotten shit, am I?"

Gyles smiled, pulling a 12-gauge shotgun and a plastic Tupperware container full of shells from the cabinet. "Nah, it's beer, bro. It's old beer, but it ain't half bad."

Brad apprehensively pulled on the refrigerator door. It popped open; with no power to run it, the light was off. When Brad opened it enough to let in the light, he could see that it was stuffed with blue beer cans. "Where in the hell...?"

"I found a delivery truck in a ditch. Booze ain't allowed at the compound, so I brought it here. I still have about forty pallets of it in a barn south of here."

Shrugging, Brad took a can and looked at the nearly three-year-old date. He popped the top and took a sip. The beer was room temperature, but it was good. "Well, I'll be..." He took a few cans and set them on the table before closing the door. "Now tell me why it is you hate this place so much," he said, looking at Palmer.

Palmer shook his head and nodded toward Gyles. "Nope; *he* can show you. I ain't leaving this room until it's time to go."

Gyles popped the Tupperware container full of shells and started loading the shotgun. "I'll show you, but let me get this loaded up first." He turned and looked at Palmer. "There's food in the cabinets and a propane stove. If you ain't leaving, how 'bout fixing us up some grub?"

"What's with the shotgun?" Brad asked.

"Drone," Gyles said. "If it comes back around, I'm going to kill it." He pushed in the last shell and stuffed others in his breast pocket. "Come on, let's make rounds before we get too comfortable." He looked at Chelsea. "Corporal, would you mind staying back? It ain't good to leave anyone alone."

Chelsea smiled and nodded. "I'll keep an eye on your

friend," she said, causing Palmer to sigh as he pulled canned goods from the cupboards.

"Let's go; we need to get this done," Gyles said, moving through a door.

CHAPTER 15

The vehicles crossed the tracks then parked on opposite sides of the road, facing north. Sean exited with the others following close behind him. Henry was on the far shoulder, kicking away the snow with his boot heel. He walked to a small depression in the earth and pointed. "There's stacked bodies over here."

Sean turned and slowly looked in all directions. They were at a railroad crossing on a north-west intersection. To the south was open road and to the north, the outskirts of a burned-out town. The railroad tracks ran parallel to the east-west road. "You sure this is where the train stopped?" Sean asked, looking to the young Baker boys.

"I found something," Henry said, not allowing the boys to answer. The man walked to a telephone pole, where a brown MRE wrapper was nailed to it. He grabbed the wrapper and removed it. Looking inside, he found a folded bit of paper in a plastic bag. "It's addressed to Sean," Henry said, holding up the folded paper.

"What's it say?" Sean asked.

Henry shook his head. "I don't feel good about reading another feller's mail."

Sean walked closer and held out his hand for the note. Henry passed it to him, and Sean carefully unfolded it. He skimmed it and stopped at the bottom before turning and looking at Brooks. "It's from Chelsea. She says her and Brad are headed north to Michigan. They stopped the train and they killed Carson. She says there's plenty of food and water in the train cars and that we shouldn't come after them."

Moving closer and inspecting the rails, Brooks looked down at the pile of bodies then turned toward Riley. "Could you identify Carson if you saw him?"

The big man shrugged and walked toward the pile. He then walked around the dead and turned back. "He's not there," he said, turning away in disgust.

"You sure?" Sean asked.

"Yeah, I'm sure. He ain't in that pile," Riley said, walking away.

"Don't mean your boy didn't kill him," Henry added. "Maybe they tossed his body off the train, or maybe the man fell off."

Rubbing his chin, Sean stared at the note then looked at the boys. "Your uncle said when you found this spot the train was still here?"

Lucas nodded. "Yes, sir; there was a couple sleeper cars hitched to the engine. Engine looked good to go, like someone just powered it down and walked away. Found dead inside and lots of food and such, just like that note said. We took as much as we could carry and headed back to camp."

"And this note?" Sean said holding it up. "You missed it?"

Lucas tipped his head to the side. "I guess with so much else to look at we didn't notice it. I mean with the train and all... But, you know, we saw the tracks headed north. There was fresh snow on the ground; you couldn't miss 'em."

"Could be a trap," Riley said.

"Nah," Brooks said, shaking his head. "Trap would make no sense. They'd just kill our people or take them. No point in leaving a note like that. Henry is right. Brad probably killed Carson miles down rail. Dumped the body." Brooks turned and looked north, toward the burned-out town. "Brad did like Chelsea said—and like Brad said he was going to do all along. He went home."

Henry moved to a rusted car and leaned against the trunk, fishing the pipe from his pocket. "So, what now then?" he asked.

"What do you mean what now? We keep east. We find my family," Riley spat.

Sean ignored Riley and looked at the boys. "Your uncle said there were tracks. Where did they go?"

"That way," Lucas said, pointing north.

"What's there?"

Lucas looked at the trucks and back to Sean. "There's a town. Depending on the roads, could be a day's drive. We might want to find a place to stay over though; it's not good to be driving after dark."

"All right, let's mount up. We're wasting daylight here."

Brooks moved between them and stopped. Lifting his rifle, he looked through the optics. "We got a problem, Chief. Road's blocked ahead."

"Blocked how?"

Brooks sighed. "I think I found that herd we were following yesterday... and it's gotten bigger."

Stepping around him, Sean moved to the front of the truck and used the scope on his own rifle. Just as Brooks had said, near the center of a group of small homes was a cluster of creepers headed in their direction. "Well damn, and just when it was about to be a productive day," Sean said. "You see any Primals?"

Brooks swept the horizon to his front then focused somewhere off to the right. "Yeah, they're out there. Good half dozen of them, at least."

Sean looked back to the road headed south then back to the front. "Shit, south is nowhere, north looks like one hell of a fight, and we aren't going back."

Henry puffed on the pipe and squinted, considering the distance. "Looks like we go east then. I'm sure we'll find another spot to cut no—" Before the old man could finish his sentence, a round pinged off the hood of the Ranger parked on the east side of the road.

"Down! Sniper!" Brooks yelled, diving into cover just before two more rounds pinged off the truck.

"You see the shooter?" Sean shouted as he squatted behind the steel rim of the vehicle. More rounds snapped off, this time hitting the pavement to their front. One of the Baker boys went to run, and Joey tackled him to the ground, the pair of them falling into the depression with the bodies. Joey recovered and rose up, firing off a salvo of rounds.

"To the north, Chief, on the rooftops," Joey shouted, ducking as more rounds rained in on them. "They're mixed in with the damn creepers."

Sean eased up and peeked over the hood of the truck. Rounds pinged in, forcing his head back down. "Shit," he shouted as bits of pavement snapped back at him. He switched positions and caught a good look. He could see there was at least one shooter on the peak of a house. The building was surrounded by the stumbling Primal mass. "What the hell are they doing? They're trapped up there."

Joey fired off another burst in the direction of the houses, and a part of the mob broke off and headed toward them at a quicker pace than before.

Sean saw the mob change directions and said, "Hold your fire; you're pulling them to us." He pushed back and rolled around to the back of the Ranger. "Brooks, you got any Mark 18s?" he asked.

"Pair of white smokes, but they're in my gear pack. Front pocket," Brooks said.

"And where is the pack?"

"Passenger side. Top of the Tahoe," Brooks answered.

"Seriously?" Sean said. Scooting forward, he leaned out and looked to the vehicle across from him. "Of course, it is." The Tahoe was on the opposite side of the street and fully exposed to the incoming fire. More rounds pinged off the concrete between the vehicles to emphasize the distance. Sean took a deep breath and readied himself. "When I pop smoke, be ready to roll; I ain't coming back to get you. We get concealment and we roll."

"We got it, Chief," Brooks shouted back.

"Then give me some cover," Sean yelled as he rolled from his position and sprinted for the Tahoe. All around him, he heard his men's rifles opened up and directing fire at the rooftop snipers. The incoming rounds stopped as he found the pack and ripped open the pouch on the front. Pulling back the pocket flap, he found the two cans. Without waiting, he popped the first and rolled it just yards in front of their position. He had the second canister on the way before the first popped and spit flame and grey smoke. Sean waited for the smoke to obstruct his view of the distant town then yelled, "Move!" He rolled out from the Tahoe and ran for his seat in the Explorer.

The men piled in, and Brooks had the vehicle running almost instantly, but with the trailer behind him, he couldn't back up. He raced forward, driving through the smoke, unable to see as the snipers' rounds pinged off the truck. Brooks powered through, knowing the snipers were firing blind into the smoke. He cut the wheel again, the tires spinning behind him and the trailer bouncing on the shoulder. Leveling out, he mashed the pedal and made for the open road heading east. Sean looked over the bench seat and could see that the others were behind them in the Tahoe.

The road arced away from the town and was quickly tucked into hills. "What the hell was that?" Brooks said.

"That, my friends, was the New Republic," Riley grunted.

"The New what?" Sean said.

"Republic; what you all call Carson's army." Riley shook his head. "I thought all the raiders would have kept pulling east, but if they're setting up Monster blocks then they're here."

"What the hell is a Monster block?" Sean said, yanking a bottle of water from his pack.

"It's what you just saw. They root out the attic of a house and let the creepers surround it," Riley said, taking the bottle from Sean as it was offered. "They use it to block traffic on a road."

"They intentionally surround themselves with those things?" Brooks asked.

Riley nodded. "It works for them. They'll stay put for a week or so, and when it's time to move on or change guards, they'll use a high truck and ladders."

Tugging on his beard, Sean looked down at his knees then across at Riley. "If they have a road—er—Monster block then they must be close."

Riley nodded. "Yeah, they'd be holed up somewhere. I'd guess north, but could be south; you never know what direction they were intending on blocking."

Sean shook his head. "Not south; there would be nothing around here to block from the north—they're looking to slow down Texas." Sean pulled a county map from his pocket and traced fingers over the roads. "Brooks, you find a spot so we can head north."

"We looking for 'em, Chief?" Brooks asked.

"Not yet, but I want to get into their backyard."

CHAPTER 16

THIRTY MILES NORTH OF COLDWATER
COMPOUND. MICHIGAN SAFE ZONE

They moved through a narrow void with a high ceiling. "Where are we?" Brad said. He looked at the floors and dark, musty walls. It reminded him of the dark access tunnels under city streets or the basements of big buildings. Ventilation ducts, water pipes, and heavy bundles of electrical wiring and computer cables hung from conduits.

Gyles stopped and looked at him, holding a finger to his lips. "Quiet," he whispered. "We're in a maintenance hallway. On the other side of this wall is the gymnasium."

"You said we were secure in here," Brad whispered.

Gyles dipped his chin and nervously scratched his shoulder. "We are, but those things are just on the other side of this wall. If they pick up on us, they'll get all riled up. It's best to not let them know we're here." Gyles turned and continued down the hall until he reached a barricaded set of double doors. Brad stood looking at them and the heavy linked chain that was wound through the handles. He began wondering how they would get through, when he saw Gyles had walked into a corner and was climbing a roof access ladder.

Gyles climbed without giving any instruction, so Brad grabbed at the ladder rungs and followed the man up. Before reaching the top, Brad watched Gyles step off onto a platform that he hadn't been able to see from the ground. The man scooted out of the way, making room for Brad to step in beside him.

"What the hell are we doing up here?"

Gyles frowned. "I wanted to tell you about this last night but thought it'd be easier if I showed you."

"Showed me what?"

Pursing his lips, Gyles looked away and moved along the catwalk that cut into a square high in the wall. Brad followed him into the space and was immediately hit with a musty stink of bad air. It reminded him of calving pens when he was a kid, but pens that had gone months without a good cleaning. He reached to his neck and pulled his balaclava up over his mouth and nose. He looked down below them and could see a false ceiling grid suspended by wires. Over their heads was a ceiling supported by black steel beams.

They shuffled along the catwalk to a narrow set of stairs that led to a door that was about two feet wide by four feet tall. Gyles stopped and knelt beside it. He looked at Brad and signed, *You ready?*

Brad shook his head and tried to hold in a frustrated glare. He grunted, and waved the man ahead to say, *Let's go.*

Gyles moved down to the door and cautiously opened it; light quickly spilled in through the opening and was followed by another blast of the dank air. The man stepped low and moved through the opening. Brad followed closely behind him then paused with his hand frozen to the handrail as he looked below. The catwalk extended out into open space. Below him was an old basketball scoreboard, and below that, a long drop to a gymnasium floor filled with Primal bodies. Not creepers, but fully functioning Primals scattered around the space in groups and clusters.

Ahead, Gyles was still creeping along the catwalk. Brad could see the things below him moving about. Others were nested together, sleeping in piles of filth. In one corner of the gymnasium, he spotted a mass of them feeding on something. It looked like a large animal—possibly a deer; they were pulling pieces off it then running away with it to their own spaces to devour it in smaller groups.

"No," Brad said, shaking his head. "Oh, hell no; I'm going back."

Brad scooted backwards and, once through the low door, turned and walked back up the narrow steps to the top of the catwalk. Once there, he didn't stop. He moved all the way back to the ladder and leaned against the wall. After a short wait, he watched Gyles return. The man moved through the doorway and closed the door then tossed up his hands at Brad.

"What the hell, man?"

"Da fuck was that?" Brad asked. "What the hell are you thinking?"

"It's what I needed to show you. I've tried telling the others, but they don't want to listen."

"What? That there's a shitload of Primals with a nest inside a school? Screw you, Gyles; that ain't some new science. There's shit like this everywhere."

"Not like this!" Gyles said with his jaw clenched. "I ain't stupid. I've seen hives before, but this is different... the numbers are doubling every day. They're pouring into the region."

"Different how?" Brad asked, still shaking his head but wanting to calm the man.

"It's not a hive. Those things are living down there; they're *thriving*. It's more than a hive, it's... it's like a home, like they're surviving here. Breeding here. And the walls to the south are keeping them here. Southern Michigan isn't safe anymore. They're migrating here for some reason, and I think that reason is us."

"Migrating? Shut up, Gyles," Brad said, unable to hide the shock in his voice.

Gyles looked down and exhaled loudly. "I can't prove it, but I think they've devoured all the food elsewhere, and this place—shielded by the wall—is a happy hunting ground. Why else would they all come here?" Gyles looked up at Brad. "Why, Sergeant? Tell me."

"What in the hell are you trying to say, Gyles? I don't know what it is you're after."

Gyles dropped to the catwalk and put his back to the wall, letting his legs hang off the steel walkway. "I've been telling people, but nobody will listen. I told it to the senator. He kicked me out of his office. I told Sergeant Brown, and he called me an asshole."

"Tell me," Brad said. "What is this about?"

"Everything has changed. All of it. It's not safe here anymore," Gyles said. "They have us outnumbered here, and it's just getting worse every day. The containment has been breached; we've lost. We can't kill our way out of this." He shook his head. "Not anymore. We need to get everyone out. Need to get the people north and away from here."

"We could burn the school," Brad said.

Gyles looked at him and smiled. "You're not getting what I'm saying. This is just one spot. Do you know how many of them are down there? There are places like this all over between here and Detroit, and it's even worse to the west. I killed a Primal last week with a Chicago driver's license. They are migrating."

"No... no way," Brad asked. "Can't be."

The young soldier shook his head. "It's true; I've seen it."

Brad examined Gyles's face then closed his eyes and looked away. "Why did you bring me here? What do you want out of me?"

"The southern part of the state is lost. We need to pack up and head north."

"You already said that." Brad could see the look of frustration in the young man's face. He paused and tried to consider the man's words. "And you told this to the senator?"

Gyles bit at his lower lip and shook his head. He leaned back against the wall and let his eyes close as he spoke softly. "He doesn't see it—or doesn't want to." Gyles sighed. "We had it clear, man—all of it. Had the Primals close to wiped out north of the wall. But that's all changed now. He hasn't really gotten a grip on what's happening. Maybe a year ago we could have held, but with what's happening with the New Republic—them knocking down the walls and walking these things to our communities, killing off the populations—we're done."

"We can fight them," Brad said.

"We can't fight both the Primals and the raiders at the same time, and still protect our people."

Brad thought about what Gyles was saying and realized he was right. They couldn't run an offensive war against the raiders while defending their homes night and day against Primals. They just didn't have the people or the resources—not yet; he knew there was help on the way, or there might be. He looked up. "What about Texas? They have the manpower to make a difference."

"They could, but it would probably be too late," Gyles said. "Even with them, the Primals have us outnumbered a hundred to one. And with the raiders already at our gates... I mean, look what they've managed to do to us in a day. All this running, you thought we were hunting them. The entire time we were being played. With that drone, they knew exactly what we were doing, and they followed us."

Brad held up his hands, having heard enough. "Listen, I'm exhausted, Gyles. Just tell me what the hell it is you want to do."

"I want you to send that corporal and Palmer back to the Coldwater compound. Tell them to pack up and move everyone to the Capital."

"And us?"

"I want you to go out with me alone. We get small and we can hurt them. I want you to help me slow down the raiders. Find out where they are and kill as many of them as we can."

"Just the two of us?"

Gyles nodded. "All we have to do is cause them problems. Keep them busy long enough so our people can move north."

Brad stopped to think about the proposition. Maybe that was the way. Get the people out of the way while they get quiet and take the fight to the raiders. Run an old-fashioned block-and-delay action while they wait for Texas. Brad shook his head and laughed.

Gyles looked at him. "You okay, Sergeant?"

Brad let his head drop, and he reached into a thigh pocket for a bottle of water. "I don't think any of us are okay anymore. The more people I kill, the closer I get to being killed. It's like there's no place to go to get away from it."

Looking down, the young man licked his teeth and nodded. "I'm sorry. I hardly know you... It's too much to ask. I can go it alone; I've been out there on my own before."

"Nah." Brad grimaced. "If there is killing to be done, I'm your man."

CHAPTER 17

L eroy Spencer woke to the sounds of gunfire. His head jerked up, and he quickly pulled on his boots.

"What is it?" he called up to the roof.

"Just travelers; we stopped 'em. They're running, scared as hell," the voice called back.

The gunfire stopped as he finished lacing up his boots. The things outside the house were still howling and banging against the exterior walls. The place had been selected well, and the man who left him there was right—the home was well-built and could hold up to the masses pushing against the walls. Well-built or not, he wasn't happy about having been put out on Monster block duty—he was a captain in the regulars; there were better things for him to do than run a three-man fire team on a blocking force.

Leroy stood from the chair and walked to a ladder leading up to a hole cut in the roof. He was in what had probably been a teenage girl's bedroom on the second floor of the home. There was a knocked-over dresser and end tables. Posters hung on the wall, there were clothes dumped on the floor, and a bed and mattress were knocked off their frame and pushed up against the only window. He stood in front of an open closet door with a mirror hanging on it, a long crack running from the top to the bottom.

He ran a hand through his greasy hair as he looked at his reflection, shaking his head at the red and wind-burnt skin on his face. For being barely thirty, he looked forty. His blue eyes were lined with dark circles and the scruff on his beard was coming in grey. "What the hell am I doing here?" he said to himself before his radio chirped. He moved back to the desk and lifted the small Motorola radio. "This is Spencer," he said.

"What's going on over there, Spence? We heard gunshots; you all okay?"

Leroy held the radio in his hand, looking at it with disgust. The man on the other side was a moron, but still technically his superior. Not of higher rank—they were both captains, but Marcus Wahl was considered senior and had been put in charge of their little group. Unlike most men in the Regulars, Marcus never served in the military. He purchased his commission after the fall, trading everything he owned for a spot in the New Republic.

Leroy looked at the radio, shaking his head and wondering if he'd made a mistake leaving his unit a year ago. Maybe he should have stayed and died with them instead of moving north. Now what was he? Was he even a soldier anymore? Maybe. He was here in uniform, a member of a recon element of the New Republic Regulars, sent out ahead of a full-strength battalion deployed to crush anything Texas sent north.

That should have meant hiding and setting up observation posts—not running Monster blocks. But Wahl was in charge, so they did things his way. And doing it Wahl's way meant they were to sit and watch for any signs of Texas approaching. If spotted, they would pursue and report back to the battalion still arriving at the train depot to the northeast.

He shook his head, thinking of the mission orders. "What the hell am I doing here?" he said again, turning back to the mirror.

Spencer keyed the radio and put it to his mouth. "Just travelers at the block; the snipers ran them off."

"Okay, sounds good, buddy. Stand by; we'll be moving along to fetch you soon. Boss wants us to pack up and move north."

"What about the road? What about Texas?"

"We've located survivors from what's left of Carson's group. Texas is on its heels; no reason for us to stick around anymore."

Spencer exhaled and clipped the radio to his shirt. "Carson's group," he mumbled to himself. "A bunch of misfit assholes doing their own thing. They deserve whatever they got." He looked back toward the door behind him, ensuring it was still barred shut. He hated guys like Carson —people who thought they made their own law. The New Republic never should have gotten involved with that lot. Now instead of being back home, eating good meals and sleeping in a warm bed, he was out here trying to shut down a war Carson's people started. And for what? A promise that they could deliver food and survivors back to the Republic? They never saw any food from Carson, and all the survivors had been moved back into Carson's district. "Survivors," he spat and shook his head. There were plenty of rumors that the survivors were really prisoners—slaves even. "Fuck Carson."

He shook his head before moving to the ladder rungs.

"So, we just surrender ground and let them have the road. I'm working with morons," he mumbled under his breath as he pulled himself up the ladder and through the hole in the roof.

At the top, he saw two men lying in a valley of the roof with a rifle rested over the peak. Spencer stepped through the hole and moved close to them, looking back toward the railroad intersection. The road was covered in thinning white smoke. The stumbling zombies had moved out and were filling the intersection, wandering aimlessly in search of the men who were no longer there.

"What's with the smoke? You all set something on fire?" he asked. In previous encounters, his shooters had put rounds into vehicles and managed to set them ablaze. It was an unintended consequence, but one he didn't mind. They preferred to not destroy functioning vehicles, but sometimes it happened. His job was to not let anyone pass the intersection. If people died in the process, it was still a win... sometimes even preferred.

"No, they popped smoke. Took off headed east."

"Popped smoke?" Spencer said. "Like they hauled ass or like they had smoke grenades?"

The sniper looked up from his rifle. He was young. Corporal Billy Adams had only been in the forces for a few months and had followed Spencer here all the way from Pittsburg. The kid was under twenty years old, still in high school when the fall happened. The boy next to Billy, Private First Class Douglas Jones, was no different. There were a lot of young men in the New Republic Regulars, young men who volunteered to join the battalions, and only the best were selected for the recon elements. It was a way to get fed, and the volunteer money went a long way toward taking care of the families they left behind.

Billy stared at Spencer and said, "Yeah, smokes and military rifles. They knew what they were doing." The boy grinned. "But they still ain't get past us. They ran just like the rest of 'em."

Spencer shook his head. "I doubt that." He stepped higher on the roof. "What direction did they come from?"

"West," the kid answered. "They used smoke and suppressing fire to keep our heads down while they ran. Most of their shots went wide though; they couldn't hit shit."

"Dammit! Those were Texas scouts!" Spencer said. "You idiots should have woken me up."

"But, sir, you said not to bother you."

"I said don't bother me for stupid shit. Texas scouts is the entire reason we're here."

He reached for the radio and keyed the button. "Hey, Marcus, you still there?"

"I'm here, buddy." Spencer rolled his eyes.

"This last group; they might be scouts. They moved in from the west, had military equipment, and fled moving east."

"You sure about that, Spence?"

He shook his head and looked at the two boys. "How many were there?"

"Buncha dudes, two trucks—one had a trailer on it," Billy said.

Spencer nodded and put the radio back to his mouth. "Yeah, I'm sure. Two vehicles; one with a trailer. Military gear. My guys shot at them, but they popped smoke and hauled ass."

"Shit! Okay, buddy. On our way; be ready to move when we get there."

Spencer cut the radio and clipped it back to his belt. He

waved a hand at the boys to gather their gear and meet him back in the bedroom below. Then he moved to the ladder and dropped back into the lower room. He stuffed his handful of things back into his assault pack then moved to the mattress and pulled it away from the window. He leaned out and looked left and right to make sure nothing had managed to get onto the lower porch roof. He found it safe and stepped out onto the roof, waiting for the boys to join him.

He could hear the two young men joking inside the room. He looked back and saw one of the boys crawling through the window with a fistful of women's underwear. "Boy, get rid of that shit! Just because we're leaving doesn't mean it's safe, so stop screwing around," Spencer scolded them.

The boys' grins vanished. Douglas tossed the women's garments underhand off the porch roof and into the zombies below.

"What about the block?" Billy asked, looking at Spencer.

Spencer stopped fumbling with his pack and looked back at the boy. "The block was set up to locate the advance Texas elements... we did that."

"So now what?"

Spencer smiled. "We're going to track down the scouts, get what information we can, and then kill them."

A rumble from up the road turned Spencer's head. A large armored car, followed by a pair of woodland-camo, two-and-a-half ton military trucks, was moving toward them. Spencer slung his pack over his shoulders and waited for the small convoy to approach. The armored car moved just past their position and stopped while the first of the military trucks drove close to the covered front porch and stopped.

"Well, this is our ride, boys," Spencer said, moving to the edge of the porch. A man in the back of the truck had already raised up an aluminum ladder for him to climb down. The zombies outside the truck had become agitated and were pushing on the vehicle. Aside from the wobble of the ladder, it didn't concern Spencer much. They'd performed the same procedure dozens of times, and the slow-moving, nearly dead Primals they called *zombies* had never been able to get into the vehicles.

He dropped down into the rear troop compartment and waited for the two boys. Billy helped the man stow the ladder, and the truck pulled away from the house. They moved onto the road and continued south toward the intersection, where they took a left turn to travel east—the direction they'd seen the earlier vehicles go. Spencer unclipped the handheld radio from his belt, watching it and expecting a call from Marcus when, instead, the trucks slowed and eventually squealed to a stop.

Spencer stood and looked out over the high rails of the vehicle. They were in the center of a cleared blacktop road. They'd moved into the cover of trees and, looking behind them, he could see no evidence of the zombies following. Spencer moved to the back of the truck and undid a latch, opening a small gate. Not bothering to drop the handmade steps, he grabbed a handle and swung down to the ground with the rest of his team following him.

He moved forward to the armored car and found it with the double rear doors opened and Marcus looking over an old road map. The man looked up as he heard Spencer approaching. "So they turned east; where you think they were headed?"

Spencer stepped up and into the armored car, the boys staying outside to stand watch like bodyguards. It was an old bank delivery vehicle. The steel shelves inside had all been removed, and a large steel table was now bolted in the center. Spencer moved around the table and grabbed a thermos that was bungee-corded to the wall. He shook it and, finding it half full, poured himself a cup of coffee. He turned back toward the map and could see that Marcus had circled the Monster block in red wax marker and had their current route traced in yellow.

He sipped at the lukewarm coffee and moved closer. "My guess is they'll take the next available route north. They weren't expecting the roadblock, or they would've fought us. We forced them to flee. They'll get away, and then try to get back on course."

Marcus nodded in agreement and traced his finger along the road, stopping at another bold line. "Here then; it'll take them right back up and into Michigan."

Sucking his teeth, Spencer leaned down over the map. He traced the route with his finger and pointed. "One Twenty-Four. It's a good route, take 'em straight to 33. It's damn near a better route than if we'd just let them pass."

"Well, we'll just have to move quickly and stop them."

Spencer smiled.

"Something funny?" Marcus asked.

"We're traveling in slow, hard-to-maneuver vehicles; they have a pair of light trucks," Spencer said matter-of-factly. "What do you think the odds are that we'll catch them?"

"So, what do you want to do then?"

"Most of that ship has sailed... the right thing to do would have been to set up an ambush, not a damn Monster block. But like I said, it's all water under the bridge now."

"Hey, Monster block worked. We spotted 'em, right? It worked, didn't it?"

"Did you think they would just see it, stop, and wait for us to go collect them? We've got nothing. The better part of recon is intel. You want to go back with what we've got?"

"Hey, you think you know so much then tell me, what do we do?"

Spencer sighed, holding back on what he really wanted to say. "Okay, yeah, it worked. We spotted the scouts, and now we need to catch them. I know of an outpost; it's just twenty miles from here. *Three Corners* they call it; drop my team off there. I'll get me a faster vehicle, take my team north, and try to cut those scouts off. You make comms with battalion and give them updated coordinates. Then, loop back and do whatever you can to get eyes on the main force that's most likely headed this way."

The man shook his head. "No, absolutely not. The scouts were the mission," Marcus said. "Not search-and-destroy the enemy's main force."

Spencer sighed and rubbed the back of his hand against his forehead, warding off a headache. "I'm not suggesting you search and destroy anything. But what good is it if we go running away with our dicks in our hands and leave the back door wide open for their main body? The battalion is at least a half day away at the railhead. A lot can change in a half day." Spencer sipped at the coffee, trying to adjust his tone. "Tell me, you think it would be better for you to report back to the railhead and tell them where you *think* Texas is headed, or call on the radio that you've got eyes on them?"

This time it was Marcus who smiled. The man looked down at the map again then up at Spencer and nodded. "I like the way you think, Spencer. That's that good army training right there. You always thinking about the shit that I miss. We make a hell of a team, you and me."

Spencer looked away, trying to hide the disgust on his face. "So... what do you think then? Three Corners, I'll procure some wheels and pursue while you go after the main body. You lead the battalion to victory this time, put an end to all of this before it even starts," he said, knowing there was no place to lead the battalion if he couldn't get useful intel from the scouts. The odds of Marcus finding anything without him were slim to none. There were hundreds of routes the main elements could be taking north; for all he knew, they could be moving through the now abandoned roadblock behind them as they sat there discussing tactics.

"Three Corners, huh? Been a bit since I been that way. They got tasty food there?" Marcus asked.

"Last I heard they had a running tavern."

Marcus nodded his head and grinned. "Okay, get back to your ride. We'll make for the outpost then."

Spencer tossed the rest of his coffee out the back door and left the cup on the table. As soon as he jumped from the back of the armored car, the driver slammed and locked the doors shut. Spencer moved between the boys on the street, who'd stood behind him during his conversation with Marcus.

"Is that how it was during the war?" Billy asked him as they walked back to the truck.

"The war?" Spencer asked. "What you mean? Iraq?"

Billy nodded his head. "Yeah. Was it like this hunting down terrorists?"

"Nah, boy, it was nothing like this. Now come on, let's try to get some rest before we hit Three Corners. I have a feeling this won't be an easy trip."

CHAPTER 18

SOUTH OF LANCASTER, OHIO. THE DEAD LANDS

S ean pulled his rifle onto his lap and dropped the magazine. He checked the tension on the rounds and reinserted it then checked the safety before placing it back between his knees. They were racing north up a two-lane county highway. Soon after entering Ohio, they found the interstate too congested and had opted for the less crowded back roads. He let his eyes drift to the abandoned homes on the sides of the route. There were no people, no wildlife, and no Primals.

"You won't see any of them," Riley said from his seat.

Sean looked at the man. "What do you mean?"

"They don't run around out in the open the way they used to. Like Dylan said, 'The times they are a-changing'."

Sean looked at the burly, bearded man. He looked more like a biker or a nightclub bouncer than someone who fit out in the wild like this. Riley presented himself as a sort of blue-collar, family man, but Sean still wasn't buying the story, and he knew Brooks had concerns of his own. He'd met enough people in the military to know that outward appearances didn't always tell the full story of a man, so he was trying to give him an honest shot.

"You ever been to one of them deer farms?" Riley asked.

Laughing, Sean shook his head. "No, why? Do people have farms just full of deer?"

Riley scratched at his matted beard. "I guess that's what they call it. Maybe it's conservation or something like that. Anyhow, back home they had this place. This old guy, he raised deer, all kinds of 'em, and you could pay to walk around the farm, and they'd eat right out of your hand. Kids loved it." Riley paused, looking down at his folded hands.

Sean watched as the man clenched his eyes and shook off a thought.

He cleared his throat and continued. "Yeah, loads of friendly deer. You could pet them, pat 'em on the back if you wanted... Just try doing that out in the woods; you won't even get close to a white-tailed deer in the forest."

Brooks looked back at him from the rearview mirror. "What, were they tied up? Or in cages?"

Riley laughed at the comment. "Nah, man, not at all. It wasn't like they were in cages or sitting in pastures. Nothing like that. But it was, ya know, they just moved around like they were secure, you know? Like when you see a peacock at the zoo. They don't run from you because they know they're safe."

"Until you shoot at them," Sean said.

Riley pointed a finger at Sean. "Exactly. And that, my friend, is why you don't see Primals just out and about anymore. They started figuring out we could hurt them, that we can kill them if we need to."

Brooks grunted. "Not exactly additional information, Riley; Primals been changing since day one."

Nodding in agreement, Riley turned to the window.

"Yeah, they been getting smarter, but things have changed. Before, it was like they were just here—just popped into the food chain where they don't belong. Like a pack of lions escaped from the zoo and ended up in some unfamiliar environment where they didn't fit. They didn't belong, like in some bad movie. Not anymore; now they're part of the balance of the food chain—top of the food chain, and they know it. Like wolves or a grizzly—they know they can hurt us, but they also know we can hurt them. That's why now you only see them when it's on their terms. Like with a grizzly."

"Been seeing a lot more of the dead ones—the creepers," Sean said. "And more of the Primals are attacking when they didn't used to."

"It's because they're starving, and that's when we need to worry," Riley said. "We saw a lot of that out east too. There's more of them than the local wildlife can sustain. Lots of Primals all summer long, but once the winter came..." He shook his head. "Well, you know how they are. Instead of lying down to die from exposure, they come out zombies. I'm not sure what it is, or how it is some evolve and know how to survive in the wild and others don't. But that's the awful thing about it—you'd think they would just go away, but no, they just become something else to terrorize us."

Brooks grunted. "They're not zombies. They do die."

"Yeah," Riley said, his voice growing quiet. "They die, but they sure take their time doing it. The thing you really need to worry about is when Primals starve, they attack."

Brooks drove the truck to the shoulder of the road, slowing as they moved past a makeshift roadblock. The vehicles used in the roadblock were burned down to their shells. There was a third vehicle pressed into the two that had formed a V to block the road. Riley lowered his window and looked out then pointed at spent brass on the ground and a badly decomposed body near one of the cars. "Someone had one hell of a fight here. Wonder how long ago this was; a year maybe?"

Sean nodded. "Year at least. You see a lot of that out on the roads," he said.

Riley sighed. "That you do."

Turning in his seat, Sean looked at the man next to him. "Tell me again how it was you found your way out here."

The bearded man shrugged nervously. "I was taken from my home, forced to work for Carson's people when they took our compound."

"So, you were a raider then," Brooks said, looking back from the front.

"I wasn't a damn raider," Riley spat back. "I was laborer. I just worked for them."

Sean pointed to Riley's gun belt. "Tell me about your six gun there."

"What about it?"

"It's a nice piece of iron, and you got a holster for it. I'm guessing you didn't steal it."

"Nah, I didn't steal it. Everyone that worked the walls had a gun," Riley scoffed.

Brooks laughed. "So you were security then. You worked the walls, you carried a gun. Hell, sounds like a raider to me."

"Screw you; you don't know shit about raiders."

Sean held up a hand, silencing Brooks. "You said you're all out of ammo."

Riley nodded. "Yeah, used it all up during the escape. Place was on fire. The walls were down, everyone was running, they had zombies and Primals inside... Things got real crazy, really fast."

"Who'd you shoot?" Sean said. "Texas was attacking, right? How many of them Texas boys did you kill?"

"I didn't kill anyone."

Sean pursed his lips and rubbed his chin. "Hell, them Texas boys were out for blood. I'm sure it was in self-defense. You or them—am I right?"

Riley clenched his hands into fists. "I told you I didn't kill anybody. I shot some of them damn zombies trying to get me, that was it. I ran and shot some more. By the time morning came, I was out of bullets, and I stumbled upon Henry. The old man shared his fire with me and gave me some food." He put his hands on his pant legs and rubbed his thighs. "You know what? If you all don't trust me, just stop. Leave me here; I'll take my chances on my own."

Sean laughed. "Don't go getting all dramatic on us. Just trying to figure you out, is all."

"You all are assholes," Riley said. "That's what I've figured out about you all so far."

Laughing harder, Sean slapped the man on his shoulder. "Damn, you're not a quick study, are you? Most folks, it takes an hour or less to figure that out."

Brooks slowed the car and moved to the center. "Hey, Chief, what do you make of this?"

Sean looked up. They were at a three-way intersection. The two-lane road continued north, but there was a road going east that branched off from it. In the northeast corner was an old billboard with a hand-painted arrow pointing east. Below it were the words *Three Corners Settlement, Traders Welcome.*

Sean turned to Riley. "Any ideas?"

Lifting his head and scratching his neck, Riley said, "Outpost; there are a bunch of them out in the territories."

"They safe?" Sean asked.

Riley puckered his lips and held out a flat hand, tipping it side to side. "Some more than others. This far out, still in Ohio, we're probably okay. Closer to the New Republic, I wouldn't risk it. These are like trading posts—supply depots, I guess you could call 'em. The New Republic uses them to get stuff. They pay the folks that live out here to gather things for them, and every now and then they truck it all back to the New Republic. Stuff that's hard to find back home, where everything's all been picked over. The New Republic let the folks that live and work here keep some of the excesses to trade with others; you know, the holdouts and survivors."

Looking back, Brooks asked, "What stops raiders from, you know, raiding them?"

Riley shook his head. "No, not at outposts. They wouldn't be welcome there."

Brooks laughed. "What difference does that make? Thought raiders do what they want."

"Outposts are under protection by the New Republic Regulars," Riley said in a tone like he was talking to idiots.

"The who?" Sean asked, cutting off Brooks's next question.

"Damn, you all really don't know shit, do you? The Regulars, son; they're like the real army. Real soldiers. Even raiders don't mess with the Regulars."

"Wait," Sean said, rubbing his forehead. "I thought General Carson's bunch were the army."

"Hell, no! Carson's lot are nothing but cutthroats and

thugs. He runs the raiders; they do the dirty work. The Regulars secure the territory, put order to the chaos."

"The Monster block back there... who was that?"

Shrugging, Riley said, "Could be either. But I'm telling you, there won't be no raiders at this outpost. I can guarantee that. They might be close, they might be watching it, but they won't be welcome inside." He paused and looked out the window. "And this far from Pennsylvania, probably no Regulars inside either, but I can't guarantee that."

Sean looked at the horizon; it was getting late in the day. "Well, hell, Three Corners it is then."

Brooks made the turn and waited to ensure the tail vehicle was following them, then eased back to the center of the road. The path ahead was clear and, unlike the road they'd turned off, there were no signs of disabled vehicles. Even downed trees and limbs were pulled back from the pavement.

"We should stash the vehicle and walk in," Riley said, looking through the windshield nervously. "Outies don't trust people with rides."

"Outies?" Sean said.

Riley shrugged. "Yeah, outies—the folks that live in the outposts. It'll be suspicious, us rolling in with these vehicles. Horse and cart maybe, but it's strange having wheels like this."

Sean considered the suggestion and slapped the seat ahead of him. "Brooks, find us a spot to stash the rides. And Riley, that's a stupid nickname. I don't want to hear it again," he said.

"Whatever," Riley sulked.

It didn't take long and Brooks was guiding them on to a two-track overgrown trail. Set back in a distant tree line was a massive red, clapboard-sided barn. The nearby farmhouse was burnt down to its skeleton of framing and foundation stones. The trail was rough, and more than once Sean thought they might get stuck. The vehicle bucked, and Brooks moved it out of the two-track and onto tall grass. The barn had double doors at one end. The left door was still secured, while the right door was broken from the hinges and lying in front of the opening. The two-vehicle convoy moved past the opening and instead pulled behind the barn, parking between an old combine and a pair of hay rakes.

Sean opened his doors and exited, stretching his tired muscles. He stepped away from the truck and walked to the barn. The floor was covered with packed clay, animal pens were empty, and hay was still stacked in a loft overhead. He looked back toward the men standing near the vehicles. "We'll set up in here. Make a bit of a base camp, store most of the military gear, and go in with the lighter duffel bags."

"Why not take it with us?" Joey asked.

Sean smiled. "If we want to look like friendly traders, we probably can't run up on this place weighed down with weapons and heavy packs," he said, moving back toward the trucks. "Let's store the rucksacks and use some of those food bags to carry our gear—anything to make us look less militant."

Joey rubbed at his forehead. "I'm not so sure, Chief. Going in there soft is an effective way to get us killed. Splitting our forces is another."

"We aren't splitting up," he said, nodding in agreement. "I'm with you on that. That's why you and Brooks aren't going in. I'll hold you two out here as a Quick Reaction Force in case we get into trouble."

"I'm not down with that, Chief," Brooks said, walking past him to drop a pair of packs inside the barn door. "I go where you go."

"Nope. I'll take Riley, Henry, and the boys. They look the part because they are the part. You and Joey look like a pair of sheepdog wolf hunters; no way anyone's going to believe you aren't shooters," Sean said. "And the fact that you *are* my only shooters is why I need you out here in case we get into trouble."

Brooks moved back toward the truck and leaned against the fender. "That's your call, but if they have booze in there, you better make a fair trade and bring me back some."

CHAPTER 19

"He wants you to do what?" Chelsea said, looking at him, not attempting to hide the anger in her voice. She let her eyes move from Brad to Gyles and then back again. They were gathered in the small maintenance break room. "Why would you want to go with them after everything they've managed to do to us in just the last day? How is any of this our fight?"

Gyles put his hands up in surrender, but he said nothing, so Chelsea turned to Brad for an answer. "We have to get the civilians out, and this might be the only way. Avoiding Primals is one thing, but combined with the attacks, it's just too much; there are women and children in there."

She shook her head. "If you all want them out, then come with us and get them out. Help us lead them north."

The young soldier nodded, gritting his teeth. "They have too good an eye on the place. If our people come out, they'll attack. They'll just wait for them to get out into the open. They'll attract the zombies to them. They only way to get them out is to hit the zombies and keep them busy while the civilians make their move."

Chelsea let out a sarcastic laugh. "Why do you know so much about the way they operate?"

Shaking his head, Gyles made a fist and shook it then turned away. "We've already been over this. I've seen what they do to communities, the way they attack them."

"And how exactly is that supposed to work? So far, all we've done is lose people and equipment. We haven't done a thing to hurt them—"

"Ahh, that ain't the case," Palmer said, raising a hand from where he stood against the kitchenette. "You were sleeping when it happened, but I know I killed a bunch when I destroyed the bookstore."

"I got blown up, you asshole. I wasn't sleeping," Chelsea snapped back.

"Well, however you explain it, we hurt them. It's not like you said."

She grunted and shook her head, moving back to Brad. "You don't have to do this," she said.

"If I don't, they might all die—all those people we saw down on that floor. I can't live with that, can you?"

"Fine," Chelsea said, turning her back to him and moving around the table to a metal folding chair. "If it's that important, I'm going with you."

Brad looked toward Gyles, who shrugged. "I mean, I thought she was injured when I suggested she go back with Palmer, but I guess if she can fight..." Chelsea grunted again and glared at him. "Well, obviously she can fight," Gyles said, correcting himself. "So yeah, three guns is better than two."

Palmer ran a hand through his hair. He was still

standing in the back of the break room, leaning against the countertop. "So where does that leave me?"

Gyles looked to Chelsea and Brad and, seeing that they weren't about to speak, cleared his throat and answered. "Well, you just wait here until we leave. Give us time to head back south, then you mount up and make it straight back to the compound. Let them know what's going on and do whatever you can to convince the captain to evacuate to Lansing."

"Why Lansing?" Chelsea asked.

"Tanks," Palmer said, answering for Gyles.

"Tanks?" Brad asked, leaning forward. "If Lansing's got tanks then let's go after these guys. You didn't tell me you had armored support."

Palmer shook his head and bit at his lower lip. "We don't, not really. Anyhow, they're hardly mobile. The few we got were tore up bad during the fall, and parts been hard to come by—not to mention the techs to work on them; replacing a tread ain't exactly something you can get done at a dealership. But they've got them dug in good all around the capital building and convention center. They might not drive, but those main guns and coax machine guns keep the bad guys away."

"Whatever. Why are we even talking about this?" Chelsea said, not impressed. She'd pushed away from the table and was standing. "Let's get our gear and get moving. If this is as critical as you all say, we're wasting time just bullshitting around this table." She turned and locked eyes with Gyles. "I assume you have a vehicle, or were you planning to make us walk?"

He nervously adjusted the hat on his head and nodded. "Hell yeah, I got one."

Chelsea lifted her backpack to her shoulders then

shrugged it higher to her back and tightened the straps. She looked at Gyles and Brad. "Well? Are we leaving or not?" Without waiting for a response, she turned and moved into the hallway.

Palmer chuckled and looked at the two remaining men. "You all better get moving; she's liable to take off without you."

Brad stood and grabbed his rifle, Gyles doing the same as they took off after Chelsea. They moved back down the long hallways to the outside door they'd entered earlier in the day. Chelsea was already there with her rifle in her hand posted up. "You said you had a ride. Where is it?"

Gyles unhooked his rifle from his chest rig and slung the 12-gauge shotgun over his back so that it lay high on his rucksack. "Back outside the way we came. Go right; it's a short bus. I've already got some gear on board."

"Short bus?" Chelsea said, her head turning sideways. "Is it going to start?"

Nodding, the young man said, "Palmer rigged it to a trickle charger; it'll crank." His lips narrowed with uncertainty. "But..."

"But what?" she said.

"It's not in the fence enclosure."

Brad stepped closer and put a hand on Gyles's arm, turning him. "Then where is it? Outside in the row of busses we passed on the way here?"

Shaking his head, Gyles cleared his throat and lifted his rifle into a low carry. "It's no big deal. It's outside and around the corner, near the high school auto shop."

Leaning forward, Chelsea looked at Gyles and asked, "Why am I thinking this is bad?"

"Well... we kinda used the shop to get the bus up and running, got new tires on it, new battery, changed the plugs, and all of that. Even rat rigged some plate steel and chain link over the windows. We got her purring good. We'd just filled her up, so she would be topped off and ready to go."

"And then?" Chelsea said sarcastically.

Gyles's face reddened. "Guess we made too much noise. Something crashed inside the school; they got into the halls. They took out the doors to the shop class, and we had to make a run for it. But no worries, the outer fence stopped them."

"No worries," Chelsea spat. "So where is your short bus now?"

Gyles moved past her and unbolted the door. He pulled it up and looked outside into the bright light then looked back at the other two. "It's parked just outside the shop's overhead doors." He looked up at the bright-blue, cloudless sky. "Cold sunny day like today, there won't be many of them outside." He finished his sentence then stepped outside with Chelsea staying close to him.

Brad cursed under his breath and reached into a nylon pouch on his chest, removing a suppressor for his M4. He threaded it onto his barrel before dropping and press checking the magazine. He looked back into the dark hallway behind him and followed the others outside.

CHAPTER 20

They walked in two columns with Henry leading the way, Riley just behind him. Sean was on the shoulder with the two Baker boys, lagging back farther behind the group. They'd lost all their military gear, all of them now carrying large duffel bags or civilian-style backpacks. Armed with shotguns and bolt-action rifles, only Sean with his M4 stood out. But this was the fall, plenty of men carried M4s now.

The road was broken, large potholes with weeds breaking through the bleached surface. They had to lift their feet and pay attention to prevent twisting ankles. Sean looked up; the sun was to his back as they approached what was determined to be the Three Corners outpost. It wasn't a walled-in compound as Sean expected it to be. It was literally a large, red-brick building at the end of a dead-end street. The type or original purpose of the building was hard to make out. Government, maybe commercial. It was tall, four stories at least, and stretched close to three football fields wide. The bottom two floors of windows were all covered in plywood. The perimeter of the building was covered with orange construction fencing, which made Sean think the building may have been closed prior to the fall.

Stepping near the intersection, Sean saw that every other building in the area had been burnt to the ground, nothing but charred remains left behind to show they were ever there. He examined the blackened beams of the buildings as they walked past them. Maybe they were burned for security purposes to not give anybody nearby a place to hide. He let his eyes scan left and right. He could see plenty of stumps but no trees. The fields as far as he could see were clear of obstructions for at least a hundred feet.

Henry stopped up front and unshouldered his pack, setting it on the ground by his right foot. He turned back toward Sean and angled his chin, signaling him forward. Sean kept his eyes on the tall building, scanning the rooflines and windows as he moved forward. He saw no signs of life. No gates, doors, or vehicle entrances. He moved up alongside Henry and stopped.

"How's this usually work?" he said, looking at Riley.

Shrugging off his own pack, Riley set it on the ground by his feet then dropped down to sit on it. The big man was sweating profusely. The Baker boys moved in close and stepped to a weed-covered street curb and dropped to the ground. Riley avoided looking at the building. "As soon as they caught sight of us, they started sizing us up. Running word to whoever is in charge. They'll call for their security guys—usually whoever it is they got that can handle a rifle. Then they'll let the people inside know they have visitors. The leader, whomever that might be, will come to some spot along the wall—or a window as this place might be—and take a long, hard look at us. Then they'll either ignore us, shoot at us, or send someone out to talk to us," he said.

As if on cue, they heard the dull ringing of a bell. The bell rang at least eight to ten times before the sounds of screeching metal joined it. Sean turned on his heels and looked toward the face of the building. Between tall windows and at the top of a set of stairs, an opening appeared in what before looked like a barricaded entrance. At first it opened into nothing but a darkened space. Soon after, a pair of figures appeared then stepped out and stopped just short of the steps. The men carried shotguns, their heads scanning the front. A third figure in a dark hide jacket walked out between them. He wore faded blue jeans and tanned leather boots, a heavy fur hat on top of his head. The man kept his thumbs in a gun belt with the wood handle of a revolver tucked into the right side. Sean could just see the grip of a second handgun in a holster under the man's right hand.

Henry looked back at Sean and grinned. "How about you let me handle this one while you take notes?"

Looking at the man approaching, Sean returned Henry's smile; he could tell this was one of Henry's type. "Carry on then."

The old man nodded and reached into his shirt pocket for his pipe. He lay his lever-action rifle over the top of his pack and stepped off in front of the group to meet the strangers. Henry had the pipe between his lips and was touching a match to it just as the man with the fur skin cap stopped to their front.

He looked at the group, his eyes studying them the same way Sean had seen chieftains study him overseas in war zones. The fights might have changed, but the people stayed the same. Once the game of looking everyone over ended, the man switched his stare to Henry and said, "What business you folks got in Three Corners?"

Henry puffed on the pipe then pulled it from his lips, exhaling the smoke. "Just looking for a place to rest our heels. We've got trades to make iffen your sign back a way holds true about traders being welcome. We can pay for our stay."

The man let his eyes search the group again, lingering a bit longer on Sean than the others. He looked back at Henry. "Where you all coming from? I haven't seen your group out this way before."

"Coming from West Virginia."

The man's brow tightened. "West Virginia, you say?" He shook his head slowly then turned to look at one of the men standing watch beside him. The man returned a cinched grin as if he didn't know what to make of it. The old man looked back at Henry. "Don't mean to appear rude, but we've had a sudden rush on travelers from West Virginia. Why in the hell would you travel north, when all we hear about is how much better things are in the south?"

"Things are changing," Henry responded just before placing the pipe back between his lips. "Just working our way north, scrapping, trying to make some trades... trying to stay above ground."

Looking over Henry's shoulder, the man again eyed the others then looked back at the same guard who this time smiled, moving one side of his mouth. The old man looked back at Henry. "Ya'll are welcome to enter. Keep your weapons holstered or on slings. No chambered rounds inside the outpost." The man removed his fur cap and looked back at the outpost. "We already made the monthly shipment back east, so the trucks are all gone. The trade boss ain't here, but we can offer you a meal and a place to stay."

"That would be right neighborly of you." Henry

grinned slyly and dropped the magazine on his 1911. He pulled the slide and caught the ejected round before returning the magazine. He turned and watched the others perform the same procedures, clearing their rifles and sidearms. Sean held steady and resisted the temptation to look behind him; he knew that Brooks and Joey would be out there somewhere perched over rifles and watching every move. He cleared his HK MK23 and holstered it in his chest rig.

The white-bearded man from the outpost looked them over and, once satisfied, nodded and signaled for everyone to follow him. Henry kept a close pace with the man, chitchatting as was his nature, while Sean lingered back and let the Baker boys move up ahead of him. He saw that the guards were scanning the outside and not particularly focused on them. Sean wasn't sure if that was a good or bad sign. Too trusting could be a fault, something to be wary of.

As he neared the building, he could make out more of the outpost's defenses. There were portholes cut into the bricks between the boarded-up windows and a narrow trench a few feet from the outer wall of the building. It was smart and well thought out, and from a distance, it was all impossible to see. He watched the others move through the entrance. One of the guards held back, waiting on him while Sean stopped at the top of the steps to take a last look around. He put his hand on the red-brick wall and rubbed the surface, noticing there were no pockmarks from bullet holes; the place seemed to have been spared any human attacks.

The guard seemed to not care about what he was doing. The man's eyes were fixed on the distant tree lines. He was stocky and dressed in jeans and heavy flannels. Sean followed the man's gaze. "Are you looking for something?"

The man lifted his eyes and looked at Sean. "Saw a group of them this morning. They've made runs for the open doors before. Can never be too careful," he said.

Sean nodded and moved toward the door. "Sorry, I didn't mean to hold you up."

Grunting a response, the man moved behind him. Two more men closed in from inside and secured the heavy door. Sean squinted; instead of entering a building as he expected, it was more of a covered walkway that led into a squared courtyard. He followed the others through to the open space that was lined with tents, shipping crates, and pallets wrapped in thick plastic. He turned in a full circle and could see that the interior windows were all intact—not covered with wood like on the outside.

He watched the guard look back at him again. This time, the man waved a hand, urging Sean to keep up with the group. They wended through the courtyard to a long, narrow building made entirely of scrap lumber. The roof was made of tarps and some large white strips of plastic, punctured by a stove pipe with a stream of white smoke escaping from it.

Just outside the door, White Beard stopped and let them bunch up. He looked at all of them before stopping to speak to Henry. "This is our community tavern, I guess you could say. If you want to grab a drink or some food, this is the place. There are a few other traders inside if you want to make some deals. Tracey inside will get you a place to sleep if you're interested in that. If not, just find the gate when you're ready to go."

Sean interrupted, putting up a hand. "Who is in charge here? I'd like to have a word, if that's possible."

The man started laughing, his stained teeth contrasting with the beard. "This ain't that kinda place. This is a community; you want to speak to the trading manager, he ain't here. Like I said, he took the last supply train east. He'll be back in a few days. You find you need something, just ask for Seth and someone will send for me."

Sean scratched at the bottom of his beard. "Tell me, Seth, where east did the trade boss go?"

The man gave Sean a sideways glance and answered, "To the railhead. Where else would he go?"

Sean tightened his brow and nodded, trying to fix his error. "The trains are running then?" he said.

"Yeah, the trains are running. Why wouldn't they be?" Seth answered, his tone hardening.

Sean shrugged and showed his palms. "No reason, we just met some folks on the road that said the trains were down." Sean could see that the guards had gained sudden interest. The man that was lingering back with his shotgun before looked up and took a step closer.

"What sort of folks?" Seth asked.

"Man and a woman. They were headed north. They said something about the trains being down," Sean said.

The white-bearded man looked puzzled and shook his head. "Not that we've heard of, but trains don't run regular no how. They run folks west then pick up goods on the way back. We don't head to the depot unless we have a full load or they call for us."

"So..." Sean asked. "No man and woman passed through here?"

"Traveling alone? They have a death wish or something? Dangerous country out there."

Sean nodded as he placed his hands in his pockets "Yeah, I reckon it is."

The man looked at Sean, his teeth clenched as he took in a deep breath, his eyes studying him. "If something was bothering you, I might be able to help you myself," the man offered.

Chomping like he was chewing a piece of grass, Sean shook his head. "Nah, I think I'll be okay. So how's the menu in here?" he said, walking away from the group and entering the tavern.

The room was dark, musty, and smelled of smoke and dry wood, the only light entering from small breaks in the roof. The floor was covered with tables made from large, empty cable spools. The outer edges of the bar were lined with longer plank tables, several of them occupied by men sitting over bowls of stew or half-empty glasses. At the end was a long bar with lights hung over it. Sean stopped and listened; he could hear the hum of a generator. He moved around the spool tables to a far corner and dropped his pack before taking a seat at a table that faced the door.

Sean watched the others enter the room behind him, but it was Riley who caught his eye. The man entered coolly then seemed to take notice of a pair on the far side of the room. The two men were wearing worn canvas shirts that were at least a size too big. One had a bright green trucker's hat turned backward on his head. The other looked to be at least fifty years old, all skin and bones with sunken eyes. Both had greasy hair and beards that hadn't been trimmed or groomed in weeks.

Riley turned away and adjusted his cap low to cover his face then followed the others in. He picked a seat on the far side of the table, away from Sean, and kept his chin tucked while his eyes stayed locked on the men in the corner. Sean let the others drop their gear and sit before he turned to Riley. "Who are they?" he asked.

Riley's head snapped toward Sean. He looked down at

the scratches and marks carved into the table. "Who are you talking about?"

"The pair your eyes are trained on; the ones you are pretending not to notice. You know them?"

Riley looked up at the distant table then back to Sean again. "I know 'em."

"How?" he asked.

"From Crabtree; they're part of Gus's crew." Riley hushed as a heavyset woman in a dark apron approached the table.

The woman set a large pitcher of water in the center and a wooden tray filled with stacked glasses and bowls next to it. She looked them over, pointed to a blackboard over the bar with scratched-on white writing, and then read aloud in a husky voice. "Rabbit stew today; there's plenty of root vegetables in it, so it ain't too bad. All the bread for today is gone." She pointed at the pitcher. "If ya want something besides water, Carl's got a batch of mead that ain't too awful for what it is. And we've always got the mash. No filling canteens from the pitcher. You need water, we got a hand pump out back you're welcome to use."

"How's the mash?" Henry asked.

She shrugged. "Keeps the generators running, so I guess it ain't so bad."

"Bring a bottle then," Sean said.

She stopped and gave Sean a stern look. "How you boys plan on paying?" she asked.

"What'll you take in trade?" he said.

She grinned, her cheeks dimpling. "Most folks pay with ammo, but we can barter on most things." She looked at the packs and slung rifles. "Say fifty rounds of .223 for the bottle of mash" —she paused and counted the men seated at the table— "and another ten for the five bowls of stew."

Henry grinned. "You got any tobacco?" he asked, holding up his pipe.

She nodded. "We got some."

Reaching inside the top flap of his pack, Henry removed two twenty-round boxes of .308 ammo from his pack and set them on the table. "Add on the tobacco, and let's make it forty rounds of real bullets for all of it."

She lifted the Winchester ammunition boxes and eyed the seals, seeing they were brand new. She nodded and dropped them into a pouch on the front of her apron. "Deal."

Before she could walk away, a large boy approached from behind the bar, holding a deep cast-iron kettle. Sean could tell be the way the kid moved that he had a quirk of some kind. He was too big for his mannerisms, and he walked with an awkward gait. He took the bowls and lined them up carefully before filling each with hearty portions from the kettle.

The boy looked back toward the kitchen the woman had just disappeared into. "I ain't 'posed to, but if you want seconds you just give me a holler, and I'll get you some more. You just say, 'Frank, I'm still hungry.' And then I'll know." He closed his mouth and looked away as he saw the woman walking back toward the table, carrying the bottle of mash.

She batted a hand at the boy and said, "Frank, go check on them fellas over in the corner." The boy nodded and moved away, still holding the kettle, and headed to the corner table. The woman handed the corked bottle to Sean then pulled a paper pouch from her apron and placed it on the table in front of Henry.

The old man let go of his spoon and wiped his chin with the sleeve of his jacket. He lifted the pouch and opened it, sniffing the contents. He looked up at the woman and grinned. "This'll do just fine, ma'am."

"Call me Tracey," she said, her eyes moving to the corner where Frank had gone.

Sean was pouring two fingers of the shine into his glass and caught the woman's concerned stare. He shifted in his seat and could see the men in the corner were increasingly harassing the boy. It went from playful to more aggressive as they caught on that the boy wouldn't fight back. "Who are they?" Sean asked her.

She looked at him, then eyed back at the corner. She shook her head. "Don't worry about it; Frank's dealt with worse than that."

"He shouldn't have too," Sean said, his jaw clenching.

Ruckus and laughter came from the corner. Sean turned to see a man pointing a hand toward their table. The man with the trucker cap yelled a jumbled slur of words that Sean couldn't make out while pointing at Frank. The boy shook his head and backed up. The man yelled again, and Frank turned and looked directly at Riley before turning back to the pair and shaking his head again. One of the men shouted toward their table as the man on the right reached out and kicked Frank away with his boot, causing the other to laugh. The man with the cap shouted for Riley by name.

"Looks like your friends have recognized you," Sean whispered.

"They ain't no friends of mine," Riley said back, his jaw locked with his lips hardly moving.

Riley pushed himself back from the table and stood, straightening his jacket before removing it and placing it over the back of his chair. With his jacket off, the revolver showed prominently on his hip. Tracey turned and looked at him. "We don't want any trouble. Just let it be, okay?"

Riley used the back of his right hand to rub at his chin. "I ain't looking for trouble either. But yet here I am, with it looking for me."

"You need some backup?" Sean asked.

The big, red-bearded man grinned and rolled his shoulders. "Just going to have a chat; go on and enjoy your rabbit," he said, stepping away from the table.

Sean watched as Riley wended across the tavern, weaving his way through the spool tabletops in the center. He'd seen enough fights in his time and the look in a fighter's eyes to know a talk wasn't coming. Others had apparently seen it too, as men were leaving tables and clearing out of the tavern. As the big man got closer to the pair, Frank used the distraction to move away from the duo.

The man with the green trucker's hat waved a hand at an empty chair, but Riley didn't sit. Instead, he stepped up close to the table, placed his flat hands on the surface, and leaned in to talk to the men. The man with the cap pointed at Riley's sidearm. The big man shrugged and, using his fingertips, removed it from the holster and placed it on the table.

Then something happened that Sean was not expecting from the big man he'd previously considered a buffoon. The man with the cap signaled for the second man to retrieve the revolver. The man pushed back his chair and leaned over the table. Once his hands had reached the gun, Riley reached out and snatched the trucker-cap-wearing man by the collar of his shirt. He pulled him forward and out of his chair then slammed his face onto the tabletop before delivering an elbow with a sickening crunch to the back of the man's neck. The second, skinny man yelped and backed away from the table, now holding Riley's own revolver leveled at his chest.

Sean pushed up from his seat, and the skinny man turned to point the gun at him. "Now ya'lls just calm down; this between us," he shouted, looking at his dead partner and then back at Riley, who was standing with his arms up and his hands balled into fists. "This between me and Riley here."

Not allowing the man to say anything more, Riley closed the distance. Sean could hear the pistol clicking on empty chambers and Riley delivering solid blows to the man's face, knocking him back and onto the floor. Riley didn't show any mercy; he stepped forward and stomped on the man's throat, filling the room with a crack as the neck broke.

A door slammed. Sean turned to see more of the tavern patrons pouring out. He could see that Tracey, now behind the bar, was holding a double-barrel shotgun in her hands. She yelled across the room at Riley to raise his hands.

Riley ignored her commands and carefully retrieved his pistol from the dead man, using his thumb and pointer finger. He then let it drop into his holster. The big man reached over the body and turned the man's pockets out, gripping the contents in his fist. Turning back to the table, Riley took the dead man's trucker hat and dropped in the fistful of contents then searched the other man's pockets. He looked up at Tracey and waved the hat at her. "Like you said, we don't want any trouble. These two did." He snorted and dropped the hat on the table. "If I was you, I'd take everything they had on them to make up for it."

"You can't just come in here busting up my place," she shouted.

Riley shook his head. "They were raiders. You know they ain't allowed in outposts as much as I do."

The woman's jaw dropped. "You sure?" she asked. "How do you know that?"

Riley moved behind the table and grabbed one of the men's packs and lifted it to the tabletop. He unzipped the rain flap and reached inside. He pursed his lips and pulled out a grey parka and a box of pistol cartridges. He dropped the parka to the table as he began loading his pistol. "You know what this is?" he asked.

"Captain's jacket," she said, frowning. "But why were they here?"

"Now that's a problem for you and your security, not me," Riley said. He turned to move back to the table when he heard the church bells sound.

"Might be your problem after all," Tracey said, now holding the shotgun down, her face held in concentration as she counted the bells.

Sean got up from his seat, watching the door as he moved toward her. "Is that security? You know this was self-defense."

She shook her head and grimaced, holding up ten fingers. "Not security, there is nobody coming for you; that's the gate bell. Ten bells is signaling *Regulars* at the gate." The big woman looked down at the floor, her jaw clenched. "We are no more friends to the raiders than we are to the Regulars that take a cut of everything we earn and call it protection fees. They can kiss my ass." She turned and saw Frank behind the bar, his eyes locked on the dead men. "Frank, get your ass up here and hide these bodies." She turned back to Sean. "I hope you got more in those sacks than ammo, because this is going to cost you."

CHAPTER 21

THREE CORNERS OUTPOST, WEST OF LANCASTER, OHIO. THE DEAD LANDS

With the rifle sling looped over his thumb, Brooks reached forward, feeling ahead with his gloved hand. He turned his head to the side then, pushing with the toe of his boot, slid ahead in the soft soil until his face was next to the base of a large oak tree. He lay motionless, listening to the faint sounds of Joey crawling up beside him. He closed his eyes tight, and when he opened them, he looked out across a large open expanse of meadow.

Three-foot-high, uncut grass blew in the breeze. Brook scanned and could see tree trunks in places where the grass was pushed down or covered with remnants of a heavy snowfall. He could tell that this was either an intentionally cut field of fire, or the people in the outpost ahead clear-cut it for firewood. Either way, it provided them with a tactical disadvantage. There would be no way to approach the building unseen in the daylight. Brooks rolled to his side and repositioned his scoped rifle so that when he dropped back to his chest it would rest in the pocket of his shoulder, and the large scope would sit at just the right relief from his eye.

Turning his head slightly, he could see that Joey was now beside him, level with his waistline. The Marine rifleman was on his right side and looking through a pair of scout binoculars. "Two on the roof; hard to see it, but there's another in that corner window to the right of the door," Joey whispered.

Brooks eased into the rifle and scanned. Ahead was the long, red-brick building. It reminded him of every movie high school he'd seen as a kid—long and red-orange with evenly spaced windows outlined in white limestone. He almost grinned, reminiscing of the time before his country was overrun with death. He pivoted and searched the knee wall along the roofline.

"Got 'em," he whispered. There were two men, equal distance apart, armed with what looked like lever-action rifles. He let his eye scan the windows. Joey had already identified a target, but he had to be sure. He panned left, stopped, and moved back to the right. "Got the man in the window," he said. The last man didn't appear to be armed, but it wouldn't make sense for him not to be.

Brooks focused hard on the scope's reticles and called out ranges to Joey, who confirmed his estimates.

"You are planning on killing these vatos?" Joey whispered.

"Planning for the worst, brother, preparing for the—"

A vehicle engine paused him. Brooks held his breath and slowly moved his eye from the scope. He paused and listened. They were loud engines; he could hear them shifting gears like trucks.

Joey heard it too. The Marine rifleman was already sliding back and changing his position so he could better angle toward the road. He settled in just as three vehicles slowly came into view—an old and badly rusted armored car followed by two deuce and a half military vehicles, painted in a woodland camouflage pattern. The armored car pulled through the intersection, turned left—followed by the first deuce and a half—and stopped directly to their front, leaving the last vehicle on the main road.

Doors slammed and hatches opened. Before Brooks could process it, there were nearly twelve armed and uniformed men standing in the street. They were dressed in ACUs—the old Army Combat Uniform. Not only that, they walked and carried themselves like soldiers. Brooks had seen enough militia groups and good ol' boys to know the difference between a boy in a surplus uniform and a professional. The hair on the back of his neck began to tingle.

"What the hell are we looking at here, hermano?" Joey whispered, the man's eyes glued to the binoculars.

"I don't know, but we can't let them get inside. Chief is in there."

Joey pulled away from the binoculars and looked at Brooks. "I'm not sure I'm okay with killing soldiers; at least, not our soldiers."

Brooks bit at the inside of his cheek. He was thinking the same thoughts but didn't want to let it move to the front of his consciousness. Right now, they were just targets, and that was how he wanted them to stay. "We don't know who they are."

Joey sighed, and Brooks looked back to the road. Men were opening a flap on one of the troop transports. Other men were removing five-gallon fuel cans, topping off the trucks. A pair of soldiers walked along the side of the road, discussing something. The pair was definitely in charge; Brooks knew it. It was all the same—the same scenes he'd seen hundreds of times on hundreds of exercises: convoys stopped and men went to work while officers planned.

The main gates of the outpost opened to reveal a pair of men who flanked an older man with a white beard. The trio exited the gate, approaching the soldiers on the road. Brooks shook his head and pulled the rifle back into his shoulder. If he was going to act, he had to be quick. But who? Who deserved a bullet? He closed his fist, blinking his eyes rapidly, trying to think.

"We can't fight them. Just give Chief a chance, bro. He's talked himself out of deeper shit than this."

Brooks clenched his fist and pulled his eye away from the scope, knowing Joey was right. Firing now would just stir a hornet's nest. His mind was flashing, trying to bounce through contingencies. What if Chief is counting on him to fire to allow his escape? What if they were inside and ready to hit them from two sides? His hand contracted and released the pistol grip. He felt Joey's hand on his shoulder. "Relax, bro. Chief's got this."

Brook took his hand off the rifle and held his empty palm toward Joey. "Okay," he whispered. He moved his eyes back to the group in front of the outpost. The trio were now in the yard in front of the building, talking to a pair of men. They appeared to be the ones in charge of the military outfit. A man turned and waved at the heavy vehicles then looked back to the white-bearded man from the outpost. The bearded man nodded his head and waved toward the outpost. One of the soldiers turned and pointed to a pair of men near a troop transport. The men grabbed large rucksacks and rifles from the back and double-timed it up the street to join the men on the lawn.

The other soldiers broke off and returned to their vehicles. Engines started and roared to life.

"They're leaving," Joey whispered.

"Not all of them," Brooks said, his eye back on the scope. His crosshair was on the tall man speaking to the white-bearded man from the outpost. When the tall man turned, Brooks could see the railroad track on the man's cover. An army captain. "They *are* military, but whose?" Brooks whispered to himself. He kept the reticle on the captain's head as he listened to doors slam and gears grind. The trucks didn't turn around; instead, they took the turn to the right, moving back toward the south. "I bet this guy has no idea I could put his lights out," Brooks whispered. "Just a few pounds off the trigger and all of his problems go away."

"Easy, killer," Joey whispered. "Let's let this convoy get out of here before doing anything rash."

Brooks kept the sight on his target. The man in the crosshairs turned back and accepted his pack from two younger soldiers. Brooks could tell these men were green; they didn't have the same posture as the veteran he was targeting. There was something about the man in charge, something that told him he should pull the trigger. The engine noise faded as the vehicles pulled away. The group of men approached the steps. Brooks was still on the glass, his finger twitching, wanting to make the shot. He pulled his hand away and exhaled as the men walked through the threshold and the gate closed behind them.

"Hey, Boss, what's that?" Joey pointed his gloved finger to the road leading to the north. Far on the distant blacktop surface, they could see wavering lines, like the ground was pulsing.

Brooks adjusted his body into the scope and tried to focus his eyes, thinking his mind was playing tricks on him —the brain seeing movement where none existed. "Can't be," he whispered. He closed his eyes tightly and slowly opened them. "We have to get back to the vehicles." When Brooks pulled his eye away from the glass, he could see that Joey had recognized it too. Ahead on the road and moving in their direction were Primals, possibly creepers stacked in shoulder-to-shoulder, and more than he could count.

"What about Chief?" Joey said.

"He'll be better off inside those walls. Right now, we need to worry about us." Brooks was already crawling backward, dragging his rifle and pack with him. "Where in the hell did they all come from? There were a couple hundred at the roadblock, but this..." he whispered and closed his eyes, thinking of the sight through the scope... the sea of bodies, the heads moving rhythmically.

"It's not the same group," Brooks grunted, moving back into the cover of the trees. He rolled to his back and sat up. Leaning down, he offered a hand to Joey and pulled the Marine to his feet.

Joey looked back over his shoulder. "We haven't seen a horde since the fall. How are they back?"

Brooks shook his head. "They aren't back. It's all of this; all the activity. The train, the vehicles, the fighting... It's bringing them all in."

"From where?" Joey asked.

Already jogging back toward the barn, Brooks said, "That group? Probably Columbus, Cincinnati, maybe even Indianapolis. There are a lot of big cities around here. Cities we don't know shit about."

Joey laughed. "We ain't in Kansas anymore, are we, Dorothy?"

"Nah," Brooks spat. "This is fucking Ohio."

CHAPTER 22

Chelsea screamed, and Brad leveled his rifle, bleeding off an entire magazine before stopping to reload. He heard Gyles's shotgun fire again, the noise echoing across the enclosed school, further enraging the Primals in all directions. Brad flinched, knowing what was coming, as another wave of infected crashed against the outer barrier fence. "We're surrounded," Brad shouted as he reloaded, and then called out for them to board the bus while he fired more suppressed rounds into the fence. His rifle barrel was sizzling, the suppressor at the end beginning to glow.

"Let's go! Let's go!" Gyles yelled, cranking the bus engine to life.

Brad heard the bus's diesel engine roar then turned and saw the door open. Brad fired off another burst into the gap in the fence then sprinted for the bus. He dove through the opening, and Gyles slammed the heavy piston that forced the door shut. Just moments later, the bus shuddered as the wave of infected collided with it.

Brad rolled to his back, breathing heavily. He could hear Gyles laughing manically, cursing at the infected as the bus ground into gear and lurched forward. Primal hands slapped at the body of the bus, their infected screams drowning out the sounds of the engine. He looked up and saw Chelsea's gloved hand. She pulled him back to his feet, and he followed her to the back, dropping heavily into a bench seat covered in green pleather. He rested his rifle against a seat's back and took in deep breaths.

Pushing farther away from the aisle, he leaned in toward the steel-covered windows. Gyles was moving fast down the access road, creating separation from the things pursuing them. He leaned back in the seat and closed his eyes. How had they closed on them so quickly? How did they find them again? He thought back to what had just happened. They'd made it through the outer gate and into the lot without being detected. Gyles moved to the bus while Brad stayed back with Chelsea to cover the auto shop's doors.

Then it happened—a low buzzing at first that quickly became a high-pitched siren. The white quad copter swooped in from overhead then blared more high-pitched beeping sounds. Like a recess bell, roars emanated from the school's hallways. Brad raised his rifle and popped off several shots at the drone—all missing—before Gyles removed the Mossberg from his back. The soldier leveled the barrel and put a blast of bird shot into the quad copter that sent it crashing to the ground.

The outer doors of the auto shop buckled as a stream of them poured out. Brad was able to stop several of the first group, killing them in the doorway and blocking the path for others. More moved past them as he reloaded, hitting the tall chain link fence that divided them from the school. Still more came, and the second wave was double the size of the first. The infected made it to the fence and were piling over by the time Gyles entered the bus. Brad had ordered Chelsea in and then he piled in behind her... He closed his eyes tightly; somehow, they made it.

But still... how the hell had they been found?

Brad lifted from the seat and moved up beside Gyles. They were racing down a snow-covered road. Moving south, the road had several vehicles pushed off to the right side, up and over the shoulder and into a ditch. "Where we going?" Brad asked him.

"A place I know. I got some friends up here."

"Friends?" Brad asked. "Then why didn't you say something about it earlier?"

Gyles shrugged and looked up into the rearview mirror before fixing his eyes back on the road. "Palmer doesn't know about them; most folks don't."

"Palmer?" Brad said. "What? You don't trust him?"

"I trust him just fine. Only he has his place and I have mine," Gyles snapped. He slowed to maneuver around a burned-out pickup truck then shifted gears as he sped onto a straightaway. "Couldn't take the risk in front of him. There was a reason Brown separated you out from the others, but we had to be sure."

"Sure?" Brad asked.

"Had to make sure you were one of us," Gyles said, glancing at him. "You don't understand what we've been up against. What Sergeant Brown told you last night about the recon to the south, what's been happening, it's all true. But the rest about being told to stand down? Well..."

"You've never stopped fighting," Brad said.

Gyles clenched his jaw and nodded before saying, "No, not all of us. But there are very few that go out and do the dirty work. We've been sending out scouts, and what we are seeing isn't good."

"You already told me about infected, how the numbers are growing."

Gyles scoffed. "It's far more than that. Most people inside the compound don't even know this war is being fought. We know the senator's plan won't work; we know it's all bullshit. Even with the best of walls, the infected will overcome us in a year."

"So you all just do your own thing. Is it mutiny or treason?" Brad asked, keeping his eyes on the road ahead.

"Fuck that noise," Gyles spat back. "The senator has no more constitutional authority than any of us do. He's a sham, only looking out for himself. If shit gets too bad in the south, he'll just jump on his chopper and head north."

"But you sent Palmer back to move the people right back to the senator."

Gyles nodded. "Yeah, and he will, and he'll tell them we were planning to find out who was attacking the compound."

"And we are?" Brad said.

Gyles nodded his head. "Mostly."

"And what does that mean?" Chelsea said, stepping closer.

Gyles looked out at the road, slowed and turned onto a dirt path crossing a snow-covered field. "We have a camp; there are people there like us."

"Military?" Chelsea asked.

Turning back in his seat to look at her, Gyles grinned. "Militia. Some were military before the fall. National Guard types, Army reservists, whole lot of veterans, but the majority are just your traditional minuteman."

"What's a minuteman?" Chelsea asked.

"Like I said..." Gyles grinned, turning back to the road. "Militia."

The road narrowed and became closed in with trees that hadn't been cut back. Overgrowth shaded and darkened the surface of the road. Gyles shifted into the lowest gear and brought the bus to a crawl, going around a steep embankment that took the bus west. The road ended and Gyles guided them onto a gravel drive that the snow had been removed from.

"Where are we?" Brad asked.

"I can't say exactly, but it's about two miles north of the wall."

Brad began to argue that point when the gravel drive ended at a tall wooden gate flanked by double-stacked shipping containers. Gyles moved the bus closer and cut the engine. He placed his hands on his lap, took a deep breath, and sighed. He reached out for the handle and released the piston, allowing the door to open.

Brad leaned toward the windshield and looked left and right, seeing no one. "Is anyone here?" he whispered.

"Oh yeah, they're here watching us. Grab your gear and follow me; someone will bring in the bus later."

Brad looked to Chelsea, who already had her ruck by the carry handle and was following Gyles off the bus. Brad shrugged and grabbed his own pack, following them out onto the gravel road. Brad saw that Gyles had his rifle slung so he did the same with his own before following the man to the large wooden gates. There was a well-worn foot path leading beyond the gate to the stack of shipping containers to the left. At the bottom left was a blue container with US STEEL stenciled on the side. Near the middle of the container was a narrow line of wooden pallets arranged like a boardwalk that led to a door cut into the side of the container.

Gyles approached the door and pounded on it with the

back of his fist. Immediately, they heard the clanging of chains and the screeching of metal from the inside. The door pushed out and revealed the face of a tall black man. He had a scar across his forehead and a crossed rifle tattoo on the side of his neck, the bottom of the tattoo barely concealed by a green-and-black patterned shemagh. The man stepped on to the pallet boardwalk and looked beyond Gyles to stare at Brad for a moment before switching to Chelsea then back to Gyles.

"Where's Brown?" the man asked.

Gyles shook his head. "We lost him last night; they hit us at Palmer's strip mall."

The man shook his head. "I told that bastard the place wasn't safe. We lose anyone else?"

"No, the rest of us made it out and holed up at the Zoo until it was safe to travel here."

"You followed?"

"Can't be certain; they were using drones. We knocked one down but could be more."

The man nodded and rubbed at his chin. "And Palmer?"

"I sent him back to Coldwater, told him to try to get them to evacuate north."

The man nodded thoughtfully. "Too late for that... had a radio chat with the captain this morning; they're already pulling up stakes and moving north. They're picking up the same Primal activity and numbers that we are. I already evacuated all the civilians and family members from here— sent them north as well. Primal activity is pegged all over the region. I haven't seen this many since right after the fall. At this rate, this camp will be surrounded in days, the roads impassable in a week."

"The Detroit breach?" Gyles asked.

Shaking his head, the black man said, "Scouts located another breach to the west near the Michigan City barrier; we got three million-plus Primals moving through it. A team tried to close the gap. It's a hundred miles from here; at the pace they estimated, they'd be here in thirty hours if we did nothing. They messaged back that they were going to try to plug the break in the wall."

Brad cleared his throat and looked at the man. "And did they?"

He looked at Brad and frowned. Brad recognized the look of a weary leader with troops in the field—troops that he didn't know were dead or alive. "Wish I knew. We lost communications with them once they started the Op." He turned to Gyles and said, "This the one you told me about? The one with the Texas friends?"

Gyles moved his jaw like he was chewing leather and nodded. "Yeah, he's up from the south, part of the Texas Army."

"That true?" the man asked.

Brad shook his head and stuck out his hand. "Nope, not at all; my name is Brad. Once, a long time ago, I was a staff sergeant in the US Army. This here is Chelsea; she's a Marine."

The man smiled and returned the handshake. "A Marine, you say? Hot damn! I'm not used to sharing my crayons in this camp, but I'll let you have some of the duller colors. Name's Luke. I served, but my last job was in a local PD." His face turned serious again. "Now what about Texas?"

Brad shook his head, and grimaced. "Sorry, I have no ties to Texas. I was with a group in West Virginia. We got hit by raiders and had people taken." Brad paused, and his eyes drifted to Chelsea before he continued. "Texas was in the area and turns out they were hating on the same folks, so, yeah, we did fight alongside them. But as far as me having an association or being able to speak for them, I'm afraid not."

Luke nodded thoughtfully. "This group you belonged to... what about them? Where are they?"

Shrugging, Brad looked down at his feet. "Can't say."

"You're here all alone then? They didn't send you?" Luke asked. "You have no backup coming?"

"Nope. I'm from up north originally; I was just passing through, trying to get home."

Luke stopped and looked at Gyles. "Is he with us or not?"

Gyles slapped Brad on the back. "He's with us."

Brad held up a hand. "I can answer that for myself. *With us...* yeah, that depends on what it is *us* are doing."

The man shook his head. "The wall is compromised; the East is here in numbers. Every colony between the freeway and the Detroit River is gone or severely damaged."

"And what are you planning to do about it?" Brad said sarcastically.

Luke brought his right hand to the back of his neck and rubbed while closing his eyes tightly. He opened them slowly and turned to look out at the surrounding forest. "I thought maybe we could draw them all here. Take them on at the walls, put up a hell of a fight. Kill off the Zombies and hide, maybe bug out in the vehicles. In the past, if you killed enough of them, eventually the Primals would figure out what time it was and fade away."

"We've fought them too, but that's not going to happen here; there are just too many for that," Chelsea said.

Luke nodded. "Yeah, once we heard about Chicago we knew it wouldn't work. Even without Chicago it was a fool's chance at best. So now the plan has changed. We know where the New Republic headquarters is and there's a good chance we can raise enough hell on the way there to draw the active Primals back through the wall and lead them south. We were just kind of hoping your Texas boys would show up to help us finish them off."

Brad scrunched his face and looked at Chelsea. "Are you kidding? And then what? Be left with a few million infected gnawing on our asses?" He shook his head and reached for his pack. "You have three million Primals moving this way west from Chicago, and another million east from Detroit, and who knows what is coming at us from the south. There is no stopping this. You lead these things south and you hit another horde—possibly wiping out whatever it is Texas has got, the same way they wiped out the Eighty-Second Airborne in D.C. There is no fighting this. We need to get our shit and run." Brad paused, locking eyes with Chelsea. He held his breath then exhaled. "There's only one way, and nobody is going to like it."

Chelsea sighed. "I'm afraid that doesn't end well for us, does it?"

Shrugging, Brad said, "We've been through worse."

Luke looked at them, his eyes moving between Brad and Chelsea. "What's your plan? We're open to suggestions."

"We have to work with them. We can't do this without their help."

"The New Republic?" Gyles said, interrupting. "Are you kidding?! You think we should work with them? They started all of this when they knocked down the walls in the first place."

"With the numbers we're facing, I don't see another way." Brad looked down. "Even with their help, this might be a one-way trip."

Luke smiled, revealing bright white teeth. He grabbed Gyles by the shoulder and squeezed. "He's smarter than you described." He laughed, and Chelsea scowled.

"That was the plan all along, wasn't it?" she interjected. "Why did you lie to us?"

Luke's face turned serious, and he looked at her. "Because most sane folks won't get it until they see it for themselves. Like you said, we cannot win it alone, and if we are going to delay long enough to get the people to safety, we need all the help we can get."

"How do we contact them?" Chelsea asked.

Luke turned out toward the setting sun. "If the scout reports from south of the wall are correct, shit is about to get crooked. All the New Republic boys are pulling back; they have to be seeing the same things we are."

"Back to where?" Brad said.

"Toledo. We have to get there before the horde, and we'll need to move quick if we want to stay ahead of it."

CHAPTER 23

THREE CORNERS OUTPOST, WEST OF LANCASTER, OHIO. THE DEAD LANDS

Sean sat like a stone at the corner table, watching the trio of men scarf down a second bowl of rabbit stew. Riley was beside him, while Henry and the other boys sat a table across the room from them playing cards. He sipped at a glass of mash, now heavily watered down. The men looked like real soldiers. Not raiders, not hardened killers like the men he'd seen on a dozen combat outposts in a half dozen countries.

The leader showed his stress on his face—the burden of command—and the two young men looked as bored as any junior enlisted he'd ever seen. They appeared to have no concern for the others in the room.

Sean looked at Riley and in a faint voice said, "You didn't quite know as much as you thought, did you?"

"Da hell are you talking about?"

"The outposts; you thought your people ran 'em," Sean said, taking another sip of the mash. "Looks to me they can't stand the fuckers any more than they could stand you and your raiders."

Riley's hand squeezed into a fist. "I'm not a raider. They are not my people."

"Well, you sure made quick work of those boys before we could figure it out. What was it they would have told us about you?"

"Those two were rapists and murderous scum."

Sean smiled with half of his face in a sarcastic grim. "What was it they said to you?"

Riley reached for his own glass and topped it off from the bottle. "They said they knew who I was, and that I would be leaving with them in the morning. That I would be carrying their gear; asked who you all were and said they were looking for recruits."

Sean put up a hand to silence the big man as Tracey approached their table. Tracey had helped hide the bodies and clean up the mess. She hadn't said much else other than making it perfectly clear she didn't want anything to do with their fight against the East. This outpost existed under neutrality agreements. Neutral to a point—if they continued to gather and make half-assed trades with the East, the East would leave them alone. She was helping them, but Sean didn't know how far that generosity would stretch. Tracey leaned over the table and removed empty bowls then pointed at the bottle. "Will you be wanting more?"

Sean shook his head and tipped his eyes toward the trio of soldiers. "So, what about them?"

"It's getting late, and they're looking to stay the night. Some convoy dropped the three of them off. Said they will need a vehicle in the morning."

"Vehicle? Why would they be dropped off if they didn't have transportation out. What are they doing here?"

She lowered her voice and looked away. "The one in

charge says they are looking for a group of men that ran a roadblock south of here." She looked at Riley. "They say these men are dangerous."

"Pfft." Riley sighed. "I'll show 'em dangerous if that's what they're really looking for."

"Well, aren't you just tougher than a two-dollar pork steak," Tracey scoffed, shaking her head. "I know damn well it's you all they're hunting. I won't say shit as long as you keep to yourselves and get out of here at sunup." She scowled down at the red-bearded man before turning back to Sean. "They're hoping to trade for a running set of wheels. Planning to pursue them—you—in the morning. They didn't say so, but I also overheard one of the kids talking about a vast group of soldiers headed to the railroad depot about fifty miles to the south."

Sean shrugged and sipped from his glass. He was lost out here. When pondering the situation, he had to come to terms with the reality that they had no intelligence on what to expect. He had no idea what the world looked like north of the Ohio River. A day earlier, he'd never heard of the Regulars and now he was sharing a tavern with a trio of them. "What's to the south then? What do you know about this depot?"

"Like I said, it's a rail yard," she said sarcastically, rolling her eyes, then saw by the look on Sean's face that he wasn't amused with her short answer. "It used to be a large railroad transportation center, all fenced in, hardened up. It's where the trade manager takes all our goods for exchange."

"What else?" Sean asked her, surprised she was being so open with him, but taking full advantage of the situation.

Tracey nodded and used a wet rag to wipe down the table. "They say Texas is moving in to slaughter all of us, and the men they're hunting could be scouts."

"Why would Texas want to slaughter us?" Riley asked, his voice almost breaking with laughter and causing Sean to kick him under the table to keep the trio of soldiers from looking in their direction.

"Look," Tracey said, leaning over them. "I know it's bullshit, but that's the propaganda they've been feeding us. They want us to believe that Texas is on some conquest mission to quell the Midwest. That the New Republic is the only answer, that them moving all those women and kids north on the trains is for their own safety."

"You know about the people and the trains?" Sean asked.

She nodded.

"Then why haven't they taken you?"

She grinned at Sean. "I grew up five miles from here. Most of the equipment in this place came from my father's bar. If they try to take it—or me—from this place, I'll fill their bellies with buckshot."

Sean smiled and tipped his head. "Fair enough. What about the rest? Have you seen people moved through here?"

"No," she said, her voice dropping to just above a whisper. "But I've heard of entire communities being uprooted... people, families, everyone being taken away."

"By Regulars?" he asked.

"No... raiders. They come first, the Regulars come later to clean up the mess and make things normal. The two groups act like the other doesn't exist. And in some ways, I think they are being honest about it. Like the Regulars don't know about the dirty work."

Riley grunted. "They don't want to know."

Sean looked around the room—dark, filled with smoke, tables and chairs filled with rough men leaning over bowls or half-empty glasses. There were plenty of empty tables, and nobody sitting at the bar. He pursed his lips and looked back to Tracey. "Is this a normal crowd for tonight?"

Tracey took a step back from the table and used the bottom of her apron to wipe her hands. She shook her head. "Word travels fast. Not many will come in tonight with them here." She looked back at Frank behind the bar. "I've got a couple tents with a few racks set up. You're welcome to them tonight, but I'd appreciate if you all were gone in the morning; don't bother saying good bye."

Sean nodded his head in agreement, and Tracey waved a hand to the boy, who grinned and came running. Sean got to his feet and looked back Tracey. "We'll get situated. Can you let Henry know to hang here for a bit before he comes along?"

She smiled at him. "Yes, I see; it's best if those fellas don't know you're all together."

Riley laughed and increased his pace to catch up with Frank, who was already at the door. Sean stepped through the open door and was surprised to see the sun had set. He looked at his watch; it was just past 1700. The temperature was dropping too, and he pulled his collar tight around his neck. He took easy steps, following Riley and the boy along the perimeter of the small tavern and then over a wooden boardwalk that led to the end of the large interior courtyard. There were three white fabric tents, the sort hunters would have purchased from sporting goods stores before the fall.

Sean did a quick turnaround to orient himself. He could see that he was surrounded by the red-brick building on all sides. They were now on the exact opposite side of the tall archway they'd originally entered. Smoke rose from barrels along the grounds of the courtyard. He searched the grounds and only saw the occasional man walking. Searching the rooftops, he could see no silhouettes; the interior did not appear to be guarded. These people were comfortable, soft. In the windows of the tall buildings, soft yellow lights glowed, and he could see bouncing shadows from the people inside.

"You coming?" Riley asked, holding aside the tent flap.

Sean took a last look then stepped through the opening. The inside of the tent made anything he'd ever spent time in while in the military look like the Ritz. It was beyond dirty; the beds were nothing more than elevated planks with worn and stained mattresses thrown over them. The wood-stove was small and made of rusted steel, and a makeshift set of pipes led through a gaping hole in the roof that was sure to let in as much cold air as the warm air the fire produced.

"It's a real nice shithole you got here, Frank. Be sure and tell your mom how we appreciate her hospitality," Sean said, tossing his back onto one of the bunks.

Frank shook his head. "Oh, she isn't my momma," he said sternly. "My aunt."

Riley reached into his pocket and handed the boy a pair of .357 rounds. "Well, however she comes to you, be sure and tell her we said thanks."

Frank held the bullets in his hand, smiling, then tucked them into a shirt pocket before turning to leave the tent. Riley moved along the wall away from the burning fire and dropped his own pack on one of the better bunks. He sat heavily next to it then looked at Sean "What do you want to do? Wait for them Regulars to fall asleep and cut their throats?"

Sean shook his head and pulled off his boots. "I tell you what I plan to do; I plan to get me some sleep then follow those boys wherever they make off to tomorrow." He pushed his pack off the bunk, rolled out a sleeping bag, and crawled inside. "You got first watch," Sean said, zipping himself into the bag. "Oh... and if you plan on doing any throat cutting, I sleep lightly and won't shed a tear if I have to put a bullet in your face."

Riley shook his head and laughed. "Damn, and all that time in the pub I thought we were bonding."

"KEEP CLIMBING," Brooks said, urging Joey higher into the rafters of the old hay barn.

The sun was dropping fast by the time they reached the barn. They could hear the things moving through the woods —not from one single direction, but from everywhere. The two men were high above the sounds, in the hayloft of the barn. Primals had moved in close and now had them surrounded but not trapped. Looking through breaks in the walls, Brooks could see them scattered in the trees, while others stood out in a distant hayfield and other old fields that had long ago been returned to nature. Joey grunted and pulled himself up over the final rafter of the barn and onto a platform. Just beside it was a large pulley that had at one time been used to raise things into the upper levels of the barn.

"They're still coming," Joey whispered. "They have to be all over the outpost too."

Brooks climbed up beside him and crowded onto the platform. He contorted his body, trying to remove his pack, seeing that Joey had already removed his own and had it strapped to a vertical beam. Brooks slid his feet back and, shrugging, freed himself from the pack straps in the confined space. He did the same as Joey and wrapped a pack strap around a beam and tied it in tight to prevent it from falling.

"They must have followed that convoy in," Joey said.

Brooks shook his head. "Too many, and they came from every direction. I don't know; none of this feels right."

They heard a loud crack and a screech below. The Primals had found the door to the barn and were pushing in against it. Brooks held his breath and listened.

"You lock the door?" Joey whispered.

Brooks looked back at the man and shook his head. "They'd get in anyway. Better to let 'em in than have the fuckers push the barn over."

Sucking in his upper lip, Joey nodded his approval. Even though the things were at least thirty feet below him, he could still hear their deep sniffs as they tried to detect their prey. Joey looked over at him, and Brooks held a finger to his lips to unnecessarily silence the man. Joey backed away, dropped to his rear, and pressed against a stubby rail on the platform. As he leaned back, the railing creaked and wobbled. Joey's eyes got big, and he shifted his weight forward, shaking his head. "This is a shitty spot to stay the night," he whispered.

Brooks frowned and pointed to the barn floor, now filling with wailing infected. "No, down there would have been a shitty place to stay the night."

A series of distant gunshots changed the pitch of howls and screams of the Primals below. Brooks tried to move so he could see through the barn's sides to the outpost, the gaps hardly wide enough to gain even a peek. He looked up and saw a square cut high into the gable end of the barn that faced the Three Corners Outpost. Brooks pointed at it, and Joey followed the SEAL's gloved finger with his eyes then shook his head no. Brooks countered and nodded his head.

Then, without arguing, he leaned out, grabbed onto the rough-cut rafters, and pulled himself onto them like a spider monkey.

Brooks didn't turn back, but he could hear Joey's muffled cursing as he moved over and under rafters toward the gable vent. He reached out for the final beam near the vent and was relieved to see another square platform was built in front of the opening. Hanging over the square frame was a large steel eyelet, probably used to hang block and tackle to get equipment high into the barn. Brooks reached down and removed his rigger's belt and used a carabiner clip to attach a loop on the belt to the eyelet. He wrapped the other end around his fist and leaned out of the square vent.

He was a good forty feet off the ground and high enough to see over the treetops. Squinting, he could make out the roofline of the outpost a bit over a mile away. He broke a rule and looked down at the ground. The base of the barn was covered with infected, the things packed in shoulder to shoulder, swarming like an organism of its own. Brooks heard another series of gunshots coming from the outpost, and the mass below reacted. Swirling, the horde curved out and away from the barn, toward the outpost.

From his high vantage point, Brooks thought the mass moved like water headed to a drain. Primals mixed in with creepers, the numbers were uncountable. He heard Joey gasp behind him. Brooks pulled on the belt and moved himself back into the barn. He looked his friend in the eye. "I've never seen this many, not since..."

"Since the fall," Joey said, finishing his thoughts. "Bro, we gotta get the hell out of here."

Brooks turned his eyes back toward the outpost. "We're okay up here; it's them I'm worried about."

SPENCER FINISHED his drink and pushed away the stew bowl. He was in the back corner of a now nearly empty tavern. He looked up to see the tavern boy walking a pair of large men out of the bar, probably leading them to the barracks tent the bartender had told him about. His own men, Billy and Doug, had sparked up a game of cards at a corner table with another trio of men. It was against regulations for them to be drinking and fraternizing with the locals while on a mission, but Spencer didn't care. He wasn't here to pursue the Texas scouts as he'd led Wahl to believe. He grinned slyly, scratching a line in his notebook. He didn't have any intention of doing that. There would be no pre-dawn wake up call for his recon team. In fact, he had no desire to break camp until well after breakfast.

He felt no guilt over it; this wasn't the US Army, and things didn't run the way they used to before the fall. Not that he didn't think it was important to the cause—he knew it was—but he knew that if he did, he and his men would probably end up dead. Another dead recon team didn't do the New Republic any good. He looked back at the road atlas, tracing his fingers over their current location then moved it back toward the railroad depot. If Wahl did as suggested, something Spencer highly doubted, he would be headed back toward the Monster block to try to find the Texas forward elements. Most likely it wouldn't work that way, and Wahl would be quickly detected and fired on by the Texas Rangers. Knowing Wahl, he would then retreat if he was lucky enough not to be killed outright.

Spencer grinned, knowing that wasn't what was about to happen. Wahl was an opportunist and a coward. Wahl would start back toward the block, heading south on the road at first, sticking to the plan until the danger started to well up in his throat. Then he would get to thinking, and his need for self-preservation would override his eagerness to please his superiors. He would stop and think up several scenarios as to why he should head to the depot instead. Once he picked the least cowardly excuse, he would inform the battalion commander that he'd sent his recon elements in pursuit of the Texas scouts, and that he was ready to *lead* the battalion right to Texas.

He looked at his wristwatch. It was just after 1730, and Wahl would be reaching the depot. He wouldn't go straight to the Battalion Commander; he'd get dinner first and make sure he had a good spot to sleep. It would be at least 1900 before Wahl checked in with headquarters. By then, the commander would be off duty for the day, and Wahl wouldn't dare disturb him. Battalion would call him for a regular SITREP at daybreak, and *then* they would know they'd split up. It would be early morning before Wahl checked in and wouldn't even attempt to get an update from Spencer until their normal noon check-in time.

He leaned back and turned to look at the radio clipped to the top of his pack. It would be sometime late afternoon before they expected any real news from him. He grinned, folded up his notebook and map, and tucked them into the top of his rucksack. Plenty of time to have another drink and recharge his own batteries.

A series of gunshots echoed from somewhere in the camp. The bar fell quiet. Spencer turned to look at the barmaid's face—he'd learned earlier that her name was Tracey, and she wasn't much of a people person. Even so, what looked like a confident woman when he'd met her, now showed fear. She looked toward the back door of the tavern, probably searching for the tavern boy. More gunshots sounded and bells began to ring. He stood and reached for his rifle leaning against the wall behind him. Billy was already moving to his side with Doug close behind. The other men from the card table began running from the tavern through the front entrance.

"Captain, what do we do?" Billy asked.

Spencer ignored the question and crossed the room to the bartender. The gunfire had increased to a steady cadence and was joined by the screams and shouting of men. "What's going on?" he yelled.

"Steady bells," she said, listening. She shook her head, her eyes still locked on the door behind her, then sighed when the young boy charged through and bolted the door. "Frank?" she called out.

The boy spun away from the door with saucer eyes; he reached down for a second locking bar and dropped it into place. "Infected at the walls. Mister Seth says he ain't seen so many of 'em together like this. He ain't sure if he can stop 'em all."

"Monster block," Spencer mumbled.

Tracey turned toward him. "What was that?"

He shook his head. "Nothing." He turned back to his men, fearing they'd brought the infected here. Whenever a large group traveled any distance, they tended to gather more, like a snowball. With the distance from the block, there could be a thousand of them out there by now. "Grab your rifles, boys; looks like our work followed us home." Spencer pointed to the tavern boy. "Take me to this Seth."

Frank hesitated to look to Tracey for an answer. She stepped between the boy and the military officer and shook her head. "No, he isn't taking you anywhere." She turned back and grabbed Frank, pushing him behind the bar.

"Where do you think you're going?" Spencer shouted.

Tracey turned back to face him. Her eyes quickly scanned the tavern; everyone was gone. Only the army officer and his two troopers remained.

"I'm taking Frank and getting the hell out of here. I suggest you do the same," she said, reaching under the bar and coming up with a nylon bag already stuffed with goods. "If Seth is worried, then you should be as well. The steady bells are only used to draw any infected to the front of the outpost so families can escape or hide, whichever is their preference."

Gunfire and ringing bells still echoed from outside. Spencer took a step toward her, but before his foot could land, Tracey had dropped the bag and a shotgun was pointed in his direction. "Now, there ain't no time for discussion. Frank and I are leaving; you boys do whatever it is you need to. Go out that front door and head to the gate. If it's Seth you want to speak with, you'll find him there."

CHAPTER 24

B rad stepped through the gate and into the interior of the camp. It wasn't what he expected. From the inside, he could see that it wasn't a ring of single-stacked shipping containers, but instead a larger stack of containers formed into a massive square with an area the size of a football field in the center. He spun, looking in all directions. The high containers had windows and porches cut into them, all facing the central open yard. It reminded him of the connex housing he'd seen in Iraq and Kuwait. He turned and looked at Gyles. "How did you get them all?"

Gyles grinned. "The freeways. Also helped when we found a train with a hundred containers. Most were empty, but the structure was what we were after."

"How big is it?" Brad asked.

"The wall sections are made up of two high and two wide. It's fifty boxes wide and fifty boxes long. Each container is twenty-foot long, and nearly ten-foot high. What you're looking at is a twenty-foot-tall and nearly a thousand-foot-long square. Took us less than a month once we had all the gear in place to move them here. Then another few months to assemble and cut holes and compartments to connect them all together."

"And you kept this a secret?"

Luke stepped forward, grinning. "Not really a 'secret.' People know about this place, but once folks find it they don't typically ask to leave, and even ones that do don't have feelings for selling us out. The camp might look safe, but it's not comfortable. It's a soldiers' camp."

Brad nodded his understanding. He looked at Chelsea and could see her attention was elsewhere. To the back of the large center square were parked vehicles, surrounded by men in packs.

Luke nodded. "We were already prepping to move when you got here. I was hoping we wouldn't have to head out without you."

"So, you'll just abandon this place?" Chelsea asked.

He shook his head. "Of course not; we have a contingent that will stay behind. Those things won't breach the walls, and even if they do, they would never get inside the container compartments."

A large steel door slid back from the container wall, revealing an opening that led to the road. Brad looked through and could see that the bus had already been moved. Several men came through the opening, followed by an open-top Jeep. The Jeep pulled off to the side, and a pair of men in faded battle dress uniforms approached Luke. Brad could see that other men in the camp had stopped what they were doing and were gathering around, forming a circle around Luke and the newcomers. "They're close; stopped a group of them just five miles away," the man from the Jeep said.

"How many?" Luke asked.

"The reports were spot-on: more than I could count. You all have to leave now, or you won't get out of the walls."

Luke pointed a finger over his head and spun it in a lasso motion. "You heard 'em, boys. Mount up." He pointed at Brad and Chelsea over the shouting of men and the starting of engines. "You two are with me."

Brad looked to Chelsea and grabbed his rucksack. They walked together, following Luke through the crowd and along the line of vehicles, until they reached a tall black MRAP. The vehicle was scarred and rusted. There were obvious signs of battle, with bullet marks and broken glass in the rear block windows. The sides and front were stenciled in bold white paint: *Vines City PD*. Over that, in blood-red letters, someone had graffiti-painted *The Beast*.

Luke walked to the back and tossed a small pack into the already opened rear hatch. Brad looked at the vehicle and back to Luke. "This thing has a story to tell."

Smiling, Luke dipped his chin. "This thing has kept me alive since the fall. It might look beat up and broken on the outside, but it's solid."

Brad tossed in his bag and went to step inside when Luke grabbed his wrist. "Come get shotgun with me. I have Gyles in the turret; Chelsea can hold down the back."

Chelsea didn't speak and instead held onto her own bag as she climbed the rear ramp, Gyles following close behind. Luke moved off to the driver's side as Brad ran up to the passenger's door. The big door opened with a clunk and Brad pulled himself up into the seat. While the outside had been sanitized to look like a law enforcement vehicle, the inside was still military with the olive-drab appearance and the equipment racks to match. Brad removed his rifle and locked it into a rifle rack next to his right knee then clicked into his harness. He looked back when he heard the rear hatch closing up and saw Gyles sticking his head up into the turret.

Gyles pulled a radio headset over his ears and said, "We good?"

Luke nodded his head and looked at Brad, who shot him a thumbs up.

"Let's roll," Luke said into the microphone.

All at once vehicles began an orderly move toward the gate. All were armored in some way, but very few were military. One by one, they broke ranks and formed a single line. A large tow truck with *Pop's Towing* written on the back pulled out ahead of them, and Luke followed it. Soon, they were back on the narrow dirt road that cut through the forest. It was dark and headlights were on. Brad could see Primal bodies in the road. Some were fresh, run down by vehicles in the front of the convoy, others were on the shoulder and had probably been there for ages.

"How many we got?" Brad asked.

Luke looked at him. "Twenty-three trucks, buck-twenty men."

The radio squelched, and Luke pulled off his headset, dropping it on the radio rack. He fumbled with a switch, diverting the sound to a speaker. "Go ahead, this is Groundhog Six."

"Groundhog?" Brad asked.

Luke laughed. "Cause every day is the fucking same out here."

The radio squelched, and a metallic voice came from the speaker. *"Groundhog Six, this is the Ranch. We've got zoms bumping into the walls; you want us to ignore them, or take action?"*

Luke paused, looking through the headlights and at the

tow truck to their front. They'd just turned onto a two-lane highway. The tow truck's tail lights were red, and the vehicles were stacking up again.

"We're at the wall," Luke said, looking at Brad before reaching for the hand mic. "Ranch, this is Groundhog Six. We are at the wall and ready to move out. Go ahead and make some noise to draw them in and around you, but conserve ammo—use flares if you need to. Be prepared to button up before."

"Groundhog Six, this is Ranch. Roger that. Ranch out."

"Good luck, Ranch. Groundhog Six out."

Before Luke had placed the handset back in its cradle, the vehicles were moving again. Before long, they were rolling through a section just wider than the MRAP. Without looking toward Brad, Luke spoke. "There were hundreds of cutouts like this in the wall; never really meant to be opened but put there just in case people needed to move through it in a hurry. I imagine the designers always figured it would be to let people in, not groups like us running our way out."

"Were you here when the wall was built?" Brad asked.

"Nah," Luke grunted. "I was with Gyles when we found this place."

"A soldier and a Marine? How'd that happen?"

Luke laughed. "I was a cop first night of the fall. Gyles's unit came in to support us."

"Support?" Brad asked. "Not evacuate?"

"Nope. No place to evacuate to. Had more people than seats, a bunch of families with us, so leaving by foot wasn't an option. We bundled up in a National Guard Armory, sealed up tight. The place was surrounded by wire fences, secure on all sides. We locked every door and put every man we had on the perimeter with a rifle.

"You know, we had two heavy infantry squads out of Fort Stewart. Two of the army's best squads with all the latest toys: light machine guns, squad automatic weapons—hell, even had a Chinook with a mini gun. On top of that, a dozen National Guardsmen, and most of my department barricaded inside with them."

"You were lucky then."

Luke looked at Brad and slowly shook his head side to side. "We held less than twenty-four hours."

Brad's jaw dropped. "I'm sorry."

"Just one story of many, brother. You know as well as I do there was no standing up to them during the fall. The fight was different then."

Swallowing and looking back toward the passenger window, Brad said, "That it was."

"What about you? What's your story?"

Brad shrugged. "I was over there when it started."

"Iraq?" Luke said.

Brad shook his head. "Afghanistan." He reached into a pocket on his left thigh and pulled a crushed water bottle and took a long drink. "We were on patrol. Lost my company, lost my forward operating base, but lived long enough to find a way home."

"Home from Afghanistan?!" Luke said with shock in his voice. "What, as part of the mass redeployment?"

"No, we were left behind. We kind of made our own way back. We made it to South Carolina then worked are way up through the Virginias. We were living well down that way the past year or so until this shit happened."

"That's how people are; they start living well then think they have to take shit from others. Like the outside problems aren't enough, they think they have to make new ones."

Brad grunted. "Assholes—always have been, always

will be."

"Amen," Luke said.

The convoy slowed again, and they entered an onramp then started traveling east on a wide highway. Brad recognized it as Interstate 90, which cut through Indiana and Ohio and ran right into Toledo. Luke moved onto the road, and the vehicles changed position, spreading out but maintaining the slow speed. Luke relaxed after reaching the steady speed. "You know how it all started?" he asked.

Brad had been over this a few times before. Every region seemed to have an answer, and they always turned into arguments with little facts to add to it. He'd heard everything from mutated Ebola from the Congo, to rabies out of Canada. Some even claimed it came from poison water deep in the Earth. And then there were the religious groups, which were the worst of all. Nobody knew the truth, but how could they? He shrugged, looked at Luke, and said, "I've heard things; what about you?"

"Was a terror attack," Luke said matter-of-factly—not as a suggestion, but as a statement. "An engineered bioweapon rapidly deployed around the world, all on a precise schedule. Some places did better than others at stopping it. Actually, the only reason we are even alive now is because the US was prepared. Well, it was half-assed and could have been better if they'd come clean with the public from the get-go, but at least they had people out in some bunker coordinating a response. If not for them, we probably would all be zombies right now."

"Bioweapon?" Brad was shocked to hear that answer, and more shocked to hear about the coordinated response team. It was a phrase he'd nearly forgotten about.

Luke looked at Brad then back at the road then back to Brad again. He saw the shock on Brad's face, and that caused him to grimace. "Wait, you aren't surprised by my answer; you're just surprised that I know. You already knew this, didn't you?"

"I knew some of it."

"How?"

Brad took another drink from the water bottle, draining it before sticking the empty bottle back into his cargo pocket. "When I was stranded over in the Stan, I ran into a pair of operators that were returning from a mission to stop the attacks."

"Stop the attacks?" Luke laughed. "They happened across the globe."

"Yeah, I get that," Brad scoffed. "They were one team of many. They failed in their mission, by the way; they never prevented their attack and the city fell apart all around them."

"Where?" Luke said, his tone serious.

Brad shook his head. "Uzbekistan. It was across the border from the place we met up. I can't remember the city name." He rubbed the scruff on his chin, scratching at his jaw line. "How about you? How did you know?"

"Close to the same, really. Gyles up there," Luke looked up and pointed a finger toward the turret. "The mission he was on wasn't really about my city. He was on some run to pick up doctors, people that were hunting for a cure. They failed too. I guess all of us did."

"Yeah, I guess we all did, even after the cure——or at least the vaccination—I thought this would all be over."

"You get the vaccine?" Luke asked.

"Yeah, I got it. You?"

Luke nodded. "Last year, a group came through here; they had a bunch of it. They said they wanted to vaccinate fighters first then the hunters, gatherers, people that left the walls and those at greater risk. They had hundreds of doses and said they'd come back."

"They didn't?" Brad asked.

"No, they didn't. Never heard from them again." Luke paused; there was a metal *thunking* on the roof. Luke strained his eyes, looking for trouble, then gunshots and muzzle flashes struck ahead.

Gyles dropped down out of the turret and shouted, "Contacts ahead. Fucking screamers are jumping down onto the convoy from the overpass." The man stood back up, and his machine gun let loose. Brad watched as tracers arced out from above. The impacts sparked and ricocheted all along the face of the overpass.

"Go, go, go, race through it!" came a garbled shout through the radio.

Brad felt the vehicle speed pick up. Gyles's fire on the overpass was effective, but the flow of Primals wasn't slowing. They were massing and flowing over, dropping onto the vehicles ahead and pouring off the sides. As they drew closer, Gyles dropped back into the MRAP and slammed the hatch shut. In a matter of seconds, a gun behind them picked up the fire, and the waterfall of bodies poured onto the MRAP. The vehicle bumped and shuddered as it rolled over a mound of the dead.

Brad turned back and saw Chelsea kneeling behind him, looking through the windshield. "There are just so many of them."

Gyles laughed. "You ain't seen nothing." He hit a switch, pouring on floodlights mounted to the top of the MRAP. The lights shone bright, illuminating the road ahead and far to the right and left of the vehicles. They were moving into a massive horde. The trucks ahead were effectively breaking a path through, but they were taking a beating.

"How the hell do we get through this?" Brad said.

"We just drive and hope it lets up."

Chelsea pointed a hand at the windshield. "This isn't a thunderstorm."

"Yeah, but it's a storm of sorts; we'll break through this mass and hope to hell Toledo is still there."

"And what if it's not?"

Luke shook his head slowly. "Like I said, let's hope to hell it is, and that they agree to let us in."

CHAPTER 25

THREE CORNERS OUTPOST, WEST OF LANCASTER, OHIO. THE DEAD LANDS

Sean heard the gunshots and sat up in the rack just as the bells began ringing. He pulled away the sleeping bag and leaped to his feet, his handgun already in his hand. He looked around the tent. Aside from Riley, who was looking directly at him, the other racks were still empty. More gunshots quickly turned into a full battle. He jumped into his clothes and saw Riley doing the same. "Where are the others?" he asked.

Riley began to speak when Henry came through the door with the boys following close behind. "Camp's under full attack. Couldn't get a look at it, but sounds serious. I saw some folks that said they was bugging out."

"Bugging out? How?" Sean said as he finished strapping on his boots and grabbed his rifle.

Henry clenched half his face. "There's a tunnel that leads to an out building; guess they think it's a way out."

Grunting, Riley was on his feet and stepping toward the still-open door. "It'll get them killed if they find Primals on the other side. Only choice is to hold this place. There's no running from this shit." The man stomped through the doorway. Henry looked to Sean for guidance. Sean waved a hand, signaling for them to move out after Riley.

The boys turned around to follow, and Sean stepped out alongside Henry. He wondered where Brooks and Joey would be if the Outpost was truly surrounded. He frowned and shook off dark thoughts; they were outside where they belonged. Nothing would get Brooks if he was in the open and had space to operate. Through the door, the interior of the courtyard was dark. Fires had been extinguished. He looked up into the windows of the buildings; all the lights were out. The only illumination was coming from the muzzle flashes of the defenders.

There were screaming and shouting groups of people running past him with packs on. Sean reached out and grabbed a frail old man in a canvas coat. "Where you going?"

The man spun toward him, his jaw was shaking, his eyes dilated with fear. "The tunnel."

"Where does it go?" Sean asked.

The man pointed toward the southwest corner of the compound. "There's an old block house that way. Used to be an auxiliary warehouse for this place. Made of concrete blocks, steel roof. Only one door and it's locked tight."

"Why?" Sean asked. "You want to go hide in a box surrounded by those things?"

The old man gave Sean a confused look. "It's a bunker; it has supplies." The old man pulled away, and Sean went to snatch him again, but the man didn't run. "It's a place to hide while the camp is defended."

Sean nodded and waved the man off. When he turned back, he could see that he'd been left alone. Henry and the others were now approaching the main gate where a wagon was positioned, and a man in dark coveralls was handing out rifles and bandoleers of ammunition. As men from the camp ran past, they took the weapons and disappeared into a doorway. Sean saw that Henry and the others had bunched up at the wagon, watching the commotion but taking no steps to do anything themselves.

Sean could see Riley standing by the entrance to the door, holding one of the rifles and with the ammo bandoleer hanging over his shoulder. Sean stepped in his direction, when he heard a shout from behind.

"Hey, you guys! Hold it right there."

Sean smiled and slowly turned back. Behind him and moving his way were the officer and his two troopers. Sean's smile faded, and his hand tightened on the grip of his rifle. The officer stomped closer then looked directly at Sean. "What's happening here?" the officer asked.

Sean looked left and right. "Well, I'm no genius, but sorta looks like the camp is under attack." Sean looked to Henry. "What do you think? An attack?"

Henry did the same twist of his head. "Aye, yeah, this seems to be your classic Primal attack."

The officer scowled. "Primal? Where the hell you from? You military? Nobody says Primal around here."

Henry shook his head, and the officer turned to face Sean. "What about you?"

Sean smiled. "I was."

The officer softened his scowl and smiled. "Listen, my name's Captain Leroy Spencer. I'm only here passing through. I need some help to find out what the hell is going on and how we can help."

Nodding, Sean pointed to the open doorway. "You can call me Sean; this is Henry and his nephews. We're in the same boat as you: just traders who heard the bells and came this way to see if we could help."

"Very well," Spencer said. "Follow me." The officer charged past them with the two younger soldiers quickly in tow.

Henry glanced at Sean. With a grin, he waved a hand. "Beauty before age."

Sean flipped the older man the bird and moved into the building. Inside, he could see groups of men standing over a bench, loading rifle magazines. At the end of the room, Spencer was talking to a bearded man in a red-and-black flannel shirt. The man pointed to a stairwell on the opposite wall. Spencer nodded and turned back to Sean, waving for them to follow as he moved out toward the stairs.

Sean and the others followed. The stairs, which were wide and made of smooth concrete, looked like they belonged in an old school building. Men were running up and down, panicked faces covered in sweat and grime. The echoes of gunshots roared into the building's confines. Sean popped in a pair of earplugs he carried in a shirt pocket and continued his trek upward, toward the fighting.

He exited from a roof access door and out into the darkness. The air was heavy with blue smoke and the stench of carbon from heavy rifle fire. Muzzle flashes refracted through the smoke like strobes. Looking down a long flat roof with men lining the outer edges, barrels of water, rubber hoses, and solar panels littered every open space. Sean pushed his way to the firing lines and looked down into the faces of thousands. The trenches that surrounded the building were already full, strands of wire and chain link fencing dragged across the yard.

Sean felt the captain standing beside him. "What's gotten into them? The infected don't mass like this anymore."

"Hunger," Spencer said. "In small groups, they do okay

in the wild. A mass like this? No. They're starving, and it drives them wild. Feeding the hunger comes first for them."

Sean leaned out and looked down. The things were pressing against the walls—some against windows and doors. He scanned the men on the perimeter. There was no organization to their firing; anyone with a rifle was firing into the mass directly to the front.

"We're losing. We need to organize our fire to the ones hitting the gates and windows," Sean said, pointing to a large mass pressed against the main entry.

Spencer nodded his head. He grabbed one of the young soldiers behind him. "Start directing fire to the attacks on the doors and windows. Don't concern yourself with those pressed against brick."

Sean still hadn't fired a shot. He stepped back and could see that Henry and the two boys were close beside him. Riley had vanished. He pulled Henry in and relayed the same instructions Spencer had just given. "We've got to organize these people or we are done."

Henry nodded and took off, grabbing men on the walls and directing their fire, giving them points of aim. Sean felt a tug on his shoulder. Spencer was pointing down the roofline to where men were pulling back from the edge. Looking below, a bit of the outer wall was buckling from the weight pressed against it. The window barriers were holding but not for long. "We've got to find out who is running this goat fuck," Spencer said just below a full yell. He pointed at the road. "Nobody will have the ammo to sustain this fight. Even if the structure does hold, we're going to have to plan an egress."

Sean nodded in agreement, the thoughts having already crossed his mind. He turned back to the fighting, scanned the terrain, and spotted the distant block building. It wasn't much, just a two-story cube with a pair of steel garage doors. He tapped Spencer and pointed. "I heard one of the civvies say there is a tunnel that leads to that building. We focus all the Primal attention here and they might have a fighting chance."

Spencer squinted and looked at Sean. The man pressed a gloved hand to his temple and grimaced before pulling back from the wall. "Let's find their leader."

Sean spotted the white-bearded man he'd met earlier in the day. He pointed him out to Spencer then they moved out together. As they drew closer, Sean could already see that things were rapidly changing. More men were leaving down the stairs than those who were coming up. Looking at the perimeter walls, the men firing were beginning to thin out. Just before they reached the leader, Sean leaned into Spencer. "Looks like these guys are starting to bail."

Spencer frowned and dipped his chin slightly. The white-bearded man had spotted them and turned toward the uniformed captain. "We need your help; can you get more soldiers here?"

Holding up his radio, Spencer shook his head. "I tried; no contact with my command."

Sean caught notice of that. He hadn't considered there being more people and this captain having potential radio communications with them. "Where is your command?" Sean said, regretting the question before the words fully left his mouth.

The captain eyed him suspiciously and tucked the radio back into his jacket. He rolled his eyes, like he was more frustrated to answer the question than concerned that Sean was gathering intel. "South, but it doesn't matter. I can't raise them on the radio."

"Is that unusual?" Sean asked.

Spencer shook his head. "No. When on mission, we only open communications every six hours unless scheduled. I have a check-in with battalion at o6oo and another at 12oo. Outside of that, it just won't work—I've tried. By the time the next check is due, it'll be way too late for this place." He stopped and looked back at Seth. "Your people are all leaving, what's the plan here?"

The old man with the white beard looked down. "I only have a dozen in my guard force, the rest are volunteers; they have families to fend for."

"If this place falls, so do their families," Sean said.

White Beard looked down and away. He started to speak, but Sean cut him off. "I know all about the tunnel. So let me ask you again, what's the plan?"

Seth's eyes grew wide. He went to speak and then closed his lips again, thinking about it. "Okay, yeah, there is a bunker of sorts. We're running a phased withdrawal." The old man pointed to the mass. "You know as well as I do, you can't beat them this way."

"Nope," Sean said, his head shaking side-to-side. "Every shot you fire draws in ten more from surrounding areas; it's a losing math battle. Your best bet is to get somewhere hard and wait it out. I don't blame you all one bit for doing it— actually, I'm surprised you've planned for it."

Seth shrugged as group of men all at once peeled off the wall and ran past him, one shouting a wish of good luck as he ran by.

"How long we got until they're all gone?" Spencer asked.

Seth looked at his watch. "Less than twenty minutes and it'll just be my guard force."

"Then what?" Sean asked.

"Then we fight and hope the roof holds."

Spencer exhaled loudly. "Not much of a plan."

"It's all I got. There are a couple hard rooms one floor down, supplies inside for a week. If they get inside the building, it'll be a race to make it there. I don't know."

"Nah, fuck that. Get your people and start peeling off. My boys can hold the roof," Sean said.

"Wait... what?" Spencer said, putting up his hand and turning.

Sean ignored the officer. "Get what magazines you have loaded up and leave me some of those battle rifles. Get your people and get the hell out." Sean turned to Captain Spencer. "You're free to go too if that's what makes you feel better."

Seth took a step back, looking at Sean. Without waiting to hear any disagreement from Spencer, he started shouting orders to his men. Within minutes, men were fleeing the roof. Rifles and magazines were dropped on a bench close by. Soon, it was only Sean's and Spencer's teams left on the rooftop. The return fire had stopped.

"Who the fuck are you?" Spencer asked.

"I was Chief Sean Rogers, United States Navy. Now I'm me—survivor of the fucking apocalypse, and I know I have a better chance at making this work than they do. I meant what I said, you can leave with the others if you want, but decide quickly because I'm about to blow the roof access. We'll be trapped up here after that."

Sean didn't wait for a response; he turned to Henry. "Can you find a way to knock that enclosure in? I need it completely blocked; nothing gets up those stairs," he said, pointing to the small structure in the center of the roof that served as the only access.

Henry grinned. "I think I can figure it out."

"Take the boys and make it happen." He turned back to

Spencer. "Clock's ticking. If you're staying, I would appreciate someone bringing all the weapons and ammo to the far end of the building. And send one of your troops to inspect the rest of the rooftop—make sure there is no other way up."

"What about them? We just stop shooting?" Spencer asked.

"That?" Sean said, pointing toward the mass. "Shooting at that would be like pissing on a volcano. We'll let them see us and keep drawing them in, but for the time being, we need to fortify our position." Sean turned away and quick-timed it to some sort of improvised greenhouse topped with a roof made of white canvas. He ripped down the canvas top and dropped it on the ground next to him. He looked over the clay flower pots—most of which were empty, probably standing by for the next growing season. He snatched a large five-gallon bucket filled with dark earth and mixed it with water then carried the muddy mixture over to the tarp and began drawing on it.

When he finished, he bundled up the canvas and moved toward the end of the building where the men were already forming fighting positions directed at what was left of the roof enclosure. Sean grabbed Riley from the group and walked to the edge of the roof that faced the distant barn. They stretched out the white canvas tarp now etched with a crude trident drawn in dark mud. Pulling the ends, they fastened it to the edge of the roof and let it hang over the side.

With the banner hanging from the building, Riley looked down at it, confused. "What is this, some sort of SOS?" he asked.

Sean looked out at the dark horizon. "Yeah, now we just hope Brooks can see it."

CHAPTER 26

TOLEDO CITY LIMITS, THE DEAD LANDS

The vehicle convoy had left the interstate and drifted north of Toledo, breaking contact with the infected hordes. They'd stopped in an abandoned neighborhood, haunted by dilapidated and burned-out homes with overgrown grass that lined the street. The convoy was all buttoned up, the engines off and the lights out. The only sounds were breathing and snoring from the occupants. Brad looked at Luke in the driver's seat; the man was sitting back, his eyes focused straight ahead.

"The power plant is in the city?" Brad whispered.

Luke shook his head. "No, just southeast on the Lake Erie shoreline."

"And they still have power?"

"Yeah, it's nuke. Place is still online with the original crew—at least that's what I'm told."

Brad turned his head sharply. "A nuke reactor? I thought all of those had been safely powered down."

"From what I understand most were, but Toledo wasn't. The crew managed to get their families inside and barricade the joint. After a few months, people started to notice Toledo had lights on, and the military sent groups in to secure and inspect it." Luke put up a finger, pausing and listening. He shook his head and continued. "Anyhow, it changed hands a few times. Was even ordered to power off by the Bunker when they were still running things, but the workers refused. Now the East owns it—well, sort of. It's in the badlands, but possession is nine-tenths, you know."

"A nuke plant in the badlands," Brad whispered. "People are living in an emerald city with all that light surrounded by darkness."

"It hasn't been all fun and games for them."

"Yeah, Gyles told me."

Luke looked at Brad and tipped his head to the side. "I'm sure he highlighted it. We have a defector on our team. He was one of the plant's original security officers."

"He defected?"

Luke nodded. "Like I said, it's not all fun and games. They have power but suffer from food shortages same as the rest of us. And being isolated brings on its own problems. The engineers have been wanting to safely power down the core for months, but the East is against it."

"Why do they want to shut it down?"

"Takes a lot of maintenance and specialized people to keep the place running. They have less than ten percent of the staff they used to, and they continue to run out of spare parts. Like any machine, things constantly need replacing. They want to put it to sleep while they can and not wait for something catastrophic."

Brad sat silently for a moment, thinking. "We sure about this, Luke?" Brad sighed. "If that horde picks up our trail, follows into the plant, and the place melts down..."

"I've thought about it," Luke said. "That's why we're

not bringing in the entire convoy. It'll just be us. They have their own mission."

"Us?" Brad said. "Why me?"

"Cause I need someone that can speak for Texas."

Brad shook his head. "I told you, I'm not with them."

"Yeah, I know that now, but they don't. You do know more about them than anybody else though. We need to convince them to work with us, and this is the only way."

A knock at Luke's door caused both men to jump. Luke released the combat lock and the door squeaked open, exposing a young man whose face was covered with a days-old beard. "We're in the clear, no infected sightings in a few hours."

Luke closed his eyes and slowly opened them. "Okay, take the convoy and do what you gotta do. Get back safe, you hear?"

The soldier extended a hand and Luke took it. "Good luck, Luke. Been good serving with you, brother," the man said before stepping away.

"Well, if that didn't sound like he was sending us to our deaths, I don't know what does," Chelsea said wearily from the back.

Luke slammed and locked the door. "You should eat those words. They're turning around and running back into the horde. They're going to try and keep them from getting to us. You're welcome to join them if this is too damning for you."

Brad put up his hand. "She didn't mean it like that, and it's on you for keeping us in the dark."

The driver put his head down then raised it back up. He turned to Chelsea. "He's right. I shouldn't have snapped." Luke powered on the MRAP and pulled the vehicle out to the shoulder of the road, leaving the lights off. "So... from here on out, it's all in the clear; you know what I know. We've got thirty miles to the power plant. We'll get as close as we can then find a spot to hole up until morning."

"And they'll just let us in?"

"I don't know."

The MRAP eased forward, the lights off and Luke driving by moonlight. Gyles was still up in the turret. Riding low, the man's head was just barely exposed now. He wasn't up there to fight but more to guide the driver. The MRAP didn't purr like a kitten and it was loud. The street was lined with cookie-cutter homes, all new construction like a yuppie development. Brad scanned out the side window, spotting green eyes reflecting at him from broken windows.

"The neighbors know we're here," Brad said.

Luke nodded. His hands relaxed and regripped the wheel. "Contact is unavoidable in the Beast, but still beats humping it out there on foot," he said.

The MRAP stayed down the center of the suburban street until it hit a hasty roadblock. Two old police cars parked nose-to-nose cut off the street. Behind them were steel barrels and wood piled up as a makeshift barricade. The shoulders of the road were stacked with piles of debris, as if the residents had used anything they could find to block the street—furniture, bicycles, old building materials. Luke turned to look at Brad. "You're up."

"Up where?" Brad asked.

Luke laughed, showing his white teeth. "Come on now, you know I can't drive through that mess. Go hook the winch cable to one of those cars. I'll back up and break a lane."

"Out there?! Hell no, there's got to be another way."

Shaking his head, Luke replied, "Not one that doesn't

bring us closer into the city. This is the route. Now go on; Gyles has got you covered up top." Luke reached into a box that was near the base of his seat, coming out with a Glock 21 equipped with a suppressor that was nearly a foot long. "You don't want to go loud out here."

Brad took the pistol, dropped the magazine, and checked the slide. Eleven rounds with one in the chamber. He looked back behind him into the crew compartment. Gyles was kneeling in the hatch and shot him a thumbs up. "Don't sweat it; I got you."

"I can do it," Chelsea said from the back.

Brad shook his head and, clenching his jaw, popped the door then eased his head out over the top edge. They'd been driving blackout with no lights, so his eyes had already adjusted to the moonlight. He looked up and noticed the sky was clear and crisp, the air cold. The yards were covered with tall grass and only patches of old snow. He scanned the homes on the right side of the road. A long ranch house was directly next to them. In the driveway of the home rested an old Chrysler mini-van on four flat tires. The house itself had all the windows broken, the curtains fluttering in a light breeze. The door to the home had been pulled free and it was lying in the front yard next to the porch.

Brad stood and looked out over the vehicle to the house on the opposite side of the street. The home was nearly identical in size and shape, yet surprisingly in better condition with no obvious signs of damage. His eyes drifted to the left, and he saw Gyles up in the turret. Brad was surprised to see him holding a SCAR rifle at the ready, the mounted M240 Bravo machine gun in the turret turned down and away from him. Gyles put two fingers to his eyes then pulled them away and spun them in a circle. He then pointed at Brad and down to the roadblock.

Brad flipped the man off in response and dropped to the ground. The sounds of his boots hitting the pavement made him cringe. He stepped away from the MRAP, his boots' soles echoing in the night. "I sound like a fucking Clydesdale," he said to himself. He pulled the pistol up with his right arm, holding it to his chest, and he took another sweep with his eyes. Nothing was moving, and there were no sounds. He walked lightly, checking every footfall, as he moved to the front of the MRAP. The winch cable was rolled up from the electric motor and hanging to an eyebolt by a large hook.

Brad grabbed the hook and went to remove it, but the tension was too tight. The hook cable was solid in place and wouldn't move. He laid the pistol on the hood of the vehicle and fought the hook with both hands, still unable to budge it.

"Release the lock," Gyles whispered.

The sound of the man's voice came at him like a hurricane-force wind in the utter silence. Brad froze and looked up at the turret. Gyles was mimicking turning his hand clockwise. "On the motor, there is a twist lock."

Brad shook his head and went back to the long, fire-extinguisher-shaped motor; below it was the spool of cable that wound out and to the hook. Brad felt along the side, finding the twist lock. He released it and immediately felt the slack in the cable. He followed the cable to the hook and was now able to easily unhook it from the eyebolt. He looked up into the windshield and saw Chelsea and Luke staring at him from the cab, Luke pointing toward the roadblock. This also warranted another one-finger salute from Brad.

He lifted the pistol from the hood, took the hook in his left hand, and began walking toward the roadblock. The cable whirred as it unwound from the spool. Brad held his breath, thankful it wasn't screeching as he thought it might. He weaved in and out of the piled wreckage to a tiny void where the two vehicles met. He could tell by the arrangement of the blockade and a pair of folding chairs that men had stood watch here. On the ground was a pile of expended shotgun shells. He knelt to find a spot to attach the cable before jumping back.

A skeletal hand with curled fingers pointed up at him from under the patrol car. The hand was attached to an arm still wearing a police officer's dark-blue jacket. Brad shook it off and moved past it to the front of the car, finding a black, steel brush guard. He pulled the cable to get slack then wrapped it around the guard. He turned back to the MRAP; Luke was waving him to return to the vehicle. He did as Luke instructed and made a direct line for the safety of the vehicle.

"You gotta lock the motor," Gyles said, stopping Brad in his tracks.

He nodded and ran back to the front of the truck and spun the winch lock back into place then quickly moved back to the cab. Chelsea already had the door open when he reached it and piled back inside.

"How was it?" Chelsea asked.

Brad shrugged. "Not so bad, I guess."

Luke laughed, causing Brad to look at him. "What's so funny?"

Dropping back into the vehicle from the turret, Gyles looked at him. "Hooking up was the easy part; unhooking after we wake the neighborhood is where it gets tricky."

"Seriously?" Brad grunted.

"What? You think it was gonna unhook itself?" Luke said. The man fired the MRAP back to life and gunned the engine then dropped the Beast into reverse. The vehicle lunged back then jerked to a halt as the cable tightened. Luke tightened his jaw and pressed on the accelerator. The roadblock began to tremor then broke free, all the garbage and rusted vehicles dragging back in one single mass. The night silence filled with the roaring engine and screeching of the debris being hauled across concrete. Luke began to laugh as he towed the island of debris behind them. The MRAP stopped, and Luke moved it forward just a hair to put slack back into the cable.

The machine gun in the turret erupted, the outside now lit by the strobes of the muzzle flashes. Brad could see the tracer rounds tearing into the house on his right, the fire moving and cutting into the doorway. "You gotta move!" Gyles yelled. "They are onto us now, buddy."

Luke threw open his door and stood in the frame, his own rifle fire directed somewhere off to his left. Brad leapt from the cab, running for the end of the cable. He saw the wire weaved through the wreckage. Brad stuffed the Glock into his belt and pulled the cable to get more slack then unhooked it from the brush guard. Screams to his front and an infected impacting with the debris jarred him back. He pulled the Glock and fired twice into the thing's face, the *clack clack* of the suppressed rounds hardly noticeable over the firing of the machine gun. He cursed himself for not grabbing his rifle.

He unwound the cable from the debris and tossed it free into the street before turning back. He spotted a cluster of infected running at him, and he raised the Glock again, but the charging infected were cut down before they could close the distance. He ducked his head and ran as Gyles provided cover fire. Once again, Chelsea had the door open for him and he ducked inside, slamming his door shut. He heard the clanging and clunking of doors and hatches being locked as the things outside impacted with the armored vehicle. Brad looked down at the Glock in his shaking hand. He took it and handed it back to Luke. "Next time you have stupid shit to be done, do it yourself," he said.

Luke laughed. "It isn't stupid if it works," he said. The man reached for a toggle on the dash and listened as the whirring motor to the front retracted the cable. "Now just hope it don't twist or tangle or you gotta go back out there."

"Fuck you," Brad said, leaning his head back as both Gyles and Luke erupted into laughter.

"I gotta come clean here; I can't stand you guys," Brad said.

The cable didn't tangle and soon the vehicle was back in gear. Luke maneuvered them forward and around the remnants of the barricade. They were out of the neighborhood and on a wide two-lane road. It wasn't as congested as they'd worried it might be; parts even looked as if they had been recently cleared. There were several cars packed tightly together, angled off and down a grade where they'd been pushed out of the way.

At another intersection was a pile of stacked corpses. The MRAP slowed as they moved past the stack. "Human or Primal?" Chelsea croaked from the back.

Brad shook his head. "Impossible to tell, but at one time they were all human."

The MRAP stopped again. The main road was blocked by many dump trucks and a fire truck, with a pair of defunct Bradley fighting vehicles on each flank. Gyles squatted back into the vehicle. "This has been here for a while. I went past it last summer. There is no way past, and even if there was, you don't want to get on the other side of it."

"Why?" Chelsea asked.

Gyles looked at her before he looked away. "Nothing but death over there. Doesn't matter, the road leads to a knocked-out bridge. Whoever defended this place made phased withdrawals from my inspection last summer. There was a massive fight here before they pulled back and blew the bridge." The soldier swallowed and looked up at the night sky from the hatch. He leaned forward and directed his words back to Luke. "Take this left up ahead here, follow it around, and we'll get closer to the lakeshore. I know a place where we can hide until morning."

"Hide?" Chelsea asked. "We're stopping again?"

Luke grunted, making the left turn. "We'll approach them in daylight. Folks are less jumpy than they are at night."

CHAPTER 27

The sun was coming up in the east, breaking through low clouds on the horizon. Sean felt the building rumble as the infected moved around the structure below them. His people were on the roof and could hear the breaking of furniture and the destruction of the building as the mass frenzied just one floor below them, sensing food just out of reach. Sean stretched and looked at his watch; it was nearly six in the morning. The creatures had broken through the walls a bit past midnight and made it to the top floors by two o'clock. By three, they were attacking the barricaded stairwell. So far, any attacks had just caused the structure to further collapse. While it prevented the infected from reaching the roof, it also made it hard to sleep.

He strained, sitting up from his spot against the far wall. He could see Captain Spencer and his two shooters farther up the roof, focusing on the collapsed enclosure. There was plenty of noise coming from below, and they knew the infected were trying to break through. Spencer seemed to feel his stare, and the man looked back at him. Concern showed on his face as he shook his head. Sean pushed himself to his feet, knowing sleep wouldn't be coming to him anyway.

Moving toward the fighting position, Spencer stood to meet him. The captain was holding the radio in his hand. He looked at Sean and again shook his head. "Nothing. I power this on at ten minutes to six, morning and night, religiously. Every time, I get an operator before five minutes to the hour." Spencer rolled his wrist to look at his watch. "It's five after."

"Is there anyone else? You have to have other protocols for emergencies."

Spencer nodded. "We have some open command nets. Nobody uses them though; they're on their own encrypted net and only for inside traffic, like truck drivers, supply drops... stuff like that. Most guys don't even carry the freqs in the field."

"Well, unless you have a better idea, you should start scanning."

"Yeah," Spencer said. He pulled a plastic map book from a sleeve pocket and flipped it over. He looked at a series of numbers written in blue pen on the back of a yellow scrap of paper. He slowly punched in the encryption key, and he hit a scan button. The backlit display began to scroll frequencies. The first it stopped on was static, so he pressed a key to continue. The scrolling stopped at two more with static before the dial halted on the voices of screaming men and automatic weapons' fire—the unmistakable sounds of desperate men pleading for help as they were overrun. The two young soldiers' heads spun back in his direction. They'd all heard it before. Spencer's arm went rigid as if he was going to toss the radio like a burning log.

"What is that?" Sean said, pointing at the number on the dial. Spencer handed the radio to Sean then tore open the map case and dug at the scraps of paper. He found one with an extensive list of frequencies and call signs. He froze, comparing the number to the back lit display and then back at the paper. He took a step back and dropped to the ground with his arm outstretched, holding the handwritten page. "It's Rapture," Spencer said.

Sean moved closer and took the paper, comparing the number on the page to the radio and confirming the call sign *Rapture*. "What is it?" Sean asked. "Who is Rapture?"

"It's the Battalion TOC at the railhead," one of the soldiers said.

Sean looked at the young man and could see the name Adams written on his right chest. Sean looked from the young soldier and back to Spencer. "What's your call sign?" Sean said.

Spencer dropped his head and looked at his boots. "I don't have one for talking to the Tactical Operations Center."

"Give me a fucking name!" Sean shouted, wanting to reach forward and slap the officer.

"They call us Recon. The Straight Six," Adams said, turning his shoulder and pointing at a patch on his sleeve with a dark six and an arrow cutting through it."

Sean nodded and keyed the radio, saying, "Any Rapture element, this is Straight Six." When he lifted his finger, he received nothing but screams in response. "Any Rapture element, this is Straight Six." Sean held the radio, listening to the screams. He took it and placed it on an empty ammo crate to his right with it pointed in Spencer's direction. The captain still had his head down, his hand shaking as the screams of his battalion poured over the open channel.

Sean looked back to the young soldier. "Adams, is it?"

"Yes, sir," the boy said back. "Corporal Bill Adams; this is PFC Doug Jones."

"Not a sir," Sean said.

"Sorry, Sergeant."

Sean grinned, trying to lighten the mood. "I'm not a sorry sergeant either. If you must, you can call me Chief, but I prefer Sean."

This time the boy just nodded.

Sean pointed to Spencer, who still had his head down. "Your captain here is rebooting. While that happens, I have a few questions to ask."

"Yes, sir—er—I mean Chief Sean."

Smiling, Sean moved closer and put a hand on the corporal's shoulder. "This battalion is at the railhead. How far away is that?"

Billy looked up like the answer was written in the clouds. "Fifty miles, maybe. Hard to estimate, but it's at least a half day's drive."

"Okay, and how many troops there?"

Billy looked at Sean suspiciously.

"I know you don't know me, and you aren't supposed to give that kind of info to strangers, but if we want to stay alive, I need to know."

Billy looked to his captain who now had his knees drawn into his chest, his head still down. "'Bout a hundred and fifty, not counting the soldiers that are garrisoned there. With them, maybe two hundred, tops."

A long scream came from the radio before it stopped suddenly, replaced by the howls and moans of the infected. Sean lifted the radio and looked at it, knowing it was hot mic'd in some dead man's grip. He found the knob and powered it off.

He looked back at Billy. "Where are you from, Billy?"

"Pittsburg."

Sean moved closer and looked the man in the eye. "Billy, what are you doing out here?"

The young soldier again looked to his leader for support but, getting none, looked back at Sean. "Texas is invading, and we got to stop them."

Sean grimaced and exhaled. "I see." He rubbed his hand through his hair and walked closer to the barricade before turning to look back at the two soldiers. "Texas isn't invading."

"They are," Billy said. "We shot at one of their scout teams yesterday—two vehicles and a bunch of guys."

Sean slowly shook his head. "That was me and my guys," Sean said.

Billy looked at him, his eyes going wide as he scanned the rest of the men on the roof... Henry sitting against the wall smoking a pipe, the two young Baker boys asleep under a flannel blanket, and Riley, who was fishing apples from a mason jar. "Why—but 'cept for you, these aren't soldiers at all."

Sean touched his finger to his temple. "Now you are starting to get it. And now I'm going to tell you why Texas isn't invading."

"You are?"

Sean grinned and dipped his chin. "They aren't invading because of this," he said, pointing toward the enclosure. "And because of this," he said, holding up the radio. "Texas has known that the infected were massing and coming in from the big cities. They've been pulling back and trying to fortify their lines while all you assholes do is make noise and draw more and more of them in."

"We didn't know," Spencer gasped, finally looking up from his stupor.

Sean glared. "You had to have known something, if that was really you shooting at us by the railroad crossing. You were surrounded by a mass. You didn't notice the numbers of infected growing? The number of large groups? The way they were becoming more aggressive?"

"Was a couple hundred," Spencer said, just above a whisper. "We attract groups like that to block roads all the time. It's not a big deal."

"You stirred them up; you brought this here," Sean said. "Now your battalion is dead, and we're trapped." He wanted to pull his pistol and shoot the man dead, but he looked at the two young soldiers and knew he would need them all if they were going to live out the day. He walked to the roofline and looked out. He knew Brooks was somewhere making a plan to get them out. "We're getting off this roof. When we do, we need a place to go. Give me a suggestion."

Sean turned to the young soldiers, who returned puzzled stares.

"Toledo," Spencer mumbled. "Toledo will be there. It's sturdy, lots of security; it'll still be there."

"Toledo?" Sean asked. "Where?"

"No," Spencer said, shaking his head. He pushed a fist to the roof and pushed himself to his feet. "No, I'll show you, but you have to get my men there. We all go."

"That was the plan," Sean said.

The splitting and cracking of wooden beams echoed from the enclosure. The roof buckled and reverberated. A blast of dust and smoke erupted as what was left of the rooftop building dropped into the floor below it. Howls filled the air, and the first hand of an infected grabbed the edge of the hole and began to pull itself up. Sean leveled his rifle and pulled the trigger. Without being given instructions, Adams and Jones were online with him, taking out targets of their own. Soon, Henry and the others were all flanking the hole and firing into the void.

They were backing up as the hole filled with the dead. Sean reloaded and continued firing. In his peripheral vision, he saw a bright fire in the distance. He took his finger off the trigger and stepped back from the hole. A cloud of black smoke was billowing through the tall trees. He moved to the building's edge as a large explosion went off near the fire and a trio of flares flew in the air.

Sean smiled. "Brooks."

Looking down, he could see that the infected on the ground were turning and running toward the distant inferno. Even those fighting to get to the roof had dropped in intensity.

Sean moved back to the troops, grabbed Spencer by the arm, and chopped an imaginary line. "Get on line and fall back to the roof's edge," he shouted. Sean pointed to ropes and guidelines that were tied together, holding down solar panels. "Get those ropes linked together and be ready to drop down."

Spencer looked at him, confused. Sean pointed to the fire on the horizon. "I got transportation inbound. We need to be ready when it gets here."

CHAPTER 28

TOLEDO CITY LIMITS, THE DEAD LANDS

The steel pole building was long and wide, filled with empty boats wrapped in plastic and tarps and now a rusted black MRAP. Brad walked from the back of the building to the front, where the rest of the crew had made themselves comfortable up on the deck of a large trailered cabin cruiser. Brad moved around to the back and pulled himself up on a ladder and climbed to the deck of the boat. From the high vantage point, he could see the long rows of plastic-wrapped boats.

Probably more than twenty boats of all types, even though the building could hold three times as many. The fall happened in the late summer, so the place probably wasn't close to capacity yet, with people trying to get every drop out of the Midwest summer before storing their pleasure boats for the winter. He could hear the men talking up in the pilot house, and Brad moved up a narrow ladder to join them. In the pilot house, he saw Chelsea sitting in the captain's chair eating an MRE.

"Seriously?" Brad said, pointing at the brown package.

"Even two years after the end of the world, I have to be tortured with that shit?"

Chelsea grinned and tossed him a package. He caught it and looked at the black writing. "Potatoes with ham; nasty. Where the hell did you find this stuff?"

She laughed and pointed to a bright-yellow Nautica bag on the deck. "There was a bag of 'em down in a storage locker. Bunch of survival stuff, first aid kit—probably gear for a lifeboat."

Brad shrugged. "Yeah, probably." He moved and dropped into a seat next to her and opened the package, dumping the contents onto the table and fishing out the entrée. He ripped the top off then scrunched his face in disgust. "With all the scientists they had working on this stuff, you'd think they could have found a way to get rid of the ass smell."

"Just eat your breakfast, Brad," Chelsea said.

He dipped the spoon in and looked through the windshield to the two men out on the bow. They held binoculars and were looking through the skylight toward the distant cooling towers of the nuke plant.

"Is it going to work?" Chelsea asked.

Brad turned his head. He could see the worry in her eyes, even though she was trying to hide it.

He swallowed down the mixture of greasy clumped potatoes and pork and blinked his eyes, pretending to choke down the food. He smiled at her. "Yes, it's going to work. It has to."

She forced a smile. "You remember that boat back in the gulf?"

"How could I forget it?" Brad said, thinking of what the military attack brought and how they sailed from the oil platform toward Oman.

"You ever wonder what would have happened if we'd just stayed on it? Found a home of our own? Every place in the world couldn't have been scarred by this disease. There must have been something out there; an island, a remote beach... something."

"I think about it all the time," he said. Brad sipped from a water bottle, trying to wash out the taste of MRE pork. "But there's no going back, Chelsea. Only forward."

She frowned. "Sometimes I feel like going forward is going back."

The bow access door opened and Gyles stepped in, carrying his SCAR. Luke was beside him with an olive painted Remington Model 700. Luke looked at them and said, "It's time."

Sighing, Brad said *okay* and put the bottle back in his rucksack. He stood and moved closer to Chelsea then looked down at her. "If you really aren't sure, we can walk away. I'll leave with you right now. I'll go wherever you want."

Her face turned red. He thought she was about to go off but, instead, she reached out and hugged his chest. She pushed back and looked him in the eyes. "Can I have a rain check?"

He pursed his lips and forced a smile, nodding. "Just let me know." Brad held in place, holding her as he watched the other two drop down the ladder and off the trailered boat. He put his hand on the back of her neck. "Let's go."

They dropped to the ground and strapped on their packs before checking their rifles. Brad moved to the tall double doors that were rust-locked into an open state. They could see out into the morning sky, blue with a few white clouds floating past, the sun just breaking the horizon. Two tall cooling towers of the nuclear plant sat in a wide field across from them. The compound was lined by double-wire fences, and in other places, hasty makeshift barriers dotted the scene.

Luke stepped through the door and pointed across the uncut field to a blacktop road. "That leads around and right to the front gate. I've spotted a half dozen watch towers on the wall. We figure it's best to just walk right up to the gate and knock on the door. Sneaking up kind of goes against us delivering a friendly message."

Brad looked at Chelsea, who dipped her chin slightly as she leaned in close. "Okay, lead the way," he said.

The road toward the power plant sitting on the banks of Lake Erie was clear. Multiple large buildings were back-dropped by two wall cooling towers, the tower farther north emitting a steady cloud of steam. The compound was lined with several rows of fencing. There, beyond the fencing, were wide fields of cut grass. Brad let his eyes scan the terrain. "Guess nobody wants to live next door to a nuclear reactor."

Gyles grinned. "At least not before, anyway. Now people want to live *in* one."

"Guess the risk of being eaten outweighs the risk of cancer."

Gyles pointed ahead on the road to a long concrete building. It gave the appearance of an administration office. Or at least it would have before the windows were boarded over and the sides lined with several layers of fencing. Even though the compound was set back from the perimeter road, the fencing extended away from the building. As they got closer, they could see that it was actually two buildings, not one. About three quarters down, a section of the building was scarred with blackened craters and crumbling concrete. Next to it was an access road and a tall, steel gate with a pair of guard towers on either side. The men in the towers were already looking their way.

"That's where I crashed the ambulance." He laughed. "That building took an entire can of forty mike-mike. I'm surprised they fixed it up."

As they walked closer, they heard no alarms, but more men entered towers and other heads popped in a gap between the fences and on the roof of the structure. "You sure about going in there? They might still be holding a grudge," Chelsea said.

Luke looked at a gap between the fences, where two men with carbines at the low ready were watching them. "Change of management," he said. "You notice something about the guards here that you didn't down in West Virginia?"

"Camo," Brad said without looking directly at the guards.

"It's more than camo," Luke answered. "They're uniforms. Military uniforms. These guys think of themselves as regular Army. These aren't the raiders we've been scrapping with."

"Wait..." Chelsea said. "The government is here?"

Luke shook his head. "Their version of it. Same as we have a version of ours. Those other people—from what I can make out from scout reports—are freelancers, scumbags and opportunists doing dirty work for their republic. The closer we get to the Republic lines, the more squared away they are."

"Interesting time to share that with us," Brad said.

"I can't teach you everything, son. If you wanted to know what's going on at home, you should have come back sooner," Luke said. "It makes no difference to us... just know that these guys think of themselves as legit, not criminals or outlaws."

"Are we?" Chelsea asked. "Are we outlaws? We wear uniforms, but they look like shit."

Luke turned his head and eyed her curiously. "You know... in their eyes, we just might be."

They walked to where the access road began, and stopped. A big sign off to the left that had once read something about a nuclear power station had now been painted over. The words *FOB Toledo, New Republic* were stenciled onto it.

Brad pointed at the sign. "That new?"

Gyles nodded. "They've really moved in and taken ownership."

They stood in a line, arm's length apart, with their weapons slung. Gyles stood on one end next to Luke, with Brad on the other end next to Chelsea, closest to the right side of the access road. "Just hold here for a few," Luke said.

Soon after, the gates of the facility began to open, and a pair of electric golf carts rolled out before the gates were closed behind them. The carts rolled toward them. The one on Brad's left carried two men in uniform while the one on the right, four. The cart with more soldiers veered off to Brad's right and stopped, the soldiers quickly exiting and spreading out, still holding their weapons at low ready. The left cart rolled right up to them and stopped when it was less than ten yards away.

The men stared them down and whispered something to each other before the driver of the cart spoke into a handheld radio. The passenger exited the cart and took a step closer. He was tall, mid-forties with grey speckling his dark hair. He wasn't carrying a rifle, but a handgun was strapped to his chest over body armor. Master Sergeant rank and the name Able, was stenciled below it.

"Huh," he grunted. "Thought you all were one of our returning patrols."

"Sorry to disappoint you, Master Sergeant," Luke said.

The man shrugged. "So if you aren't my boys, who the hell are you?"

Luke pointed a finger to Gyles. "We're from Michigan, these two from Texas."

"Texas?" the man said.

Brad waved a hand. "Not exactly. We're from a survivors' compound in the Virginias run by Lieutenant Colonel Dan Cloud. It was set up with help from Rangers out of Savanah Georgia."

"Rangers, you say?" the man said, looking at a Ranger scroll on his own left sleeve. "If that's true, give me a name."

"Colonel Erickson," Brad said.

The master sergeant held his expression and looked back at the soldier in the golf cart behind him. "Seventy-Fifth, Master Sergeant," the soldier said.

Able scowled. "I know who in the hell he is; I just thought the ornery son of a bitch was dead. Been a bit since I'd heard that name." He looked back at Brad. "Where is Ericson now?"

Brad shook his head. "It was over two years ago. Last I know, he moved what was left of the Third and the Seventy-Fifth down to Fort Sam Houston to help deliver the vaccine."

Laughing, Able dropped his hands to his hips. "You mean Erickson and my own Bat were responsible for delivering the vaccine?"

"Yeah, we secured it, and he delivered it to Sam Huston for production. I guess you know the rest," Brad said.

"You know… I always wondered why the vaccine went out the way it did; how it went to everyone with no questions asked. When we heard there was a cure, I thought for sure some asshole would try and keep it to himself and use it for a shitty power trip."

"Erickson and Cloud wanted to make sure everyone had access to it."

Able nodded. "Still, your man there says you're with Texas, but you say you're not."

Brad looked at the man in front of him and let his eyes scan to the four standing over watch farther back. He looked at Luke, and the man flashed his palms in mock surrender. "To hell with it," Brad said to himself. He looked back to Abel. "We had some scumbags attack our compound; they killed a lot of our people. Took a lot more— women and children—before they burned our compound."

Able nodded. "I see. And Texas?"

"They came to our assistance."

"And the ones that attacked you?" Able asked.

"We killed them—all of them. I put a bullet in their leader's face myself," Brad said.

"This one you killed, he have a name?" Able asked.

Chelsea turned, looked at him harshly, and shook her head.

Brad winked at her. "He called himself a general, but he was more of a coward and a rapist. He went down hiding behind a woman. His people called him Carson."

"Well, hell," Able said. "Erickson is alive, and Carson is confirmed dead. And they said Christmas don't come to the deadlands." Able stepped forward and looked at Brad harshly. "I got another question for you, and how you answer will determine what comes next."

"Go for it," Brad said.

"We're missing a battalion that didn't check in last night; you know anything about that?" the man asked.

"What the hell are the four of us going to do to a battalion?" Brad said, smirking.

Able laughed. "Yeah, I thought so. Communications from the south have been shit for a while." The man stepped closer and extended his hand. Brad hesitated but returned the handshake.

Able looked at him close and spoke lower so his men behind him couldn't hear. "Carson *was* a rapist and a murderer. He had a lot of control in the Republic, but he in no way spoke for us."

"But they said he *was* the Republic," Chelsea said.

Able looked at her and pursed his lips. "No—he was not. In fact, the only reason we now have troops in this reactor is because he's vanished. Regular army are starting to move into all his former holdings. You should see the faces of the folks when we arrive; they act like we are their liberators."

"Then what about the attacks on Michigan?" Gyles spat out, breaking the mood.

Able sighed. "They are still out there, lots of raiders still in the badlands, and not everyone at home agrees with how the country is supposed to look. It's hard to explain."

Luke stepped forward. "I don't think we'll have time for it. Fighting over what's left of the country isn't why we're here."

"Why are you here then?"

Luke rubbed his chin with his left hand. "The Primals are massing in numbers we've never seen before—they're hording, and they're on the move."

Able nodded. "We know that already; millions are migrating up the East Coast from DC and out of New York.

We've already sent the last of our regular units that way. It's half the reason they are so worried about the battalion down south; they want them recalled back to Philly. If shit gets hairy, they're all we'll have in reserve besides some local militias."

Gyles frowned and shook his head. "It's more than that... we're tracking other masses from Chicago and Detroit, and we don't even know about the other big cities like Columbus and Indy. Master Sergeant, you've got a horde right on your city limits west of Toronto. If we don't do something, we're talking about a second fall."

"What kind of numbers?" Able asked.

"My scouts estimated three million moving by way of Chicago, maybe another million out of Detroit."

"Hell, we haven't even got a thousand soldiers total." Able lifted the handheld radio to his lips. "Open the gate, we're coming in." He turned to Luke. "I've had scouts in the city the last week. They're showing an increase in activity, but nothing like that. Come on, we need to compare notes."

CHAPTER 29

THREE CORNERS OUTPOST, WEST OF
LANCASTER, OHIO. THE DEAD LANDS

S pencer fired into the face of a charging creature; the
thing's head snapped back, and he adjusted fire to the
left, clipping a female and another male just pulling out of
the hole. His bolt locked back, and he pressed the magazine
release, letting the empty drop to the deck before reaching
for another in his vest. The pouches were all empty. He
reached to his back and pulled out one of the three he kept
there. Locking in the mag and letting the bolt fly forward,
he was back in the fight. He turned and yelled at Sean, "If
you have a ride, it better hurry; I'm drying up on
ammo here."

Grunting, Sean took the last bandoleers of .223 from an
ammo can then threw the empty steel box toward the hole,
smacking an infected in the head. He dropped the
bandoleers on a table near the Baker boys, who were fever-
ishly reloading the empties. Turning back toward the
distant barn fire, he scanned with his optics. There were no
signs of Brooks and Joey. He second-guessed himself; maybe
the fire was their demise and not a signal or a distraction to
draw the infected away.

His eyes moved away to the left and toward the distant block building ringed with the tiny perimeter fence that was more for show than purpose. He could see no sign of the people he knew were hiding inside. Regardless of what happened up here on this roof, those people would be okay. Well, as okay as being surrounded in a sea of Primals can be. But once this fight was over, the Primals would move on. He turned and looked back into the courtyard. The infected had thinned out—even in the areas surrounding them, the infected had moved on toward the barn. Only those inside the building still determined to get at them on the roof remained.

"There!" he heard Billy yell. "Chief, are those your guys?"

Sean spun toward Billy, who'd positioned himself high on an air-conditioning unit so that he could fire down into the hole. The young soldier was pointing toward the back approach to the compound. Two SUVs were racing across the field, one pulling a trailer. "That's them. Let's go, boys. Peel out of the fight and get set up down below!"

Spencer turned toward the Bakers and stuffed filled mags back into his vest. "You all go first; I got this."

Sean moved around and pushed up next to Henry and Riley, who were working carbines of their own. "Go secure the ground and get loaded. As soon as I see your asses go over that roofline, look out because I'll be coming in hot."

Riley grunted. "I'll be looking for you."

Moving up beside Spencer, Sean fired slow, methodical shots into the hole, taking down an infected with every trigger pull. When he turned back, he could see that all the men were off the roof, and Henry was straddling the edge. "Let's go, Chief," Henry shouted, raising his rifle and ready to cover them.

Sean nodded and put a hand on Spencer's shoulder. He guided the man back to the roof, allowing him to fire as they moved backward together. Sean reached the ropes, and the old man fired off the rest of his rounds and let the AR-15 drop. "See ya on the ground, boys," Henry shouted, falling over the edge.

As soon as Spencer stopped firing, they could hear the gunfire pick up below them and see the infected climbing from the hole. They tried to ignore the urge to keep fighting and gripped the rope, tossing their legs over the sides. They weren't in rappelling gear, and there was nothing to slow them down except the friction on their worn shooting gloves. Sean burned down the three stories and collapsed in a heap in over-grown shrubbery. He kicked off the wall and rolled backward and onto the ground, looking up into the face of Riley, who was laughing at him. "Real graceful, buddy," the red-bearded man shouted, reaching down and pulling him to his feet.

"Stop playing grab ass; we gotta roll!" Brooks yelled from the Ford Explorer.

Sean flipped him the bird and, looking to the vehicles, he could see the men had already piled into the overstuffed Tahoe and Ranger. He ran and jumped into the towed trailer with Spencer and Riley. He attempted to yell *Go!* but before he could, the vehicle was lunging forward, the trailer bouncing violently over the uneven ground. The air knocked out of him, he grabbed onto the sides of the trailer, being flung up and down. He saw Riley go airborne and dared letting go enough to grab the man and pull him back down into the trailer.

"Holy shit, your boy can drive," Riley grunted as the trailer finally evened out onto a blacktop road.

Sean pivoted around to his backside, throwing coolers

and canvas bags off him. He pushed up, twisted he neck, and could see Joey driving the Tahoe close behind them. "I'd like to say Brooks didn't hit every bump to show his affection for me, but I don't want to lie."

Spencer was on his hip gasping and sucking water from a drinking tube. Sean looked at him and the man nodded. "How far to Toledo?" Sean asked.

"Three hours with open roads and we keep the pedal down."

Sean looked back down the road and could see it was clear; nothing was following them. That wouldn't hold though. He knew from experience the things at the outpost would already be gathering around their departure point and would soon be headed in their last known direction. It was good news for those hiding in the block building, but bad for them. Brooks had fled north, not knowing the plan to go that way to Toledo. If he'd been privy, he would have escaped to the south or east. *Spilled milk at this point,* Sean thought. He shifted up to sit against the edge of the trailer and caught Brooks's eye in the rearview mirror. Sean held up a fist, signaling for the driver to stop. Brooks nodded, and the vehicle slowed.

The Explorer eased over with the Tahoe pulling up on the left side. As soon as they came to a halt, a rear door flung open in the Tahoe and Doug Jones dropped out, vomiting on the ground. Sean leapt out of the trailer. Walking past the ill man, he looked down at him and said, "Thanks for saving it for when we weren't busy."

"You're welcome, Chief," the man coughed between gags.

Sean moved to the front of the Explorer. Brooks had his window down but was still in the driver's seat with the engine running, "Cut it a bit close back there, didn't ya, Chief?"

Sean shrugged. "You were running late. I thought you'd never show up."

"Yeah, forgot to set my alarm clock. You get me that bottle of booze ya promised?"

Shaking his head, Sean showed his empty palms. "Maybe next time. We drank the last bottle waiting on you."

"I see," Brooks said, flipping him off. "What's the call?"

"Toledo," Spencer said, walking forward.

"Who's your new friend?" Brooks asked.

"Long story, but we've got solid intel of a horde to the south... could be far bigger than the one we just ran away from."

"Larger? How much larger?"

Spencer exhaled through pursed lips. "Large enough to wipe out a two-hundred-man battalion."

Brooks held his hand over his eyes then reached across the vehicle and unfolded a map. "Toledo is due north—straight shot. We should get going if that's the plan."

"Nope," someone said from the back.

Sean turned around and saw Riley. He had a pack on his back and was stuffing spare magazines from the trailer into his pockets. Sean looked at him, trying to gauge if he was a threat. "What do you mean nope?"

"We're going back," Riley said, the Baker boys moving up next to him. Henry stood behind them, stuffing tobacco into his pipe.

"Back where?" Sean asked.

"The ranch first, then the Three Corners," Lucas, the older of the two Baker boys, said. "We aren't leaving those people back there to die."

Sean looked at the boy's determination then to Henry. "You in on this, old timer?"

Henry finished packing and lit the pipe, exhaling deeply. "I'll stick with 'em—at least until they get to the ranch. You got yourself a good mission here; I think you all have enough to keep busy without me."

"And you, Riley?" Sean asked the red-bearded man. "You're not the type to be giving a shit about others."

Smirking, he stared back at Sean. "I've left folks to die before. Not fixing on doing it again."

"That's not what this is," Sean said. "If anything, we saved them and gave 'em time to get away."

Riley nodded. "I get that, but we got to go back for 'em now, and I know that's not in the cards if we stick with you."

"Boss," Brooks said from the driver's seat. He pointed at the rearview mirror. Sean looked back down the road and could see the first of several Primals moving toward them.

"Bastards are fast," Sean said. He looked at the men on the road facing him then pointed to the Tahoe. "Okay, take the truck and go. Stick to the main roads, and don't stop until you get back to the Baker ranch. Once we wrap up, we'll send help if we can."

Henry shot a mock salute. "Don't worry about us; no need to come back. I'll make my way back down to Crabtree and send word to you somehow. Boys like us know as much about surviving as you all do."

Sean returned the salute and told them to go before he changed his mind. He watched them pile into the Tahoe and drive off to the north, looking for a new route to get south. When they were gone, Sean found himself on the street, looking at Spencer and his troops.

"Captain," Sean said. "Put your boys in the trailer. I'm not giving Brooks another chance to kill me."

Spencer smiled and pointed at Bill, who pulled Doug back to his feet and helped him climb in. "Any luck on the radio?" Sean asked.

The man shook his head. "Every freq is dead. I'll try pinging Toledo when we get closer."

Sean moved and boarded the Explorer behind Brooks, with Spencer climbing in beside him. Joey was looking back at him with a toothy grin, and Sean almost laughed. "Damn, son, you happy to see me, or what?"

"Thought you were done for, Chief," Joey said.

"Well, I'm not."

Joey nodded and laughed. "Brooks said you were too mean and ugly for a Primal to bite. But I was still worried."

Sean looked over his shoulder and could see that the jogging infected were within a hundred yards. "Well, as much as I appreciate the concern, Brooks, would you mind getting out of here before those things take a bite out of my ass?"

The Explorer raced ahead. Spencer reached into his pack and pulled out a canvas map bag. Removing a notebook, he flipped through it and turned to a page. He leaned forward between the seats and showed it to Brooks. "The camp is a nuclear reactor on Lake Erie. This is the most direct route to avoid built up areas."

"A nuke power plant?" Sean said. "I thought all of them were shut down and evacuated during the fall."

"Not all," Spencer said. "About a half dozen are still running under military control, and we just got this one back."

"What do you mean you just got it back?" Sean asked. "Who had it?"

"It was sorta between hands," Spencer said. "Carson's people had it—sort of. They were using it as a staging area for some of their operations toward the Michigan Safe Zone. With Carson gone, we pushed back in and secured it for the New Republic."

"What do you know about Carson?" Brooks said, looking back in the mirror.

"Not much," Spencer said. "We never operated close to his people. They always pushed out far ahead of us, secured the terrain, then we would come in to hold it. They had some things going on up around Michigan, and more recently, were pushing south, following the railroad. It's all tapered off now and the military is moving in to secure the ground."

Sean looked at him. "You know that's not what they were doing."

"There were rumors."

Brooks laughed. "Had to have been more than that. They were murdering families and kidnapping people. Nobody wondered where all the single ladies and unaccompanied children were coming from?"

"It's complicated."

"Going to be a long drive; we gotta talk about something."

Spencer pressed his back into the seat and clenched his fists then looked up at the ceiling. "The Civilian Authority runs things in the New Republic. It covers most of Pennsylvania, Ohio, and parts of Upstate New York. It should be part of Michigan and Indiana too but..."

"But what?" Sean asked.

"Well, Michigan has their wall, and being surrounded by the Great Lakes, they weren't as quick to leave what they had built and join the Republic. They are still part of the Alliance though, or they are if one still exists."

Sean scratched at his beard. "And Indiana?"

"No," Spencer said. "Indiana ceased to exist almost a year ago, along with most of Ohio. It was just too much territory to protect, and we don't have a wall like Michigan. Every one of those communities had to be individually fenced and defended."

Joey turned back in his seat. "That's how we ran in Virginia; it works."

Nodding his head, Spencer looked away from the man and stared out the window. "Maybe... but it didn't work for us. Eventually, the Indiana and Ohio leadership agreed to shutter their outposts and consolidate in the east."

"And the people just moved?" Sean said.

Spencer shrugged. "With some convincing."

"And that's where Carson came into play."

"I'm afraid so. We were all busy in the east, trying to keep the New York hordes from overrunning us. The military doesn't have a voice and is really nothing more than a backdrop. After the fall, shit just went sideways; everyone wanted control. What was left of the military was focused on setting up and holding perimeters, trying to defend the FEMA camps and rescue civilians. By the time things shook out, it was chaos. If you think Afghanistan was confusing with a tribal system, the Midwest was worse."

"Who was the Civilian Authority?" Sean asked.

"Every mayor with a hometown militia thought they were in charge. Most of the federal government that had escaped D.C. ended up around Philadelphia, where they tried to start a new congress by proxy. It was how they drafted the Midwest Alliance. But there was still a lot of infighting. I'm telling you, everyone wanted a piece. Everyone thought they knew what was best for the survivors. Hell, as far as that goes, not much has changed."

"And the military? Who's in command?"

Spencer shook his head. "Just as bad. There are a lot of National Guard units that came in fully intact. Others like me, we found our way there when our units were overrun. I was part of Tenth Mountain, sent up to secure Boston." Spencer looked down and shook his head. "There were only a few dozen of us that made it out. I know of a couple no-name generals, loads of staff officers. Nothing ever really got organized beyond a battalion here and there, and we still all reported up to the Civilian Authority."

Brooks looked up again. "So it's all regionalized, nobody talks higher than battalions?"

Spencer nodded. "That's correct. No brigades, no divisions. Every battalion—which are hardly company strength—reports to a regional leader. It's like the Civil War Union. And local commanders are just as bad. A mayor had a food distribution center in his district. He would give access to it, and in exchange, one of his local militia bosses would get promoted to colonel. A state senator had some of the most prime farming land. His nephew gets a commission and a battalion posted in his hometown. Like I said, it all became tribal, with us out on the perimeter holding the line."

"And who were you with?" Sean asked.

"That's a bit trickier," Spencer said. "Some of us officers off active duty got special assignments. I'm in a recon unit. Rather than tasked with defending some isolated city or securing perimeters, we go out and recon."

Sean looked at him and nodded. "And what were you reconnoitering when we bumped into you?"

Spencer sighed. "We've been over this. We were told by fleeing units that Texas was on the move and looking to take out territories."

"And what fleeing units were these?"

"Raiders."

"Carson's raiders," Sean said.

"The same ones."

Sean grinned. "Carson's raiders—who had just had their asses handed to them after attacking our home, you mean."

"Look," Spencer said. "We aren't enemies here; I can see that now. All along, I thought it was messed up for us to be picking fights with the west while we were losing ground to the infected, but what the hell am I supposed to do about it?" The man shook his head in frustration. "I'm not in charge, and those men with me are just kids. I spend most of my days just trying to keep them alive. What the hell was I supposed to do?"

"Hey," Sean said. "I believe you. None that matters anyhow if we don't live to report these hordes."

Brooks pulled the vehicle to the shoulder and cut the engine.

"You see something?" Sean asked.

"No... I gotta take a shit."

CHAPTER 30

B rad followed Luke and Gyles down a long corridor. Chelsea remained close beside him. They'd been allowed to keep their weapons but were forced to unload and clear them once they entered the building's interior. A trio of soldiers led the way, and another trio tailed behind them. Able walked them through a barricaded lobby. The interior of the room was scorched black from fire damage, while holes and shrapnel marks scarred the walls and floor. Beyond it was a long hallway where Able took a right and led them into a conference room.

Maps hung on the walls, and stacked papers covered every available tabletop. Able moved directly to the back and pulled down a white sheet that revealed a tactical overlay of the region. It showed the powerplant on the lakeshore and several bold-lined roads going west and south with route names over the tops of them. On the map, Brad could see squares with the names of battalions over them and stars showing the locations of communities. As the man had said, nearly every square was situated in the East, near

New York, with one to the south and a few scattered among the communities.

Able pointed at the map and looked at Luke. "Now, show me where you spotted these hordes."

Luke moved closer and looked at the area of Toledo and traced the highway back. "They were here when we broke contact." He looked down and found a marker then pointed it to the map, looking for permission. Able nodded, and Luke traced a finger along a dark-blue line labeled *The Wall*. Then he drew a series of hash marks in it. "The wall has been breached in these spots."

"The infected broke through your wall? I was told it was twenty feet high and poured concrete," Able said.

Luke looked at the man hard. "What do you think? You ever seen an infected use a shaped charge."

Able shook his head. "Carson."

Nodding, Luke continued. He drew more hash marks around Detroit, close to Michigan City, and finally drew a star where Brad knew their camp was located. "The Detroit containment wall is gone, and another hole is near Chicago. I've got people at a camp here, and they already reported being surrounded by heavy populations."

"What is Michigan doing with their communities?" Able asked, his voice going somber with the realization that the raiders had blown the containment.

Luke pointed at the map. "They'll head north. If all else fails, they'll cross the bridge into the UP and blow the bridge. Last word we had, the Upper Peninsula is clear of infected."

"Clear?" Brad asked.

Luke stopped and looked at him. "Yes, clear."

Brad sucked in his lower lip and looked at Chelsea, who squeezed his hand, knowing his home was on the

Superior Lakeshore. There was still a chance for his family.

Luke finished speaking and turned to Able. "There is no fighting this; we need to talk evacuation."

"Evacuation means shutting down the reactor," Able said.

"We shut it down or the infected do. I had an up-close look at your defenses. They're impressive, but even you know they won't hold against that."

Able paced across the room and dropped into a chair behind a long, steel desk. He looked down at a corded phone and lifted it from the cradle. He didn't dial, but after a pause he shifted his grip on the phone and said, "This is Master Sergeant Able; any word from Straight Six?" He paused and flipped open a leader's book on the corner of his desk. "And when was their last contact?" He sat flipping through pages in the book before stopping. Then he folded the page over and set it aside. "Okay, I need you to call and get Philly on the line for me."

Able held up the book and showed it to the strangers in the room. "These are my orders for this place. It says I'll do whatever I can to keep the lights on."

Luke shook his head then moved to a table and shoved papers away, making himself a seat. "If you stay, you'll all die and the reactor will still go dark."

The phone rang, and Able held up a finger and answered it. "This is Master Sergeant Able, I need Secretary Gimble. Yes, I'll hold."

"Gimble?" Chelsea said. "Wasn't he the Treasury secretary?"

Able dipped his chin. "Was. Now he's the Chair of the Civilian Authority in Philadelphia."

"What is that, like a President?" she asked.

"No, lot lower than that, but he has the know on everything in the NR. He runs the agen—" Able put up his finger again.

"Mister Secretary, this is Able from down in Toledo." Able turned his chair to look at the map, still holding the leader's book in his left hand. "Yeah, we're okay, but I have a problem here. We've lost contact with the battalion to the south, and I have scouts showing large numbers of infected on the freeway, moving east." Able shook his head. "No, sir, these are city-strength numbers. Some say millions."

Able placed the book on the desk and clenched his fist. "No, of course I don't have air assets to confirm the size... No, they are not at the reactor site... Yes, I understand there are no available reinforcements..." Able pulled the phone from his ear then snapped it back. "Yes, sir... We can give it twenty-four hours to observe. Please contact me if the situation changes." Able dropped the receiver, removed his soft cover, and scratched the top of his head.

The phone rang again. "Well, that didn't take long," Able said. He lifted the receiver to his ear. "I said—wait... *who* is at the gate?" Able looked at Luke then at Brad. "Get their asses in here."

BRAD AND CHELSEA sat in the corner of the room, sipping from paper cups when the conference room door opened and a tall, blue-eyed, blonde-haired officer with captain's brass and a unit patch Brad didn't recognize entered the room. Behind him were two younger soldiers wearing the same patch, the last of the two closing the door once he'd entered.

The captain stopped when Able crossed the room and

met him halfway. "It's good to see you, Captain. Where is the rest of your battalion? We'd just about given up hope on you all." Able smiled with half his face and shot an awkward glance toward Luke.

"They're gone," Spencer said.

"What do you mean 'gone'?" Able asked, his back going rigid. Brad could see that Luke and Gyles had sat up in their seats. The captain moved away from Able and approached a tray with pots of coffee on it. He lifted and rattled a pot before filling a cup. He looked down at the black liquid.

"Battalion was lost last night—overrun by infected. I was at Three Corners less than fifty miles north with my team. We were hit also. The battalion is gone, Three Corners is gone, and we've got a hostile mass moving this way from the south."

"Wiped out by infected?" Able turned to Luke then looked at the map. He moved closer to it and took the marker from the table. "You came from Three Corners?"

Spencer sipped the coffee and nodded.

"And the Straight Six was at the old railyard?"

"They were."

"You saw them? You can confirm the battalion is lost?"

Spencer reached to his hip and tossed the handheld radio onto the table. "I listened to them die," he said through clenched teeth. "If we don't want to join them, we need to get the hell out of here. You need to call command and ask for reinforcements, demand transportation."

"They won't send anyone; they don't have anyone to send," Able protested. He moved back to the desk and picked up the phone. This time he dialed a direct number. He held the phone to his ear and waited for an answer. "This is Master Sergeant Able at the Toledo Reactor. I am calling an evacuation of the facility. I'm going to order the reactor core be shut down." He laughed. "You heard correct." He laughed again. "So you'll send a team to arrest me, but not to reinforce the facility? But you don't have men for reinforcements? Well, I suggest you all get your affairs in order because I'm turning the lights off and bugging out." He slammed the phone into the cradle then looked at Spencer.

"Better hope you're right."

"I'd rather be wrong; if I'm right, we're all dead."

Able grimaced and looked at Luke. "I know you boys came here hoping to get help for back home. I can't offer that to you, but I'd appreciate your help here if you could spare it. I'll need every shooter I can to get these civilians out."

Luke scanned the room and stopped at Brad. "I've got commitments at home."

Brad looked at Chelsea, who reached out and took his hand. He turned back to Able. "Get us some proper chow, and we'll fling bullets for you."

Able pointed to a soldier who'd been standing by the door. "Escort these folks to the mess hall then get them set up with security." He turned back to Luke and the others. "Get some chow and get outfitted; I'll come find you. If you decide to leave, I won't hold it against you."

THINGS WERE MOVING FAST NOW. Moments after they'd left the conference room, lights on the wall began to flash red, and soon after, a dull alarm pulsed. The soldier escorting them down the corridor pointed to a speaker. "It's the core alarm. They're shutting down the reactor. I've heard it a hundred times in drills, but I kept hoping to hear it for real."

"Hoping?" Brad asked.

"Hell, yeah, shutting this place down means we can go home." The man stopped and turned around. "I was kind of hoping we would go home on our own though and not be chased." He pointed to a door. "Mess hall is in there. It's self-serve and the food sucks."

Luke pushed past them to get inside. As the door opened, Brad caught sight of three uniformed men talking to a pair of civilians in white shirts. Unlike the men on the gate, their uniforms were soiled and ripped. Brad moved closer, and one of the men turned back to see who had entered.

"SON OF A BITCH," Brooks shouted. He bounded across the room and lifted Brad into a tight bear hug, only dropping him so that he could apply the same torture to Chelsea. He stepped back and stared at them, shaking his head as Sean and Joey moved in. "I thought you'd be up in Michigan raising babies by now," Brooks said, Chelsea throwing a punch at him that he barely dodged.

Brad grinned and then frowned. "It wasn't good there. What are you guys doing here? It's not safe."

Sean smiled and shrugged as one of the civilians stepped toward them and said, "What do you mean it's not safe?"

Brad looked at the man, wondering if it was his place to say anything. He pointed at one of the flashing red lights. "We're about to be overrun by the infected. They are ordering the place to be evacuated and the reactor core shut down."

The man gulped and took a step back. "Are you sure about this? They're really shutting down the reactor? It's not another drill?"

Brad shook his head.

The man looked at the other civilian next to him "Then they'll trigger the NERT."

The second man said, "We'll be okay."

"Da fuck is a NERT?" Brooks asked.

"Nuclear Emergency Response Team," the man said, his feet shuffling, already eager to leave the room.

"I heard them say nobody is coming; your friends in the north said no. And by bad counts, they are looking at a million visitors on the way here."

The first man pulled at the second civilian's shoulder. He took a step then looked back. "NERT is bigger than that. It goes out to anyone listening. Uses the satellites—well, the ones left, anyway. If a reactor is about to go down, there are people that will do whatever they can to keep it from melting down." The man turned and stepped to the door before looking back a last time. "If anyone listening can help, they will." The man left the room with the other close behind him. The door shut and suddenly the strangers were the only ones left in the cafeteria.

"It's bullshit, right?" Brooks said.

Sean looked away and moved back to the deli counter. There were stacks of thawed cold cuts and stale bread. He smacked them together into a sandwich and looked back to the group. Brad moved next to him and loaded a plate of his own. "I'm sure a thing once existed called NERT, but who is out there now that would come to the aid of a nuclear reactor? Anyone that knows about this stuff is dead."

"Not necessarily," Sean said, finding a seat and sitting down heavily. He slid the tray close to him and took a huge bite then gulped down a glass of water. "There could still be bunkers of people out there, and Captain Spencer said there were other nuke sites. Maybe someone is listening."

"But enough to fight the infected and save the reactor?" Chelsea asked.

Sean shook his head side to side. "Nope, nobody for that. Best case, I say we gotta just keep the place secure long enough for them to softly shut it down and put her to sleep."

"Then what?" Brad asked.

"Why are you asking me? You all didn't have a plan of your own before you came out here?"

Brad and Chelsea turned their eyes toward Luke. The man put up his hands. "Hey, I was on the assumption they would be able to help us... do something to fight back the infected. This is all sad news on my end, and to be honest with you, I got my own war and my own people back home."

Brad shook his head and looked at Gyles. The man looked down at his tray, not speaking.

"I'm here to kill Primals, makes no difference to me where they at," Joey said, shoving his tray away from him. He stood and began walking toward the door. "I don't care what you other pussies decide."

Brad, Chelsea, and Brooks all quickly exchanged glances and, shoving away their own trays, headed for the door.

"YOU'VE each got three hundred rounds on you. The Kevlar is light but will protect you from most of what the infected can throw at you." Able pointed to a table of gear then held up a fabric shirt. "I'm sure you are familiar with bite shirts. Personally, I don't wear one. Seen more than one man go out by being chewed to death, but it's up to you."

"Chief Rogers tells me they've done some sniping, so I'll leave you all to that. I'm giving you all a tower on the Lake Erie side. Hold the line as long as you can, then make your egress. We're already shuttling civilians to the coast and loading boats. If you see flares over the main gate, drop whatever it is you are doing and haul ass, 'cause it's all over."

"How long?" Brad asked.

Able shook his head. "You all's intel was spot-on. My Rangers came back and said there are thousands on the highway. They set up roadblocks and are already fighting them inside the city. They'll be here by last light."

"They're worse in the dark," Sean said.

Able nodded. "My boys will stall as long as we can, but we won't get another day."

Brad looked at Able. "Have you heard from the two men we came in with?"

The master sergeant shook his head. "They didn't tell you? They left a while ago, said they had to get back to their camp, people counting on them and all of that. To each his own. I won't hold anyone here even though I do appreciate your help." Able frowned then handed Sean a handheld radio before turning to walk away. Sean and Brooks grabbed their gear and stood next to Joey. The time for debate was over. They left the building and followed a trail to their designated tower. In the distance, they could hear gunfire.

The tower on the lakeshore side of the camp was tall and well-built. The trail stopped at the base of the tower then continued to the lake at the far side. They opened a door at the base and climbed to the top. They entered a large circular room with sliding glass windows on all sides. At both the lake side and plant side were doors that opened onto a wide catwalk. The tower wasn't pre-fall, but Brad could tell that whoever built it had put in the time to do it right. He walked across the tower floor and joined the others on the catwalk. The sun was just beginning to set. They turned and looked toward the plant and places where the perimeter was nothing more than strands of chain link fence.

"It was generous of them to give us this tower and put their own people in the trenches," Chelsea said.

Brooks laughed.

"Something funny?" she asked.

Sean slapped the younger SEAL's back then looked at Chelsea and pointed in the distance at the line of vehicles rolling to the lakeshore. "You see them out there?"

She nodded.

"That's at least a thousand yards through open terrain on the wrong side of the fence." Sean turned and pointed to the trenches. "And over there, still a long haul, but it's inside the wire and if—"

"If?" Chelsea said, her eyes getting big.

"*If* we do our job, they just might make it to the boats."

"What's our job?" Chelsea asked.

"We have overwatch. Once all the civilians are loaded, they'll call to pull out the troops, and when they decide to pull back from those trenches, we'll provide them cover. This tower is like a clock. The twelve faces the main approach the infected will use to attack the wire; I'll set up here with Brooks. Three, six, and nine will be covered by you three. Don't worry about defending the camp; you just defend this tower. Nothing gets up."

Chelsea nodded and went to speak again, but Sean cut her off. "But if it gets too rough and those flares pop, then it's shit sandwich time and we must make it to that shoreline. We already discussed the distance and the side of the fence we are on."

Chelsea's head scanned to all the places Sean hand pointed out. "Did you tell Master Sergeant Able about this?"

"Oh yeah, I volunteered us for the tower duty."

"Why would you do that?" she asked.

Sean put a hand on her shoulder. "Because it keeps us all together and not spread out along some wall. If we must fight our way out, we'll do it together."

She reached in and hugged Sean. When she pulled back, her eyes were wet. She turned and quickly walked to the other side of the tower.

Sean looked at Brad and Joey. "Brooks and I will stay quiet and take long shots as long as we can; you guys try to not draw fire unless you have to. The less they think about this tower the better."

"You got it, Chief," Joey said, walking over to his side of the tower.

Brad stayed, looking at Sean, but he couldn't speak so he turned and walked to his own spot on the tower and knelt. He pulled up his rifle and looked through the Trijicon optic. It was magnified, and the dot illuminated. He scanned the terrain in his sector. It was mostly gravel lots and buildings—all fenced in, all within his rifle's range. He heard gunfire from the front of the camp, and he adjusted his position. Looking out into the sunset, he could see tracer fire as the Rangers made a fighting withdrawal from the city.

"They should just keep running," Chelsea said, startling Brad. He found her standing just beside him, watching the same events. "They should just keep running—no point in stopping here."

He wanted to argue with her and to reassure her, but he

didn't have the words. Instead, he bit at his lower lip and nodded. She moved closer to him, put a hand on his shoulder, and together they watched. The Rangers were in armored HUMVEEs, moving in leapfrog patterns, two racing away while two others held position and let loose with their turret-mounted machine guns. Once a pair of HUMVEEs had fled far enough back, they would stop, the gunners opening up, and the pair of trucks they'd left behind raced forward.

They watched the vehicles move in the coordinated fashion. It was dark, and all they could see were the headlights and muzzle flashes. Brad was about to comment on the possibility of the convoy doing nothing more than leading the infected directly to them when he saw the first of the Primal ranks. It wasn't a ball of them on the road, or a horde—it was a massive wall stretching across the horizon. As the vehicles entered the gates, the soldiers on the roofline opened fire, doing little to stop the hordes from moving against them. Explosions erupted from the field with bright flashes and white smoke as fireballs erupted into the sky.

"They had the field mined?" Chelsea said, watching in fascination as fireballs rolled upward.

"I guess it's good we stuck to the road earlier and didn't wander onto the lawn."

Chelsea squeezed his shoulder and jumped when a suppressed gunshot came from the front of the tower. Brad leaned out and saw that the infected had already begun to surround the perimeter and were attacking the trench line. Another shot and soon Sean and Brooks were rapid firing. Brad looked down below and saw a single figure in a bloody, white shirt running across the gravel lot toward the trail leading to the escape boats. "They are already inside the wire," he stuttered.

Chelsea looked down, following his finger. She didn't speak; instead, she ran to her position. Brad raised his rifle and focused on the man, aiming down at his legs to compensate for the speed. He watched the man stumble, and then pulled the trigger twice, seeing the thing roll into the gravel. He looked up and saw two more on the same path. He heard Joey's and Chelsea's rifles.

Looking through his sights, Brad fired on the first then shifted fire to the second. He looked over the optic and now saw waves of them coming. The air was filled with gunfire, making it impossible to distinguish who it was coming from. He fired into the wave to his front, dropping and replacing magazines. Explosions erupted in the field and along the trench line. He scanned to the roof and spotted a mortar pit he hadn't seen before. They were dropping rounds at max rate but were doing little to affect the waves of infected throwing themselves at the plant.

Brad heard Joey scream something, and he took his eyes off the rifle long enough to look at the man through the glass enclosure. He was pointing down. Brad moved to the railing and could see infected piled around the exit door. The mass of their bodies was pressing it closed. He leaned over the rail and fired into the tops of their heads, adding a mass of bodies in front of the door. As the bodies dropped, he shuddered with the realization that they wouldn't be able to open the door if they had to run.

Like a cruel joke being played after it was too late, the flare popped into the air. Chelsea looked up at it and backed away from the railing. She moved toward Brad. "It's time to go," she shouted.

Brad shook his head and pointed to the ground. "The door's blocked." He pointed to the distant trail that Sean had shown them earlier. It was now full of the infected;

there would be no fighting through it. Out on the lake they could see the navigation lights of boats pulling away. Chelsea spun back toward the trench lines and the soldiers on the buildings. Everyone was still fighting. There would be no retreat. The flare was pulling more infected toward the buildings and away from the fleeing families of the camp. She shook her head rapidly. Brad let his rifle drop on its sling and pulled her in.

CHAPTER 31

TOLEDO CITY LIMITS, THE DEAD LANDS

The fighting and screams of the infected dragged on for hours. The team was now in the tower enclosure, hiding. There was no point in wasting rounds; the fighting was over. The plant was lost, every man for himself, fighting their own way out. They knew some had made it—they'd watched vehicles loaded with troops race out of the gate, firing. Others left rooftops into the buildings to barricade themselves inside. They had watched the navigation lights on the lake fade as the boats pulled away.

Night became morning, the gunfire stopped, and the screams of the infected turned into moans. Brad was awake with Chelsea sleeping beside him. Sean sat in a chair in a corner, staring straight ahead, hardly moving as his eyes watched the horizon. He started when a chirp emanated from his pack. He looked at Brad then at the bag. "What the hell?"

There was another chirp, and the others were awake, trying to identify the source of the sound. Sean yanked his bag close, reached into a front pouch, and pulled out a radio with a green light on the top. The light timed out and faded.

The team looked at each other. When the radio chirped again, Sean bolted upright, nearly dropping it.

"Any station, any station, this is Navy Helo Twelve Twenty-Six. Please respond."

Sean stared at the radio. He closed his eyes tight then opened them, pressing the button. "Uhh, Twelve Twenty-Six, uhh, we're here."

"Last calling station, please identify. Over."

Sean looked at Brad, who tossed up his hands. Brooks was on his feet; he pointed at a sign that read Tower Five. Sean nodded and pressed the transmit button. "Twelve Twenty-Six, this is Tower Five of the Toledo Nuclear Reactor."

"Understood, Tower Five. What is the status of your reactor?"

Sean stood and looked toward the plant. The trenches were gone and overrun, but he could still see soldiers stranded on the roof. The cooling towers were cold, with no steam leaving them. Sean pressed the button. "The reactor was safely shut down. Listen, we got people here on the roof and in my tower."

"Understood, Tower Five. We received your NERT call. We are coming to get you out."

THANK YOU FOR READING

Please leave a review on Amazon.
About WJ Lundy
W. J. Lundy is a still serving Veteran of the U.S. Military with service in Afghanistan. He has over 16 years of combined service with the Army and Navy in Europe, the Balkans and Southwest Asia. W.J. is an avid athlete, writer, backpacker and shooting enthusiast. He currently resides with his wife and daughter in Central Michigan.
Find WJ Lundy on facebook:

WHISKEY TANGO FOXTROT CONTINUES IN BOOK 9 COMING SOON!
For More from the World of Whiskey Tango Foxtrot

TORMENT
Available now!

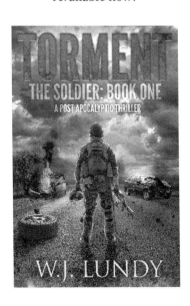

Join the WJ Lundy mailing list for news, updates and contest giveaways.

Whiskey Tango Foxtrot Series.

Whiskey Tango Foxtrot is an introduction into the apocalyptic world of Staff Sergeant Brad Thompson. A series with over 1,500 five-star reviews on Amazon.

Alone in a foreign land. The radio goes quiet while on convoy in Afghanistan, a lost patrol alone in the desert. With his unit and his home base destroyed, Staff Sergeant Brad Thompson suddenly finds himself isolated and in command of a small group of men trying to survive in the Afghan wasteland.

Every turn leads to danger. The local population has been afflicted with an illness that turns them into rabid animals. They pursue him and his men at every corner and stop. Struggling to hold his team together and unite survivors, he must fight and evade his way to safety.

A fast paced zombie war story like no other.

Escaping The Dead
    Tales of The Forgotten
    Only The Dead Live Forever
    Walking In The Shadow Of Death
    Something To Fight For
    Divided We Fall
    Bound By Honor
    Primal Resurrection

Praise for Whiskey Tango Foxtrot:
"The beginning of a fantastic story. Action packed and

full of likeable characters. If you want military authenticity, look no further. You won't be sorry."

-Owen Baillie, Author of Best-selling series, Invasion of the Dead.

"A brilliantly entertaining post-apocalyptic thriller. You'll find it hard to putdown"

-Darren Wearmouth, Best-selling author of First Activation, Critical Dawn, Sixth Cycle

"W.J. Lundy captured two things I love in one novel-- military and zombies!"

-Terri King, Editor Death Throes Webzine

"War is horror and having a horror set during wartime works well in this story. Highly recommended!"

-Allen Gamboa, Author of Dead Island: Operation Zulu

"There are good books in this genre, and then there are the ones that stand out from the rest-- the ones that make me want to purchase all the books in the series in one shot and keep reading. W.J. Lundy's Whiskey Tango Foxtrot falls into the latter category."

-Under the Oaks reviews

"The author's unique skills set this one apart from the masses of other zombie novels making it one of the most exciting that I have read so far."

-HJ Harry, of Author Splinter

The Invasion Trilogy

The Darkness is a fast-paced story of survival that brings the apocalypse to Main Street USA.

While the world falls apart, Jacob Anderson barricades his family behind locked doors. News reports tell of civil unrest in the streets, murders, and disappearances; citizens are warned to remain behind locked doors. When Jacob becomes witness to horrible events and the alarming actions of his neighbors, he and his family realize everything is far worse than being reported.

Every father's nightmare comes true as Jacob's normal life--and a promise to protect his family--is torn apart.

From the Best-Selling Author of **Whiskey Tango Foxtrot comes a new telling of Armageddon.**

The Darkness

The Shadows

The Light

Praise for the Invasion Trilogy:

"The Darkness is like an air raid siren that won't shut off; thrilling and downright horrifying!" ***Nicholas Sansbury Smith, Best Selling Author of Orbs and The Extinction Cycle.***

"Absolutely amazing. This story hooked me from the first page and didn't let up. I read the story in one sitting and now I am desperate for more. ...Mr. Lundy has definitely broken new ground with this tale of humanity, sacrifice and love of family ... In short, read this book." ***William Allen, Author of Walking in the Rain.***

"First book I've pre-ordered before it was published. Well done story of survival with a relentless pace, great action, and characters I cared about! Some scenes are still in my head!" ***Stephen A. North, Author of Dead Tide and The Drifter.***

A new military thriller from WJ Lundy

Donovan's War

With everything around, him gone. Tommy Donovan must return to the war he has been hiding from. When his sister is taken, the Government fails to act. Tommy Donovan will take the law into his own hands. But, this time he isn't a soldier, and there will be no laws to protect evil. This time it's personal and he is making the rules.

Resigned to never finding peace from the war long behind him, retired warrior, Thomas Donovan, is now faced with an even deadlier conflict... one that could cost him the last of his humanity.

Once a member of an elite underground unit, the only wars Thomas knows now are the ones that rage inside him. All he wants is to stay under the radar of existence, trying to forget the past and isolating himself from the present.

OTHER BOOKS FROM UNDER THE
SHIELD OF PHALANX PRESS

FIVE ROADS TO TEXAS

| LUNDY | PARKER | BAKER | HANSEN | GAMBOA |

From the best story tellers of Phalanx Press comes a frightening tale of Armageddon.

It spread fast, no time to understand it, let alone learn how to fight it.

Once it reached you, it was too late. All you could do is run.

Rumored safe zones and potential for a cure drifted across the populace, forcing tough decisions to be made.

They say only the strong survive. Well they forgot about the smart, the inventive and the lucky.

Follow five different groups from across the U.S.A. as they make their way to what could be America's last stand in the Lone Star State.

AVAILABLE ON AMAZON NOW

SIXTH CYCLE

CARL SINCLAIR | DARREN WEARMOUTH

Nuclear war has destroyed human civilization.

Captain Jake Phillips wakes into a dangerous new world, where he finds the remaining fragments of the population living in a series of strongholds, connected across the country. Uneasy alliances have maintained their safety, but things are about to change. -- Discovery leads to danger. -- Skye Reed, a tracker from the Omega stronghold, uncovers a threat that could spell the end for their fragile society. With friends and enemies revealing truths about the past, she will need to decide who to trust.

Sixth Cycle *is a gritty post-apocalyptic story of survival and adventure.*

AVAILABLE NOW

THE INVASION TRILOGY

DARREN WEARMOUTH

**Aliens have planned against us for centuries…
And now the attack is ready.**
Charlie Jackson's archaeological team find advanced
technology in an undisturbed 16th Century graves. While
investigating the discovery, giant sinkholes appear across
planet, marking the start of Earth's colonization and the
descent of civilization.
Charlie and the rest of humanity will have to fight for
survival, sacrificing the life they've known to protect
themselves from an ancient and previously dormant enemy.
Even that might not be enough as aliens exact a plan that
will change the course of history.

DEAD ISLAND: OPERATION ZULU

ALLEN GAMBOA

DEAD ISLAND: Operation Zulu

Ten years after the world was nearly brought to its knees by a zombie Armageddon, there is a race for the antidote! On a remote Caribbean island, surrounded by a horde of hungry living dead, a team of American and Australian commandos must rescue the Antidotes' scientist. Filled with zombies, guns, Russian bad guys, shady government types, serial killers and elevator muzak. Dead Island is an action packed blood soaked horror adventure.

Dead Island: Dos and ***Dead Island: Ravenous*** are available now!

INVASION OF THE DEAD SERIES

OWEN BAILLIE

INVASION OF THE DEAD SERIES

This is the first book in a series of nine, about an ordinary
bunch of friends, and their plight to survive an apocalypse
in Australia. -- Deep beneath defense headquarters in the
Australian Capital Territory, the last ranking Army chief
and a brilliant scientist struggle with answers to the collapse
of the world, and the aftermath of an unprecedented virus.
Is it a natural mutation, or does the infection contain -- more
sinister roots? -- One hundred and fifty miles away, five
friends returning from a month-long camping trip slowly
discover that death has swept through the country. What
greets them in a gradual revelation is an enemy beyond
compare. -- Armed with dwindling ammunition, the friends
must overcome their disagreements, utilize their individual
skills, and face unimaginable horrors as they battle to reach
their hometown...

WHISKEY TANGO FOXTROT

W.J LUNDY

Alone in a foreign land. The radio goes quiet while on convoy in Afghanistan, a lost patrol alone in the desert. With his unit and his home base destroyed, Staff Sergeant Brad Thompson suddenly finds himself isolated and in command of a small group of men trying to survive in the Afghan wasteland. Every turn leads to danger.
The local population has been afflicted with an illness that turns them into rabid animals. They pursue him and his men at every corner and stop. Struggling to hold his team together and unite survivors, he must fight and evade his way to safety. A fast paced zombie war story like no other.

ZOMBIE RUSH

JOSEPH HANSEN

ZOMBIE RUSH

New to the Hot Springs PD Lisa Reynolds was not all that welcomed by her coworkers especially those who were passed over for the position. It didn't matter, her thirty days probation ended on the same day of the Z-poc's arrival. Overnight the world goes from bad to worse as thousands die in the initial onslaught. National Guard and regular military unit deployed the day before to the north leaves the city in mayhem. All directions lead to death until one unlikely candidate steps forward with a plan. A plan that became an avalanche raging down the mountain culminating in the salvation or destruction of them all.

ZED'S WORLD

RICH BAKER

BOOK ONE: THE GATHERING HORDE

The most ambitious terrorist plot ever undertaken is about to be put into motion, releasing an unstoppable force against humanity. Ordinary people – A group of students celebrating the end of the semester, suburban and rural families – are about to themselves in the center of something that threatens the survival of the human species. As they battle the dead – and the living – it's going to take every bit of skill, knowledge and luck for them to survive in Zed's World.

BOOK TWO: ROADS LESS TRAVELED

A terrible plague has been loosed upon the earth. In the course of one night, mankind teeters on the brink of extinction. Fighting through gathering hordes of undead, a group of friends brave military checkpoints, armed civilians, and forced allegiances in an attempt to reach loved ones. Thwarted at every turn, they press forward. But taking roads less traveled, could cost them everything.

BOOK THREE: NO WAY OUT

For Kyle Puckett, Earth has become a savage place. As the world continues to decay, the survivors of the viral plague have started choosing sides. With each encounter the stakes - and the body count - continue to rise. With the skies growing darker and the dead pressing in, both sides may soon find out that there is No Way Out.

GRUDGE

BRIAN PARKER

The United States Navy led an expedition to Antarctica in December 1946, called Operation Highjump. Officially, the men were tasked with evaluating the effect of cold weather on US equipment; secretly their mission was to investigate reports of a hidden Nazi base buried beneath the ice. After engaging unknown forces in aerial combat, weather forced the Navy to abandon operations. Undeterred, the US returned every Antarctic summer until finally the government detonated three nuclear missiles over the atmosphere in 1958. Unfortunately, the desperate gamble to rid the world of the Nazi scourge failed. The enemy burrowed deeper into the ice, using alien technologies for cryogenic freezing to amass a genetically superior army, indoctrinated from birth to hate Americans. Now they've returned, intent on exacting revenge for the destruction of their homeland and banishment to the icy wastes.

THE PATH OF ASHES

BRIAN PARKER

Evil doesn't become extinct, it evolves. Our world is a
violent place. Murder, terrorism, racism and social
inequality, these are some of the forces that attempt to
destroy our society while the State is forced to increase its
response to these actions. Our own annihilation is barely
held at bay by the belief that we've somehow evolved
beyond our ancestors' base desires.
From this cesspool of emotions emerges a madman, intent
on leading the world into anarchy. When his group of
computer hackers infiltrate the Department of Defense
network, they initiate a nuclear war that will irrevocably
alter our world.
Aeric Gaines and his roommate, Tyler, survive the
devastation of the war, only to find that the politically
correct world where they'd been raised was a lie. All
humans have basic needs such as food, water and shelter...
but we will fight for what we *desire*.
A Path of Ashes is a three-book series about life in post-
apocalyptic America, a nation devoid of leadership,

electricity and human rights. The world as we know it may have burned, but humanity found a way to survive and this is their story.

AS THE ASH FELL

AJ POWERS

Life in the frozen wastelands of Texas is anything but easy, but for Clay Whitaker there is always more at stake than mere survival.

It's been seven years since the ash billowed into the atmosphere, triggering some of the harshest winters in recorded history. Populations are thinning. Food is scarce. Despair overwhelming. With no way to sustain order, societies collapsed, leaving people to fend for themselves. Clay and his sister Megan have taken a handful of orphaned children into their home--a home soaring sixteen stories into the sky. With roughly six short months a year to gather enough food and supplies to last the long, brutal winter, Clay must spend most of his time away from his family to scavenge, hunt, and barter.

When Clay rescues a young woman named Kelsey from a group of Screamers, his life is catapulted into a new direction, forcing him to make decisions he never thought he would have to make.

Now, with winter rolling in earlier than ever, Clay's divided attention is putting him, and his family, at risk.

HUMAN ELEMENT

AJ POWERS

Human Element

The Neuroweb began as the greatest invention since written language. A simple brain implant that allowed the user to access information, entertainment, and even pain relief. The Neuroweb was the beginning of a golden age for mankind...

Until it was compromised.

Everyone with the implant lost their most important commodity: their free will. The collective human consciousness was hacked, and now directed by artificial intelligence. Only those without the Neuroweb have a chance of resisting...If they dare.

Aaran has legitimate reason to believe he's the last free-thinking human alive. After his family was killed in the purge, he fled for his life. Now, he aimlessly wanders through the suburbs of Cincinnati alone, desperate to find a reason to live.

When he meets a girl like him - another free thinker - they search together for a cause worth fighting for. Worth dying for.

THIS BOOK WAS FORMATTED BY

CARL SINCLAIR

Looking for book formatting?

carlsinclair.net/formatting

Made in the USA
Columbia, SC
19 January 2019